Embers of You

AMITY

MADI DANIELLE

To my Booha. Jameson and Sutton have always been and always will be for you.

Content Trigger Warnings

This book has many fun moments, however does deal with some heavy topics. These do contain spoilers so, but if you have triggers please take care of yourself.

Triggers include:

- Discussions of cancer
- Death of a parent

Playlist

This is how I learn to say no - EMELINE
Plot Twist - Ashley Kutcher
Cowboy Side of You - Clare Dunn
Runnin' Out of Air - Love and Theft
John Wayne - Lady Gaga
Strip It Down - Luke Bryan
Sand - Dove Cameron
My tears ricochet - Taylor Swift
I love you, I'm Sorry - Gracie Abrams
Innocent (Taylor's Version) - Taylor Swift
Ordinary - Alex Warren

Hardware Store
GROCERIES
Food Mart
JAMESON'S HOUSE
Roasted Bean Coffee
Barkin Pups
Grooming
AMITY
Fire Co.
MAIN STREET
SUTTON'S HOUSE
SCENIC DRIVE
AMITY
WES'S HOUSE
BAILEY'S HOUSE

CHAPTER 1

Sutton

SITTING ON A HARD, scratchy hotel bed in the middle of nowhere, I can't help but wonder where I went wrong in my life to end up here. Was it the people I chose to associate with? My supposed best friend and even my family.

Bennet, my Landseer Newfoundland lays next to me on the bed, looking up with his big, dark brown eyes almost like he's asking the same internal question.

What are we doing?

"I don't even know, buddy," I tell him while I brush my fingers through his thick fur and scratch behind his ear. "But I'm figuring it out."

Dogs are so expressive, and I can tell he trusts me. Unconditional loyalty is something only a dog can give. Humans can be such shit. They lie and cheat, a dog would never. At the end of the day most people are only looking out for themselves.

Sighing, I open my laptop to search for a place that would be a good fit for us. I've driven us over seven hundred miles away from Los Angeles. I think we are just outside of Medford, Oregon, at least that's the last sign I remember seeing. I have no idea where we're going, or what we'll do when we get there. I just know that staying in L.A. wasn't an option anymore. As far as I'm concerned, there isn't a place on the planet that could be far enough from the people I've chosen to leave in my past.

As soon as I found out just how deeply the betrayal ran, I packed up everything, including Bennet, and left my parents' house. Living there while I saved money for a place of my own wasn't worth having to accept that level of deception.

I open up the dog groomer group I'm a part of to look for any job openings. Anything will do; I just need to find something soon because I don't want to stay in this motel room much longer.

One particular post catches my eye, and I'm not even sure why. Some posts have fancy pictures, big words, exciting language. Not this one. This one is simple.

DOG GROOMER WANTED
We're a small shop in a small town in Washington.
Great view while you work.
Flexible schedule.
Message if you're interested.
P.S. We have a bird.

A good view, flexible, and a bird? Why not?

I send a message and see the owner of the post is located in Amity, Washington. I assume that's where the shop is located and decide to look up places to rent nearby.

After researching the town, I realize it's on the coast, but several pictures include a lot of mountains. I wonder if the 'great view' is either one of those. My last shop was in the middle of the L.A. chaos and a small beachside town sounds way calmer. Exactly what I need.

Considering it's close to the middle of the night, I don't expect a response from the grooming salon owner, Trish, but I'm proven wrong when my phone lights up while I'm scanning through rentals.

Trish: When can you start?

She doesn't even know anything about me, and wants to offer me the job already?

Sutton: Do you want to see any of my grooms first?

Trish: Sure.

I hit send on some pictures of a few of my favorite grooms I've done. There was a regular standard poodle whose owner let me get really creative. I add a couple more basic grooms with a Schnauzer, Cocker Spaniel, and a Scottish Terrier.

The pictures have just barely gone through when another message pops up.

Trish: When can you start?

There's no way she looked at the pictures yet, but I'm not about to give up this opportunity.

Sutton: Friday?

Trish: See you then!

She sends me the address to the salon, and I double down on my effort to find a place to rent.

"I guess we're moving to Washington," I tell Bennet. He snuggles his head against my leg as though he's giving me reassurance.

The next morning, I wake up to Bennet whining next to my face from where he sits on the floor. The sun's shining through the cheap curtains, and I know we should get back on the road. I must've fallen asleep while looking at places to rent last night. I emailed a few potential properties, but since I start my new job tomorrow, I don't have time to wait around to hear back.

After taking Bennet out to do his business, I feed him breakfast and pack up the few belongings we have. We get loaded up into the car, and just like that we're back on the road, heading toward our new beginning. I just hope it's a good one.

ANOTHER FIVE HUNDRED MILES DRIVEN, and I'm exhausted. The sign that indicates we're now in Amity is the only thing that keeps me going to the tiny motel and dragging myself into the front office to request a room. The receptionist looks at Bennet skeptically as she hands me the room key.

"He won't do any damage, I promise," I tell her, but the look she gives me in return indicates that she doesn't believe me.

I'm too tired to try and defend my dog anymore, so I take the key and head to the room; falling face first onto the bed as soon as the door is closed.

Despite being completely exhausted I'm assaulted by nightmares. The flashes of what I saw. The reason I left L.A. robs my peaceful night sleep.

My best friend. My best. Fucking. Friend. And...*ugh.* I see them together. My mom is there. She knows and I can never seem to forget.

I wake with a jolt, and it's still dark out. Bennet is lying next to me, his head on my chest looking at me like he knows everything that was just running through my mind. Maybe he does know since he was there, and he witnessed it all right along with me.

I pet his head, hoping to soothe both of us. It works and before I know it, I've drifted off to dreamless sleep.

The next morning, I drive over to the grooming salon taking in the charm that comes with such a small town, knowing I need to find a more permanent place to live. My goal after work is to look at the two properties for rent that emailed me back. They both said immediate move in, and even though it will take up almost all my savings for the deposit, I can't keep sleeping in motels.

I didn't ask Trish about bringing Bennet to work with me, but I hope she won't mind. This is just another reason we need our own place as soon as possible. I have my bag of supplies slung over my shoulder as I walk inside. The salon looks like a cute little house, separate rooms, art on the walls that are painted in a variety of calming colors.

Once inside, I'm immediately greeted, but not by a person.

"Hi." I look over to see a white Cockatoo who's currently perched on top of a large cage.

"Um...hi." I don't want to be rude and not respond...to a bird.

Oh God, I'm already losing it.

"That's Jerry Lee." A voice that is definitely human comes out from the back, and I assume it's Trish. I'd guess she's probably in her fifties, with her light brown hair pulled back in a messy ponytail. She's wearing a faded T-shirt and jeans. "I'm Trish."

"Nice to meet you. I'm Sutton." We shake hands, and she looks down at Bennet.

"What a beautiful Newfie," she beams, and I sigh with relief.

"Thank you, his name is Bennet."

"Cute. Come on, I'll show you where your station is."

Since it's my first day, I'm not very busy, so I answer the phone to book some appointments, and take a couple walk-in nail trims and baths before Trish says I'm good to go for the day.

I put away all my equipment in the special vanity that was already set up at my workstation. I like the space, and it turns out it's a converted house so both Trish and I have our own grooming rooms. The bathing area is centered between our two rooms and provides just enough privacy so I can listen to music while I work.

My old salon was a large, well-known place in L.A. where a lot of people, including some celebrities, came to get their dogs groomed. It was crowded, loud, and full of drama. Unfortunately, that seems to be what happens when you stick a bunch of women together in a confined space for a long period of time.

What made it worse is that at one time I also lived with some of those women. I made good money, but it wasn't enough to comfortably afford a decent place on my own, which resulted in me renting a room in a four-bedroom house with three other groomers.

Talk about drama.

Which is why I ended up moving back in with my parents to save up. Until that was ruined.

This new pace of life is refreshing to say the least.

I walk outside with Bennet sticking close to my side on his leash when suddenly a siren rings out in the air making me jump. I look over to the building next door to the salon where a fire truck is pulling out and driving off. That's when I realize the window by my station inside looks directly toward the fire station. It looks like a typical brick building; one I didn't even notice until now. I just hope the sirens don't scare me while I'm grooming.

Or at least that I'll get used to it.

MY NEW HOME is a small mix between a cabin and a cottage just outside of the main area of Amity. It's hidden by some trees and is only a short walk from the beach so I'm not complaining about the small size. It's essentially a glorified studio. There isn't a separate door to the bedroom which could be considered more of a den.

Good news is I have a place to stay for the foreseeable future. Bad news is it has no furniture.

I love it.

The outside resembles a log cabin, but the inside has simple white walls and wood floors. The kitchen isn't big, but it has full sized appliances, and I'm glad I have the option to cook again.

I end up going to the local store in town to get an air mattress, pillows, blankets, and some food. The amount of money from my savings that I've burned through in renting this place stresses me out, and I just know I'm going to have to use more to get furniture. But I'll take that one day at a time, because at least I'm not in a hotel anymore.

This is the place I'm going to be able to start over.

CHAPTER 2

Jameson

"HEY *CHIEF*," my coworker, Parker, says sarcastically as I walk in for my shift.

"Shut up, I'm not the chief here."

I adjust the heavy bag slung over my shoulder, its weight a familiar presence as I make my way toward my locker. I spin the combination lock and pull open the door, the metal creaking slightly. I shove my bag in, and take a deep breath, knowing the next forty-eight hours of my shift will be unpredictable.

I just got back to Amity a couple of months ago after being away for the last ten years. During that time, I became the fire chief in Tampa where I moved when I was twenty-six and wanted to get away from this small town.

Then my life got flipped upside down with a single phone call from my mom, and I knew I needed to come back to be here for her. Even though she insisted I didn't need to uproot my life and move. My dad still hasn't forgiven me for leaving in the first place, and it seems like he couldn't care less that I'm back. But I didn't come back for him. I came back for her.

She's the reason I voluntarily stepped down from chief back to a firefighter, and my sudden return back to the station I started my career at as soon as I was able to. The biggest adjustment to coming back here in comparison to Florida is that since we're a slower station, we work forty-eight hours on, ninety-six hours off. Back in Florida it was twenty-four on and forty-eight off.

"Not yet," Parker says, following behind me. "Old man Gary will retire soon, and you'll take his spot."

I shrug. "I don't even know if I want that again, it's kind of nice to not have as much responsibility."

"Suit yourself. Though I'm sure you'll miss having that nice cushy office job." Parker slaps my shoulder before walking back out into the common area of the station.

"I like being a part of the action."

I go out to the common area with him, the familiar hum of the fire station's daily rhythm filling the space. I notice three other crew members are doing various activities ranging from laying on the couch, cooking, and organizing equipment. Some of my coworkers are meticulous when it comes to how the equipment is arranged. Josephine, or Jo as we call her, always likes to make sure everything is in perfect order. She's also notorious for hating how Gerald on the other shift has all the gear set up. It's probably one of the longest running feuds I've seen on the job.

"Did you hear about the newbie in town?" Parker asks from the couch. He's the youngest at our station, only twenty, and always likes to know what's going on around town and sharing with the rest of us. Even if we don't care. Especially me.

"Girl or guy?" Dave asks from the kitchen.

"Chick," Parker answers easily.

I go into the kitchen to grab some water and try to tune out this conversation because I really don't need to know about some new girl coming into town. I have enough to worry about.

"Heard she's working over at Trish's place and looking for a place to stay. Maybe I should go over there and offer up my bed," Parker says, and I know he's joking, but I throw a towel at his head for it.

"Don't be a douche, Parker, show some respect," I scold him.

He holds his hands up in surrender, but he's still chuckling.

"This is why you're single," Jo calls from the other room. She's the only woman on our shift, and I know it can be annoying dealing with all this testosterone all the time.

"I'm single by choice," Parker announces, which results in a few different reactions. Mostly chuckles, snorts, and various mumblings. "Okay, fuck you guys," Parker snaps.

We all laugh as Parker storms off somewhere. He's young and still so immature. He has a lot to learn in life, but I don't doubt that if he sticks around here with this group that he'll end up okay.

I'M EXHAUSTED by the end of shift. I never sleep well at the station, I'm always on guard for a call and one would think I would be used to it after years of doing this job, but it still affects me.

When I pull up to my parents' property, the familiar sight of the old farmhouse puts me at ease. I swing my car door open and make my way up the creaky porch steps, the screen door clicking as I push it open and step inside. The house smells like home— freshly baked bread, a hint of lavender, and that comforting, warm scent of wood and dust. As I make my way further into the house, I find my mom wiping down the kitchen, and I furrow my brow at her.

"Ma, what are you doing?" I say softly, stepping closer.

"Hi, sweetie, I needed to move around. I was going crazy just sitting."

"You're supposed to be resting." I gently take the rag from her and try to lead her back to the living room.

"I feel like I'm always *resting* Jameson." She sighs.

"As you should be, considering you're going through *chemo.*"

She waves me off like what I'm saying is ridiculous.

That's the reason I came back, though. She was diagnosed with stage three ovarian cancer, and even though the doctors gave her a somewhat positive prognosis I just knew I needed to be back to help her. She has my dad, but they live on a large property with a lot of farm animals. Even though my dad and I are barely speaking I know he needed the help as well.

Once I have my mom settled on her recliner, I go back into the kitchen to get her some water.

"What else do you need, Ma?" I ask after I hand her the glass.

"My son to get married and stop worrying about me so much."

"Glad to hear your sense of humor isn't affected by your medication."

"I'm fine, I can get whatever I need myself, and you look like you could use a nap. Rough night?"

I shake my head. "No, it was fine, I just prefer sleeping in a real bed compared to a cot."

"Understandable. Go get some sleep, then you can cook dinner tonight since you want to be so helpful."

I chuckle before giving her a kiss on the cheek. "Bye, Ma." I head out to walk down to the guest house on the property that's been mine since I was a teenager and wanted more space. I had to renovate it quite a bit, which my parents told me if I did then I could have it as my room. There wasn't a better motivator as a sixteen year old kid who had dreams of sneaking girls in and throwing secret parties.

Both of which I did once it was done, of course, but now it's just nice to not have to constantly face my dad's disapproving glare.

After my nap I work on some projects around the property, cleaning the horse stalls, and making note of the various repairs that need to be done to the barn. I feed the cows and goats before heading back to the main house to do what Mom said and make her dinner.

I cooked some simple barbeque chicken, mashed potatoes, and vegetables. Mom tries to encourage conversation between Dad and me, but it goes nowhere. Just as it always does.

Dad grunts in response to me and doesn't ask anything about my life. I can see how it wears on Mom, and I wish it could be different, but I can't force him to forgive me or at least pretend for her. I've tried.

After dinner I realize I left my bag at the station because I was so tired I completely spaced out. I know I should just wait to get it on my next shift, but it has my toothbrush and toothpaste. I can't stand the feeling of going to sleep without brushing my teeth, and I don't have a backup.

My parents might, but at this point I would rather drive back into town than deal with the possibility of an awkward confrontation with Dad again.

With that, I go to my truck and drive back to the station. It's already pitch-black outside with the street barely lit by the dim street lamps.

I do my best to sneak inside without drawing attention to myself because I know the rest of the guys will give me shit for coming back. They know how meticulous I can be about things and admitting this would be the perfect opportunity for them to give me shit.

Luckily, I make it out without anyone seeing me. As I'm walking back to my truck, I see someone I don't recognize standing by an old looking Jeep in one of the parking spaces at

Trish's. That must be the woman Parker was talking about. I'm about to get into my truck when I notice she's just standing at the driver's side door, and it looks like her head is against the window.

I can tell something's wrong, so I go over to check on her because I doubt she wants to be standing in an empty parking lot in the dark in a place she doesn't know.

"Hey," I call softly as I approach to not scare her.

She lifts her head before turning to face me, and I feel like I just got smacked in the face. I don't know what I was expecting, but it wasn't to come across the most beautiful woman I've ever laid eyes on. I'm not a dramatic man, either. She's extraordinary. Her chocolate brown hair whips around her shoulders. Her eyes shine with unshed tears. Plush lips, straight nose. She looks younger than me, probably mid-twenties, but she looks tired, and not just from lack of sleep. There's something about her that just seems exhausted, and it makes me want to wrap her in my arms and give her everything she needs from here on out.

The compulsion is so powerful it almost knocks me back. I've been attracted to women before, obviously, I've dated in the past. But it has never felt so strong, so potent, and it makes me want to shut it down because it scares me at the same time.

"H-hi," she stutters as I approach, and her voice is almost melodic, and wraps around me with just the one simple word.

"Are you okay?" I ask once I'm closer to her. Even in the dim light I can see that her eyes are green, the shade like a dark moss, so unique and perfect. Just like her.

"Yeah…well, okay no." She sighs. "I locked my keys in my car."

She sounds so defeated, and it makes my chest ache.

"Well," I set my bag down on the ground, "it's a good thing I'm a professional locksmith."

Her head snaps up as she looks at me. "You are?"

I chuckle. "No, but I do know how to get keys out of a locked car."

She looks at me skeptically. "Please don't break the window. I know it's an old car, but I love this thing."

"Don't worry, I won't need to break any windows."

"Is this some sort of trick and you're going to rob or kidnap me?"

I'm taken aback at her question. "Is that something that's common where you come from?"

"Considering I'm from Los Angeles...yes."

I nod. Big city, impossibly high crime rate. Makes sense that she's uneasy about a random guy approaching her claiming to help.

"Well, welcome to Amity, we tend to keep the robbing and kidnapping to a minimum."

That actually earns me a light laugh from her, and I immediately want to hear more of it.

"I'm Jameson," I introduce, mostly because I really need to know her name. I stretch my hand out for her to take, which she does. I try to control my reaction to the feeling of her perfectly small fingers wrapping around mine, and how perfectly our hands fit together for those few moments.

"Sutton."

Of course her name is beautiful. Everything about her is.

"Nice to meet you, Sutton." I test out her name on my tongue, and it feels so right. I want to keep saying it. I give her a smile before remembering that she needs my help. "Let me go get a couple tools, and I'll be right back."

She worries her lip, and I can tell she doesn't want to be left alone, despite what I told her about being safe here.

"I'll be back in less than a minute, there are tools at the fire station right there." I point to the building.

"Won't you get in trouble for stealing tools from there?"

I chuckle. "They can try."

I leave it at that as I jog over to grab the tools I'll need without getting the attention of anyone inside, knowing if any of them hear me, I won't have Sutton all to myself anymore. Luckily, they all must be eating or cleaning or sleeping because I'm able to slip out again without drawing attention to myself.

Sutton has her jacket wrapped around herself tightly as she looks around nervously when I come back. The cool ocean wind is strong right now, and I feel bad for not considering how cold she must be standing out here.

Shrugging off my own jacket I hand it to her.

"No, thanks, I'm okay." She waves me off.

"I'd feel better if you took it." I hold it open for her so she can easily slip her arms inside.

She hesitates before realizing I'm not going to give up, and lets me slide the coat onto her small frame. She's drowning in the fabric, and for some reason a possessive side of me rears its head at the sight.

Once I've noticed she isn't shivering, I get to work on getting her keys out. It doesn't take me long as I slip the slim-jim tool down into her door, and the lock gives easily. I open the door, and grab her keys, holding them out to her. Our hands graze as I hand them over.

"Thank you so much." She hugs her keys to her chest.

"You're welcome. I'll give you my phone number in case you need help again." It's an excuse, and a pretty weak one, but I want some reason to talk to her more.

"Oh, um, that's okay. I won't do this again, I promise."

Ouch.

"Well, how about you have it just to have it then?" I smile.

Sutton starts to remove my jacket from her shoulders. "Thank you for your help, but I'm not looking for anything right now."

I stop her before the article of clothing has slid down her arms. "You're not looking for friends in your new town?"

She looks at me skeptically. "I don't think I could be friends with you."

"Suit yourself." I shrug. "I'm a great friend, you'll see."

I turn to head back toward the station to return the tools.

"Bye, Jameson," I hear her call from behind me and it makes me smile.

"Bye, Sutton." I don't turn around as I give a small wave, knowing she still has my jacket, and that she doesn't believe I'm going to keep trying to be her friend.

Yeah, sure. Just a friend.

CHAPTER 3

Sutton

"SHUT UP, VERN!"

I glance over to Jerry Lee who's just squawked that phrase for the third time today. The first time I wasn't sure if I heard him right. The second time I began to wonder if he was saying "Vern". Now, the third time I'm definitely sure I've heard him right.

"Who's Vern?" I call out to Trish who's cleaning her station in the other room.

She walks in, making the Shih Tzu puppy on my table start to wag her tail aggressively in excitement. I hold on to her so she doesn't end up flying off the table toward Trish.

"No idea. He's said that since I got him."

"Weird."

Jerry Lee also barks. Yes. Barks. Like a dog.

That I've just assumed comes from living at a grooming salon, but it still doesn't cease to amaze me, and I really want to see what else he can say.

"Oh, look at that, it must be truck washing day," Trish says with a nod toward the window.

"What?" I ask, turning to see what she's looking at, and then I see it.

"I told you about the view here, pretty nice, isn't it?"

The firetruck is pulled out onto the driveway of the station, and jumping out of the front seat is none other than the man I met the other day when I locked my keys in my car.

Jameson.

I watch his large frame as he walks around the truck, along with four other people carrying various supplies. My eyes can't leave him. No matter how much I tell myself to look away, to stop staring. I just can't. He's wearing a navy T-shirt that hugs his large arms, and the back has "AFD" on it, assumingely for Amity Fire Department.

His back is to me as he gets to work, and I continue to watch the way his muscles bunch along his back as he cleans the truck. His shirt is tight against his body, and it makes me wish it could disappear. I could tell when he came up to me, he's a big guy. He has to be about six foot two. He's muscular, but not in a body-builder way, more like his strength is derived from hard labor.

Jameson's arms stretch up as he continues to work on the truck, and I feel like I'm in a trance. Hypnotized. I can't stop watching the way his body is moving, and imagining how it would move against mine.

A loud bark knocks me out of my daydream of wandering hands, sweaty bodies, and loud moans. I remember where I am, and the little dog on my table is just looking up at me. The bark was courtesy of Jerry Lee, who has now flown into this room with me.

"You wanted to come stare at that hot guy, Jameson, too?" I ask him. He just barks in response.

As much as I try to focus on grooming the dogs on my schedule, I can't go more than a minute before I'm staring out the window again. Eventually they're done cleaning the truck, and I watch as Jameson climbs back inside to put the truck back inside the station.

I wasn't lying when I told him I'm not looking for anything right now. I'm really not. Getting involved with a man at this point in my life isn't on my list of priorities, especially while I'm still reeling from everything that happened back home. I don't need to become involved with anyone and create any more complications if I could ever bring myself to trust someone else. No, I'm more than content being on my own with just my dog.

That's also how I know I couldn't be friends with Jameson. He's too good looking. Seemingly too nice, which is probably just an act. That's been my experience, anyway. They're always nice in the beginning.

My distraction is finally gone, and I can finally focus back on my actual job. I'm finishing up the haircut on the Shih Tzu when the front door opens.

Jerry Lee flies out to return to his perch on the cage.

"Shut up, Vern!"

I smother my laughter. I'm sure at some point that might get annoying, but as of right now it's pretty funny.

After I set the Shih Tzu down, I go to greet the person who just came in. It's a woman, probably in her early thirties. She's pretty; blonde hair, blue eyes. She looks like someone who I would've expected to see coming into the salon back in L.A. She looks like she's done up enough to walk down the red carpet at a fancy event, not Main Street in this small town.

"Hey, how can I help you?" I ask, wiping my hands down my jeans, self-conscious at how much of a mess I look compared to this woman.

"Oh, hi. Where's Trish?" she asks, giving me a once over, and I stand taller because I refuse to let her think she's going to intimidate me.

"She's bathing a dog right now; I can help you."

"Are you new?"

"Here? Yes. To dog grooming? No."

"Hm." She seems to consider me for a moment. "Fine. Have you ever groomed an Australian Goldendoodle before?"

It physically pains me to hold back the eye roll I want to let loose. Australian Goldendoodles are not a real breed. They're marketed as "mini" goldendoodles, and breeders charge obscenely for them. They're a mutt. Which is fine, I have nothing against mixed breeds. But I do have something against lying breeders. In my experience, the people that believe those breeders and act like they're better than everyone else even though their dog is the same as a mix from the shelter. It's frustrating.

"Yes, I've groomed Goldendoodles before." I try to keep the bite out of my tone, but it's getting harder by the second.

"Okay, but my breeder has very specific instructions on how to care for these dogs, and I think it should be Trish...no offense."

I smile wider, and I probably look crazed. "I'm sure I can handle it, and if I can't then I won't touch your dog again."

She purses her lips before reluctantly saying, "Fine."

"What's your name and phone number so I can call you when she's done?"

"Her name is Daisy, and mine is Mallory." She rattles off her phone number so fast I struggle to write it down. I hope Trish actually knows it because I'm not confident that I gathered it correctly.

"Not too short, I just want a puppy cut," she says, and I feel my eye twitch.

A puppy cut is not a specific haircut. It just means the same length all over, but it could be a puppy cut shaved bald or half an inch all over. That. Means. Nothing.

"So just a trim all over?" I ask, widening my smile to painful levels.

"Yeah, a puppy cut."

"Okay, I'll call you when she's all finished."

I can tell Mallory wants to say more and doesn't want to leave her dog with me, but she finally decides to walk out. As soon as the door is shut, I drop my fake smile and look down at the dog at my feet. Daisy is cute, she's wagging her tail looking up at me, almost like she knows her mom is insane too.

"Come on, Daisy, let's get you all cleaned up for your crazy mom."

"Crazy mom. Shut up, Vern!" Jerry Lee calls from his perch.

Okay, so maybe Jerry Lee is annoying.

CHAPTER 4

Jameson

"DID you see Mallory leaving Trish's place? She's looking good," Parker says with a pointed look in my direction as I finish my last round of checking the truck.

"Go for it, bud. She'll eat you alive."

"I wouldn't mind her mouth all over me." He winks.

I shake my head. She's ten years older than him and my ex. We dated for about a year when I was in my twenties. We broke up when I moved to Florida. It wasn't that serious, and I never saw it going in that direction, so if Parker thinks he can handle her he can be my guest.

While Parker continues to talk about how good Mallory looks to anyone who will listen, my mind is stuck on the mysterious brunette that just moved into town. I can't help but look out the one window that faces the little grooming shop and think about what she might be doing right now.

I want some sort of excuse to talk to her again, anything that will give me a reason to hear her voice one more time. Maybe I'll pretend as if I forgot to ask her something, or that I need her opinion on something ridiculous. Obviously, our first meeting was completely by chance, and I want it to happen again. I don't have a dog, so the most obvious idea is out of the question. I mean I could get a dog; I have been wanting one for a while.

"What do you think, Jameson?" Parker's voice pulls me from my thoughts.

"About what?"

Parker and Dave chuckle, both clearly amused by how distracted I clearly was.

"How long until Mallory is throwing herself at you again?" Dave clarifies.

"Why are you two gossiping like teenagers?" I ask, not wanting to give into this useless conversation.

I zone out whatever they're saying once again when movement in the window catches my eye. It's Sutton, and it's clear that she's focused on whatever it is she's doing at this moment. Without much more thought I'm moving toward the door of the firehouse.

"I'll be right back, guys," I call out to no one in particular.

"What are you doing?" Dave questions.

"Where are you going?" Parker presses.

"You can't just leave in the middle of shift!" Jo hollers.

They call after me, but I ignore them. I'm just going next door for a second.

I step in the building I've never stepped foot in before, looking around for the new mysterious woman.

"Hi." I look around for who greeted me, and see a white bird perched near the door.

"Hi?"

"One second," another voice calls out. This one is certainly human.

I look back at the bird; he turns his head like he's examining me before he barks.

"Sorry, how can I–" She cuts herself off as soon as I turn to look at her.

"Hi again." I smile.

Sutton looks around like she's expecting someone else to appear, but I think it's just the two of us. And the bird.

"What—" She clears her throat. "What're you doing here?"

"I'm actually here for professional matters," I lie.

"Professional matters?"

I nod. "I have to do some fire safety checks; did Trish not tell you one of us would be by for this?"

She shakes her head.

"It shouldn't take me long, unless you'd prefer I come back when Trish is here?" I offer, though I'm holding my breath.

"No, no, it's fine. Do what you need to do." She waves me off.

"*Shut up, Vern,*" the bird squawks.

"What did he just say?" I ask Sutton who looks like she's trying to hold back her laughter.

She just shrugs before turning and walking down a short hallway to another room. I pretend to busy myself with checking things around the shop. I have absolutely no real reason for being over here other than trying to talk to Sutton, so once I've spent a fair amount of time in the other rooms to not seem too obvious, I enter the room she's in.

While I pretend to check outlets and lights around this room, I catch her subtly trying to look at me. I smother my smile before breaking the silence between us.

"So, how're you liking it here so far?" I ask, glancing over at her as she brushes out a scruffy looking dog on the table.

"It's fine. Quiet."

"Do you like the quiet?"

She shrugs. "I guess."

I walk a little closer to her and lean against the wall next to where she's working. "Have you thought more about having a friend in town?"

She snorts out a small laugh, and it's extremely adorable. "I'm not against friends here."

"You just don't want to be *my* friend," I taunt.

She turns slightly to look at me, her green eyes locking on me with intensity. "I said I don't think I could be friends with you, not that I don't want to."

"Sounds like the same thing to me."

"It's not." She turns back to the dog, taking some scissors and cutting around the dog's legs.

"Then why not give it a shot," I try.

"Are you done with your check?" she asks, ignoring me.

"Almost. Can I see your keys?'

She furrows her brows at me. "Why?'

"It's the last thing I need to check."

She opens a drawer behind her and jingles her keys in front of me.

"Just had to make sure you weren't going to need me to rescue you again." I wink at her before she rolls her eyes.

"I'll make sure to only lock keys in my car when you're not around," she sasses.

"Sounds like a good reason to have my number, then."

"Goodbye, Jameson." She shakes her head, going back to the dog she's grooming.

"Hot guy, Jameson," the bird says from the perch in the room; I didn't even notice when he flew in here.

Sutton's face immediately flushes, and I bite back my smile.

"Talking about me?" I ask the flustered woman who's avoiding eye contact.

"He said that before I started working here."

"Sure, he did. Bye Sutton." As I'm closing the door behind me, I hear her scolding the bird.

I hold back my laughter until I'm almost back at the firehouse where I'm greeted with curious stares, but I refuse to answer any of their questions as to what I was doing. It doesn't matter, and besides, I don't even think I would know how to answer.

CHAPTER 5

Sutton

"I'M GOING to open every door and window in this place and let you fly free, Jerry Lee." I can't even appreciate my accidental rhyme as I threaten the bird who happily flies back to his perch by the front door after Jameson leaves.

As I try to focus on grooming the dog still on my table, I can't shake the interaction I just had. Especially the mortifying ending. I finish up grooming Daisy, figuring it's as good as she's going to get with what her mom was wanting. I send her a quick text as I clean up my area while Daisy runs around the shop.

The front door opens, and when I look up, I see it's Trish walking in.

"Hey, that guy Jameson came over here to do his fire check safety thing," I tell her while I continue sweeping up fur.

"The what?"

"I don't know, he said you knew about it."

"Jameson did?"

I stop sweeping, leaning on the broom to look up at her smirking face.

"Yes?" I say slowly, not understanding why she's questioning this.

"Interesting, what exactly was he checking?"

"Uh, I don't know I didn't watch him."

She just nods without saying much else, her expression unreadable. There's something in her eyes—hesitation, maybe, or something deeper that I can't quite put my finger on. The silence between us stretches, not exactly uncomfortable but weighted, as if there's more she wants to say but won't.

"*Hot guy, Jameson,*" Jerry Lee pipes in, and I strangle the broom handle as Trish smiles in my direction.

"He's a good guy," Trish says simply.

"Oh, I'm not—"

She holds her hand up to silence me before giving me a small smile and walking toward her own station on the other side of the salon.

I go back to my task of cleaning up my area. When I'm dumping the last bit of fur into the garbage by the window I look up and see the garage to the fire station is open, and Jameson's out there with a younger looking guy. He looks like he's explaining something to him, and I can't help but watch.

Jameson's large arms are folded across his broad chest, his baseball cap flipped backwards on his head. He stands at least a few inches above the younger man, and his perfectly straight teeth show as he smiles through whatever speech he's giving.

I'm so lost in my distraction that I don't even hear when the front door opens or notice when Daisy starts running toward it. The only thing that pulls me out of my haze is the voice speaking to me.

"Hello?" I snap up and look over to where Mallory is now standing in the front while Daisy dances around her feet.

"Hi, sorry, I was...sorry." I shake my head while grabbing my card reader that plugs into my phone.

"Checking out the view over there?" she asks with a smirk. "Hard to not miss, huh?"

I shake my head. "No, I was just cleaning up. How does she look?" I bring the conversation back to her dog.

Mallory crouches down to examine the excited puppy who won't stay still long enough for her to get a good look. "She's decent."

"Glad you approve, it'll just be fifty today," I tell her, entering the information into my phone so she can pay.

She hands over her card, and I start to run it when she starts talking again.

"Looks like Jameson's working today."

I give a small hum of agreeance while focusing on the phone.

"He and I used to date."

I can tell she's trying to get a reaction from me, and I have to work to hide the pang of jealousy I'm feeling though, I don't know why. I have nothing to be jealous of, the man is at least ten years older than me and clearly has a past. I'm not even in his present or future so it doesn't matter.

"Then he left, and I didn't want to do long distance. He was so torn up over our breakup, but I just couldn't do it. Maybe now that he's back, I'll give him another chance."

I finally finish ringing her up, handing her card back while trying to hide the slight tremble of my hands. I refuse to acknowledge anything she's saying to me.

"Thank you for coming in, I hope you have a good rest of your day," I say through a fake smile.

She looks me up and down, her gaze slow and deliberate, and I can't help but shift uncomfortably under the weight of it. I know I look like a mess—disheveled hair, rumpled clothes, exhaustion written all over me—but somehow, I feel even worse under her judgmental stare. "Let me know if you want to meet up for coffee sometime. I can fill you in on all the info you need in this town."

With that as her parting words, she scoops up her dog before leaving.

I will most definitely be passing on that invitation. I think back to what Jameson said about not wanting friends in my new town. It's not that I don't want friends, it's that I don't think I can trust anyone to let them in like that.

Trish is nice. I don't think we're necessarily friends, but I'm not completely alone here. Which is also why I quickly finish cleaning up the salon so I can get home to Bennet. I've been here all day, and I know he's going to need to go outside.

As I'm leaving, I look over at the fire station without much thought, and see Jameson is still outside with a few other people. He catches me looking and waves. I feel my cheeks warm as I return the wave with a small one of my own before getting into my Jeep and taking off.

Bennet greets me with a wagging tail as I walk through the front door. I immediately open up the back door for him, and he runs out to do his business. The cool ocean air whips at my hair, and I can't help the feelings that seem to take over as I let the reality of what my life is crash over me.

I left everything I've ever known to come to this place where I don't know anyone or anything to start fresh. But that was the point, wasn't it? A fresh start. A chance to escape the past that had unraveled so brutally before me. The people closest to me betrayed me in a way I never would have expected, so trusting anyone after that is not something that will come easily.

Walking into my parents' house. My house. Seeing my best friend, and...I let out a loud sound of disgust. Bennet looks up at me like he's wondering what I'm doing. I wave him off.

"Don't worry about me, bud, do what you need to do."

He goes back to sniffing to find the perfect spot to go to the bathroom and I just look up at the sky. Everything will work out. I have to believe that. I didn't walk away from everything just to crumble now. I don't need any of them in my life, not after that.

CHAPTER 6

Jameson

I'M EXHAUSTED at the end of my shift, but I need to go to the grocery store and do some stuff around my parent's property before I'm going to get a chance to sleep. The first thing I do when I walk in the store is grab an energy drink out of the small fridge before I grab the few items I need for myself and others for my parents.

I push the cart through the aisles, gulping down the energy drink as I go. I turn down another aisle, and that's when I see her holding a basket in the crook of her arm. She's chewing at her thumb while staring at the shelves in front of her.

Smiling, I watch her for a beat before approaching. I just saw her yesterday but seeing her again so soon has an unfamiliar feeling bubbling up.

"We've gotta stop meeting like this," I joke.

Sutton jumps slightly before turning toward me, a smile she tries to suppress on her lips. "Stalker, much?"

I chuckle and turn to pretend like I'm interested in the wall of canned vegetables she was staring at before. "In a town this small, you don't really need to stalk anyone."

She quietly hums in agreement before grabbing two cans of corn, then turning to walk away.

"Sutton?" She turns back to look at me.

"Since this is the third random encounter we've had, I think it's time I get your number."

She smirks. "Pretty sure it's only the second since yesterday doesn't count."

"Why not?"

She just smiles. "Goodbye, Jameson."

I finish up my shopping without running into her again, and I have a feeling that's because she didn't want me to. I'm too tired to dwell too much on it as the caffeine from the drink I consumed isn't waking me up like I was hoping.

"Ma?" I call out as I balance all the shopping bags on my arms.

"In here," she calls back without any other clue.

My mother greets me with a wide smile that's quickly replaced by a disapproving glare as she eyes the bags I set on the counter.

"We can shop for ourselves, you know?" She folds her arms across her chest.

"And I like helping, which you know," I tell her as I start putting the items away.

"And I like being independent, which *you* know." The look she gives me makes me feel like she wants to burn a hole in my brain. I just shake my head as I continue to put the groceries away, despite her effort to help me. "Jameson, I can see how tired you are, go get some rest."

"I'm fine."

"You're always fine. Listen to your mother for once."

I chuckle, reaching around her to grab the last of the items off the counter, kissing her cheek as I turn back to the fridge. "I always listen to you, Ma."

"Your sweet talking gets you nowhere with me, and you know it," she scolds.

I finish putting the groceries away, then glance around the kitchen to see if she might need help with anything else. When my eyes land on hers again, she's playfully glaring at me.

"Do any of the animals need to be fed?" I ask.

"No."

"Any cleaning in the barn?'

"No."

"Lawn needing—"

"No."

"Anything—"

"No."

"Ma—"

"No."

I can't help the laugh I let out at her insistence. I know there are things that need to be done around the property. Dad can't do them all, and despite how Ma tries to help, I know it wears her out. She can't do as much as she would like me to believe she does.

Holding my hands up in surrender, I tell her, "Fine, I'll go rest for a little."

She nods her approval before I reluctantly leave to go to my own small house. As I'm walking the short distance, I see Dad out on one of the riding mowers, but he's just sitting on it without actually moving. He looks like he's staring out at something in the distance, but when I try to figure out what he could be looking at all I see is the vast landscape of the property. Nothing in particular, just the land.

I wonder what he could be thinking about. What's going through his mind that made him stop and just...stare. I watch him for a few moments, wondering if I should make my way out there to see if he's okay. Maybe offer him some help if he's stuck or ask if the mower broke down on him.

Just as I'm about to walk over to check on him he seems to come out of his trance, starting up the mower without a problem and continuing with what he was doing. I debate meeting up with him at the barn to ask what that was about but decide to put off the potential fight for another day.

Plus, I really am exhausted. As soon as my head hits my pillow, I'm asleep.

When I wake up it's dark out, and I know I've slept longer than I meant to and now my whole schedule is thrown off. This isn't the first time this has happened and won't be the last. I stretch out my stiff limbs as I get out of bed.

I get dressed, readying myself for what has become routine tending to the property, just as I always do. It's the perfect time because Ma isn't around to yell at me to stop helping, and Dad isn't around to fight with me about anything else.

Since Amity is so close to the ocean, it's always on the colder side, especially at night, no matter what time of year it is. So, I throw on my jacket once I'm dressed and head out to the barn. It's around midnight, and the only light outside is from the moon and the stars. I've walked this entire property so many times over my life I can do it with my eyes closed.

The barn illuminates with the motion sensored lights, and a couple of the horses shuffle around in their stalls. Ma used to give horseback riding lessons to children before she got sick. Growing up, I would help out, but my real passion was barrel racing. I spent my time training and working with other riders whenever they wanted to learn. We still have all the horses because she couldn't part with them and swears they have therapeutic powers for her, even though she doesn't ride anymore.

I approach Sandy, Ma's main horse for her lessons. She was born here when I was young, and we raised her. She's twenty-eight now, and her age is starting to show, or maybe Ma is right, and they just have some special connection. She's always said that about her and Sandy. She said she could feel when Sandy was sick, and maybe it's the same the other way around.

The Palomino mare huffs as I approach. She already knows about the peppermints I've got stashed in my pocket because I give her one every time I come out here.

"Hey girl," I say with my hand outstretched toward her.

She takes the offered peppermint from my hand before I rub her nose as she chews on it. "I'm back to help out. I want to help take care of you all."

She huffs again like she understands, and I'd like to think she's thankful I'm here. I give the other horses treats as I make my way down to the biggest stall on the end where my old barrel horse stays. Juniper, my Appaloosa, nods her head at me as soon as I'm in view and I chuckle, handing over a peppermint, rubbing her nose as she chews.

I've missed riding horses, either leisurely around the property or from the pure rush of adrenaline that comes with a barrel race. It's been too long since I've felt that, too long since I've let myself sink into the familiar comfort of the saddle. One day soon, I'm going to have to get back on a horse again. Running my hand through the fluffy fur that's starting to shed off Juniper I get an idea to try and spend more time with Sutton. We'll just have to see if she'll go for it.

CHAPTER 7

Sutton

MY PHONE RINGS, and I look at the screen, scoff at the name, flip it over, and put it down while getting back to grooming the excitable yorkie on my table.

"There's no way I'm talking to her, no I'm not," I coo at the little dog currently wiggling her butt at me.

My ex-best friend seems to be switching off with my parents on who's trying to get a hold of me. I refuse to talk to any of them after what happened. I need to process, and even then, I'm not sure I'll ever really understand or see them the same.

I continue to run my clippers on the dog's coat while she tries to give me kisses and jump onto my shoulder, and I chuckle at her persistence. Jerry Lee has been fairly quiet all morning, but I realize now he may have been sleeping. Because when he suddenly starts barking, I just shake my head.

"Who's going to tell him he's not a dog?" I ask the yorkie. She tries to sneak a wet kiss again, and I laugh.

The door to the salon opens, but I don't think it's Trish, because she's not scheduled with any clients today, and the next dog on my schedule isn't due to be dropped off for another hour. Immediately, I think it's this dog's mom coming early. I walk around the table, making sure the dog, who thinks she's a jumping bean, doesn't go flying off as I greet whoever it is.

"Hot guy," Jerry Lee squawks and I freeze. He's only said that when it's—

"Good morning, Sutton," Jameson greets with a wide smile as he comes into view.

My mouth goes dry at the sight of him here again. My eyes rake over his distressed jeans, navy T-shirt, and backwards cap on his head. Everyone knows that is every woman's kryptonite and how dare he come in here looking like that. He has to know what he's doing.

"Shut up, Vern," Jerry Lee's squawk pulls me out of my frozen state, and I attempt to fix my face to hide the fact that I'm probably practically drooling over this man who just walked in.

"Uh, good morning. How can I help you?"

"I actually had a question for you." He smiles, and I expect his question to be asking for my number again. I don't know if I have the strength to turn him down again. Especially with him looking like that, even though I know I should. I'm not here to fall in bed with the first local who's nice to me.

"Sure, what's your question?" I try to sound cheery, putting on my best customer service voice.

"Do you only groom dogs or do you do other animals?"

My face scrunches up in a grimace. This man better not ruin the sweet image I have of him in my head and ask me about grooming him.

"Uh, only dogs and cats. I'll trim bunny's nails though." I give him a skeptical look, waiting for the other shoe to drop. Or punch line to this inevitable joke.

"What about horses?"

I look around, down to the yorkie, and then up to Jameson. "There's no way a horse would fit in here."

He laughs, it's deep, guttural, and sends a wave of pleasure between my thighs, where I should not be feeling anything for anyone right now. "No, the horse wouldn't come here, you would have to come to the ranch."

"Oh." It's all I can say, my cheeks flaring slightly at my initial thought and how dumb I probably seem. "I don't...um, I wouldn't know how to groom a horse."

"Doesn't seem much different than grooming a dog, just a bit bigger." He lets out a small laugh, almost like he's nervous. Especially when he takes off his hat, running his hand through his dark hair before replacing the hat back on his head.

I shake my head. "I don't know if I could do that, I'm sorry. You could ask Trish when she's here, maybe she will."

"I'd rather it be you." He smiles.

"Why's that?"

"Hot guy, Jameson," Jerry Lee calls out, and I drop my head to hide the red spreading onto my cheeks.

"Well, for one, you taught him that." He chuckles.

"I didn't. He said that when I started here, someone else taught him," I insist.

"Right." His tone is disbelieving, and I roll my eyes. "But I think you would do well. The horses are sweet, and I can pay double whatever you would want to charge me."

I narrow my eyes at him, the persistence has me feeling like there's an ulterior motive hiding somewhere in his words. On one hand he seems sweet and genuine, but on the other hand he could be planning to kidnap me and hold me hostage on his ranch.

Stranger danger and all that.

"I don't think I can do that, I'm sorry. If you have a dog that needs groomed though, you're more than welcome to bring them to me here." I smile widely, though it's fake.

"I don't have a dog, but I was thinking of getting one. Is there a breed you'd recommend?"

"Um..." Again, I look down at the yorkie who's sat down and is looking up at me wiggling her tail like she's extremely enter-tained by all of this. "I would say get whatever dog speaks to you. There's no better bond or love from a dog."

He nods. "I'll remember that. Think about the offer, though, because it'll stand."

"Okay," I agree, though I don't know if I could ever groom a horse, or what that even means.

"Have a good day, Sutton." He smiles as he leaves, and I watch, though the second he's out the door I let out a long breath I didn't realize I was holding.

Looking down at the dog again, I shake my head. "Do you know what that was about?"

I wish she could answer and give her two cents on what she just witnessed, but instead, she's jumping up trying to give me kisses again and I laugh. "Okay, let's get you finished so you can smother your mommy with your kisses."

AFTER I GET HOME from work, I go check the mail and see an extremely tall woman with dark blonde hair at the bank of mailboxes. Walking up, I smile. "Hi."

She looks up, doesn't smile, but doesn't frown either, her face remains passive. "Hey."

"I'm Sutton, I just moved here," I greet, attempting to socialize with someone other than the good-looking firefighter or my boss.

"Bailey," she introduces.

"Nice to meet you." I smile wider.

"You too." She nods, her lips spreading in a small smile before walking toward a house across the street from mine.

Hm. Not sure if that could turn into a friendship, but at least I know one neighbor. I'm looking through my mail as I walk back and see there's something addressed to a "Bailey Collee." I debate bringing it over to the house where I saw her walk to. I decide I should; it could be a good way to break the ice a bit more.

I knock hesitantly and when she opens the door, she's frowning.

"Sorry, this was accidentally delivered to my box," I tell her, holding out the envelope.

She looks down at it, then me, taking it carefully from my grasp. "Thanks."

I nod, then turn away to go back home because she doesn't seem like the talkative type, and I feel like I've already overstepped with her somehow. She seems even more closed off than me, and I don't want to piss her off.

"Sutton," she calls out, and I stop, turning back to face her. "We could hang out sometime. If you want."

I hear the hesitance in her voice, but I smile at the effort. "That sounds great. I work at the grooming salon down the road, but I'm usually done by five most days."

"Sounds good, we'll plan something." She turns her mouth up in the slightest smile.

I hear a door shut next door to her and turn to see a large man with a frown on his face walking toward his car parked in the driveway. When I turn back to Bailey she's scowling in his direction. I can't help but think there's a story there that I would love to know more about.

"I can't wait," I say, pulling her attention away from the neighbor who is driving off.

She nods, and we go our separate ways. I'm glad to possibly be making a friend while also hoping I'm not getting in the middle of any drama. I left all of that back home; I came here to restart my life away from the toxicity I found myself in.

It's why I'm not entertaining Jameson in any way. Any sort of relationship has drama written all over it.

CHAPTER 8

Jameson

MY INITIAL PLAN TO spend more time with Sutton didn't exactly work out like I thought it would. Which is okay, it was a long shot since she clearly hasn't been around horses before, and I get her being hesitant.

So, I choose to take her up on her other idea. I've wanted a dog for a while, but back in Florida I lived alone and worked too much. I knew it wouldn't be fair to the dog or to myself. Even now I work too much, but I know my mom will enjoy having a dog around. Just not a puppy, which is why I drive down to the local animal shelter.

I'm greeted instantly when I walk in. "What're you looking for today?" the friendly older woman at the front desk asks.

"I'm hoping to adopt a dog," I tell her.

She chuckles. "Well we have plenty of those. Did you have any specifics in mind? Breed, age or anything like that?"

I shake my head. "Nothing like that. Who's been here the longest?"

She smiles widely. "That would be Duke, I'll take you to meet him."

The woman leads me to the kennels where they line both sides of the aisle, each with at least one dog in it, there's a litter of puppies with their mom, a couple bonded pairs, and my heart breaks at every one of their faces looking out at me. I want to take them all home, they don't deserve to be stuck in a place like this.

We finally reach a kennel toward the end, and the nameplate is a laminated piece of paper with "Duke" written in dry erase marker. It's faded and it goes to show just how long he's been here.

"Here he is, he's been here for about eight months, he's a blue nose Pit, ten years old, and the sweetest boy," she introduces.

The bulky dog has a large head, and with his mouth open and panting, it looks like he's smiling. He wags his tail just slightly, and I already know I can't leave him here even a minute longer after he's already been waiting for a home this long.

"Why has he been here so long?" I ask.

"Well, he has a slight issue with his...um...male part."

I furrow my brow, and look at her, questioningly.

"When he gets excited, sometimes it gets...stuck."

"Stuck?" I cough.

"Yes, it doesn't go back to how it should and when it's really bad the vet has to fix it surgically."

I have so many questions, but I need them both to know that he's coming home with me. His issue doesn't worry me, if he has to go to the vet for a penis surgery, I'll make sure it happens.

"I can handle that," I tell her, turning back toward Duke who is still looking up at me with his wide smile. "You want to come home with me, bud?"

🦅

DUKE and I get back to my house, and my first order of business is introducing him to Ma. We stopped at the pet store on the way home to get him everything he needs. I may have overloaded on toys and bones for him, but he was stuck in that cage for eight months, and he deserves to live the rest of his life spoiled beyond belief. And that's exactly what I plan on doing.

"Ma?" I call out, walking through the front door.

"In here," she calls back from a little further in the house.

I follow her voice and find her in her bedroom with photo albums open in front of her, and stacks of photos she's putting in them next to her.

"Hi, sweetie. Oh, who's your friend?" she asks as soon as she sees Duke. I keep him on the leash because I don't want him to jump up on the bed and ruin her project.

"This is Duke, my new dog." I smile.

"What a sweet boy." She smiles, slowly getting off the bed.

When I try to help her, she waves me off and slaps my hand playfully.

"Aw, thanks Ma," I joke, which earns me a playful glare.

"I meant Duke. You're about to be replaced by him you know," she teases right back, and I act offended.

"I'm hurt. If I had known it was that easy to replace me, I would've gotten a dog years ago."

"Oh hush." She leans over to pet Duke, but I don't like the way she's hunched over. It isn't good for her back. I know that if I try to say anything to her, she'll just get mad at me, so I bite my tongue.

"I hope it's okay for him to stay here with you when I'm working."

"Of course, he's welcome any time. In fact, he can just stay here when you're not working, too."

"Ma," I scold jokingly, and she laughs.

"You're over here hovering over me whenever you're home anyway, I'm sure he'll be with you."

She's not wrong about that. Though, I try to make excuses to be here around her rather than just being here to check on her, which is what it really is. Plus, I just want to help. I want her to know I'm here to support her, since I have been so absent for the last ten years. Even though we talked often, it's different to actually be here.

"I am not," I insist anyway. "I'm usually out doing work on

the ranch."

"Right," she placates me, sitting on the edge of the bed while Duke rests his head lightly on her leg. "Speaking of helping, I do actually have a job for you."

I perk up at the sound of that, only because she hasn't asked me to do anything to help, despite my instance and I feel like this is progress.

"Yeah? What do you need?"

"My friend's daughter, Summer, is going to camp and her horse she barrel races with is going to stay here and will need to be worked while she's gone."

"I haven't run barrels in years," I hesitate. I'd do anything for her, and she knows it. I'm just a bit worried about how out of practice I am.

"It's like riding a bike, or a horse, rather." She chuckles at herself, and I can't help but smile. "It'll be fine though; he's a sweet gelding who shouldn't test you too much."

"Great, thank you for making me feel so much better," I say sarcastically.

"Oh stop." She swats me lightly. "You'll be fine. Maybe you can even show off a bit at the rodeo in a couple weeks."

I forgot the local Amity rodeo will be happening at the beginning of July. I used to always be in them, even though I never wanted to pursue a career in the rodeo. I never wanted to travel around or live that life. But the one time a year I would participate gave me a rush that I loved. Though, I'm older now and the thought of it makes me hesitate a bit.

"I'll think about it," I tell her, not wanting to completely shoot her down, but also thinking it's not likely to happen either.

"Great, I got you all signed up this morning." She smiles widely.

"Ma, that's not me thinking about it."

She shrugs with a smile, and it's impossible for me to be mad at her when I know she's just doing what she thinks is best for me. And honestly the thought makes me excited.

"Okay, well do you have anything else you volun-told me for that I should know about?"

She shakes her head with a smile.

"Okay, is there anything you need done around here before I get Duke all set up down at my house?"

"No, you do enough around here. Your father and I have managed just fine, you know?" She isn't upset that I haven't been around, and I know she means well, but I can't help the way it stings that I haven't been here.

"I'll probably still check in with him, see if he needs anything." I hide my grimace at the thought. I'm sure the last thing he's going to want is my help, but at least I'm offering.

She sends me a small smile like she knows exactly how that conversation will go but doesn't voice it.

"Let me know if you need anything or if something comes up. I'm just down the hill," I tell her.

She's waving her hand, shooing me out of the house. I take Duke, and we head toward the barn.

Once we get there, I look in to see my dad getting the dinner ready for the horses. I take in a silent breath of air, grounding myself before saying anything. "Hey, Pop, you need any help?"

He grunts in a way that isn't an answer, and I grind my teeth slightly. He won't even look at me.

"I can get more bales down if you need," I offer, because the hay loft can be a bitch to deal with and I know it would be a lot easier for me.

"I got it."

I want to argue with him, but know it won't lead to anything good, so instead I just nod my head and take Duke to my house. I'm going to end up coming out here after dark and getting things done for him anyway.

He can be mad about it when I'm not around, but I'm here to help, so that's exactly what I'm going to do.

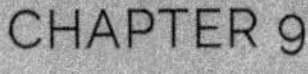

CHAPTER 9

I **ENDED** up researching how to groom a horse, and it isn't that complicated. At least it's not when the horse just stands there and lets it happen. Though, I'm not sure how common that is. I love grooming big dogs, but a horse is another level.

I'm also still unsure about spending any time alone with Jameson. He seems sweet, which is a scary thought because it would be so easy to fall into him. That's something I can't afford to do. It's best to keep my distance and eliminate any risk of getting too close so I don't fall into his trap.

I might be overthinking this. In fact, I know I'm overthinking this. I just can't find it in me to care because it's better to be safe than sorry.

Jerry Lee starts barking in the other room pulling my attention back again, and I realize I have a very large dog on my table that's been standing patiently as I've been brushing the same spot for way too long.

"Sorry, buddy," I apologize, though he just wags his fluffy tail like it didn't bother him one bit.

The front door opens, and this time I'm not even surprised when I see who just walked in, but I am a little surprised to see that he has a dog with him this time.

Jameson looks over at me with a wide smile and I fight to return it with one of my own and probably end up scowling or making some ridiculous face in return.

"Whose dog did you kidnap?" I joke.

"No one's, he's mine," he answers easily.

I lead the large St. Bernard off my table and put him in the back room to greet the cute pitty with the extremely hot firefighter.

I kneel down, extending my hand and the dog immediately licks it, coating me in too much dog saliva and I chuckle, wiping my hand off on my pants. "What's your name?"

"It's Duke, I just adopted him yesterday," Jameson answers with an even wider smile.

"He's so sweet. What made you decide to get a dog? Please don't tell me it was because of me."

He shakes his head. "No. I've wanted one for a while, just have always been too busy. But it also helps to know of a groomer to take him to."

"I'm sure you've known Trish." I stand up, narrowing my eyes at him slightly.

"Anyway," he diverts. "How often do I need to bring him to you then? Once a week or more often?"

I rear back slightly. "Whoa, no. If you're wanting him to get baths, maybe bring him in once every two months. If that."

He looks genuinely confused. "He doesn't need to be bathed more than that?"

I shake my head adamantly. "No, that'll dry out his skin. I mean he may need his nails trimmed every four to six weeks if you really wanted to keep up on it."

"I'll bring him in as often as he needs."

I go back to petting the adorable dog's head while hiding my smile from him because I don't want him to know how amusing I find this interaction.

"If you'd like. You don't need to make an appointment. Just come in any time."

"You know I will." His eyes shine in a way that makes my stomach swoop. "I guess I'll let you get back to work then."

I nod. "Yeah, okay."

Standing, I let them head toward the door. And of course, because I can't have a single time where Jerry Lee doesn't do the absolute most in trying to embarrass me, he squawks, *"Hot guy Jameson."*

I rush to grab the St. Bernard again and hide the redness that's taken over my face and neck, not wanting him to see me and the effect he has on me.

"This bird is pretty opinionated, you know that?" he calls out, the humor evident in his voice.

"Have a great day," I squeak out weakly. I swear I hear him laughing before the door closes, and I drop down, sitting on the floor as the St. Bernard comes up to my face, staring at me and I swear I see the judgment there. "I don't want to hear about it from you."

He huffs and I drop my head back against the wall. I have a feeling keeping him at arm's length is going to be harder than I thought.

WHEN I GET HOME, I notice that my neighbor, Bailey, is outside again. I wave in her direction as she's getting stuff out of her car. She sends a small one back, then balances the bags on her arms carrying them inside. I hesitate for a minute, wondering if I should offer to help but she doesn't seem like she would accept it if I did.

After an awkward amount of hesitation, I turn to go inside.

"Hey," she calls out. I almost don't turn around, convinced she's not talking to me. When she calls out again, I turn.

"Sorry, I didn't want to say the wrong name. It's...Sutton, right?" She hesitates.

I nod. "Yeah, sorry I wasn't sure if you were talking to me."

"Yeah, I wanted to see if you've heard about the local rodeo in a couple weeks."

I shake my head. "No, I haven't." I don't admit that I've never been to any rodeo or know anything about them.

"It's kind of a big deal around here. A yearly tradition that everyone turns out for. If you wanted to, I thought we could maybe go together? If you wanted."

"Oh." I'm taken aback slightly that she's inviting me somewhere. "Yeah, uh, sure that seems fun."

"Cool." She nods.

I smile widely, and she returns it with a small one of her own. After having an awkward parting we head into our own houses. I appreciate the fact that she's not overly friendly or mean. She seems to be somewhat awkward like myself and seems like she would make a good friend for me.

Maybe someone who wouldn't betray me in an awful and weird as fuck way.

CHAPTER 10

Jameson

DUKE JOGS ALONGSIDE me as I go down to the barn to meet with the new gelding I'm apparently taking care of for the summer. I don't mind helping out, it's why I'm here. But I don't really want to barrel race in the rodeo. I'm older, out of practice, and worry that I'll look ridiculous compared to the young riders.

I know if Mom is signing me up it's because she believes in me—because she wants to see me out there. So I'll do it. For her. Because she's given me everything, and this—this is how I give back. I'd do anything for her.

Duke walks up to the front of a stall, and when Sandy leans through the opening and lets out a huff Duke jumps back. I chuckle. "She won't hurt you, bud, don't worry."

He still keeps his distance away from the stalls while the horses each try to stretch as far as they can to reach him with their noses. I find Jasper, the unfamiliar bay gelding, munching on some hay peacefully.

"Hey bud," I greet. He turns his head slightly but doesn't take his attention away from his food. "Guess we're going to become friends this summer, huh?"

He seems to perk up slightly at the name of his real owner, Summer, and I feel bad he's probably going to miss her, but hopefully he'll tolerate me. I brought some peppermints in my pocket to try and win him over. Entering his stall, he still doesn't move as I approach with one of the mints in my outstretched hand.

It doesn't take him long to notice I'm in here. When I step fully inside, he turns to face me, slow and deliberate. He flares his nostrils once, taking me in, and sniffs out the candy I have for him, taking it gently from my palm. I pet his face while he chews. "Take it easy on me, would ya? It's been a while since I've raced."

He lets out a huff and I'm choosing to believe that is his way of telling me that he will.

I put a halter on him and lead him out to the cross ties. I take my time grooming him before putting the saddle on. I guide him to the outdoor training ring where I make sure to set up some beginner barrels to practice.

After lunging Jasper for a few minutes to warm him up, I hop onto his back while Duke keeps his distance, sitting well outside of the ring.

"If anything happens to me, your job is to run and get help," I tell Duke, only half joking before addressing the horse. "You, don't hurt me."

I have Jasper walk around the perimeter of the ring a couple of times before moving him up to a trot, then finally a canter.

"Alright, ready to do this?" I ask him as we take the position to do a run. I let out a breath, and signal Jasper to go, knowing this is just a practice and that time doesn't matter. The only thing that does is not getting bucked off or having him fall and hurt us both.

And we're off. Jasper knows exactly what he's doing as he takes off under me, I stay low while guiding him around the barrels he runs toward quickly. We navigate our way through the pattern quicker than I anticipated, and I pull on the reins, signaling him to stop.

It isn't going to be my best time, but the adrenaline of riding again feels good.

We end up running the pattern a couple more times, but I don't want to wear him out too much. That, and I already feel the muscles in my legs beginning to ache from the lack of use over the last several years. I ride Jasper around the arena slowly for a few minutes to cool him down.

Duke follows as I lead Jasper back in to untack him, making sure to feed him a little extra hay in his stall. We may not be perfect in time for the rodeo. Our turns might be a little wide, our timing a little off. Maybe we'll knock a barrel or two, or maybe my nerves will get the best of me for a second out there in the ring. But that's okay as long as Mom enjoys watching me because that's the whole reason I'm doing this.

I look at the time, seeing that Duke and I have an appointment to get to. One with a particularly beautiful dog groomer. We get to my truck and I help Duke into the front seat before climbing in myself.

As we're driving, I rub the top of his head. "You're lucky you get to spend a few hours with the pretty girl. Want to put in a good word for me?"

His tongue is hanging out of his mouth as he looks at me like he's smiling. He probably knows how lucky he is and is taunting me.

We get to the grooming salon; I look over at the fire station where some of my coworkers are outside with the truck. I send a small wave in their direction before bringing Duke into the neighboring building.

We're greeted, but again, not by a human. *"Hot guy, Jameson."*

I chuckle, especially when I hear Sutton in the other room say, "Jerry Lee, I swear to God I'm gonna—" She freezes as soon as she sees me standing here. "Oh, hi."

"I think the bird likes me."

"Or hates me," she grumbles. Her tone changes as she smiles while greeting my dog. "Hi, Duke."

"It doesn't seem fair that he gets such a warm greeting from you," I tease.

"He's cuter."

"Ouch." I hold my hand against my chest like she hit me.

Sutton looks up with a small smile, and I can't help but give her one back. She's so beautiful it's hard to not be completely mesmerized by her. Especially with the way she's looking at me right now. Until she shakes her head and looks back down at Duke.

"So, what're we doing today?" she asks.

"Anything you think he needs. I want him to get the full treatment, he deserves the best."

She chuckles softly. "We can certainly do that, it'll cost you."

"I'll pay it."

"Is your daddy trying to impress me?" Sutton squishes Duke's face as she asks him.

"Not at all, if I was trying to impress you, I'd have much more elaborate plans to do so," I tell her. "If you'd like to find out what those are, I'd be happy to show you."

She ignores the comment. "I'll call you when he's ready, in about two hours."

"I'll be ready."

She nods, and neither of us move.

"Anything else you need from me?" I ask.

"Your dog." She gestures for me to hand her the leash. "And your phone number."

"Of course." I chuckle, handing over the leash, and when I do our hands graze each other just like the night I gave her keys back. There's a shot of electricity that runs through me. The way her dark green eyes shoot up to mine I know she feels it too. I want to say something about it. I want to try asking her out again, but before I can form any words the bird starts barking and she drops her gaze from mine.

She holds onto Duke's leash, and he trots happily over to her. I write down my number on a piece of paper on the desk, and hand it over.

"Okay, see you when he's all ready."

"See you soon." I watch as she takes my dog to the bathing area. As I walk out the door, I hear the bird squawk, *"Shut up, Vern."* And I can't hold back my laughter. Especially when I hear Sutton shouting out another threat to him about opening up a window to set him free.

"Look who can't stay away," my coworker, Will, calls out.

"Believe it or not, you're not the one I can't stay away from."

"Aw, don't play hard to get."

I shake my head with a small laugh as I start to get in my car. "I'll be back later to get my dog. Try not to miss me too much."

Will waves me off, and I look toward the window at the grooming salon one more time and swear I catch sight of Sutton looking out, but she disappears quickly. Talk about playing hard to get.

CHAPTER 11

Sutton

"SUTTON, ARE YOU HERE?" Trish calls out while I'm bathing Duke, who keeps trying to give me kisses when I lean over to scrub his belly.

"Yeah," I call back, and look over at the doorway to see her standing with an unfamiliar blonde girl who doesn't look like she's a day over twenty.

"I don't think I got a chance to tell you about my niece, Lily. She helps me out around here at the salon during the summer while she's home from college."

"Hi, nice to meet you." I go to stretch my hand out, but then see it's covered in suds and send a wave in her direction instead.

"You, too." Lily smiles.

"She helps out with bathing some dogs and nail trims but only comes around a couple times a week." Trish gives Lily a pointed look like she's supposed to help out a bit more.

"Hey, I just like to make sure there's plenty of me to go around, I'm busy. Lots of people to see, things to do, I work when I can." Lilly giggles. She seems bubbly and nice, though they clearly have a relationship that consists of teasing as a form of love language.

"We'll let you get back to it, I just didn't want you confused whenever Lily makes her appearance around here," Trish tells me.

They walk away and I go back to rinsing Duke and learning that he's sweet until the dryer turns on. Then, he attempts to eat the air that comes out of it.

"That's really not helpful," I try to tell him over the loud dryer, but he doesn't listen and continues to chase the nozzle with his open mouth.

Eventually, I manage to get him dry, trim his nails, and brushed with a rubber brush since he barely has any fur.

"Guess I should call your dad," I tell him while he smiles with his tongue out. "Jerry Lee, you better not say a damn word."

The traitorous bird doesn't make a noise, and I assume he's sleeping, but something tells me he'll make sure he's awake to embarrass me once again when Jameson shows up. Since that seems to be his specialty.

I let Duke run around the empty salon as I call his dad, who picks up on the second ring.

"Hello?"

"Hi, Duke is all ready for you to come get him."

"Perfect. Are you hungry?"

"Okay, I'll see you-what?"

"Are you hungry?" he repeats.

"No?"

"Okay, it can be for later then. Do you like sandwiches? Or pizza?"

"What're you talking about?"

"If you don't pick, then I'm going to choose for you, and we can both hope I guess correctly."

I open and close my mouth a couple of times unsure of what to say.

"Okay, my choice, then. Hope you like anchovies and pineapple."

"You really don't—" My phone beeps signaling that he hung up and I scowl at the screen. Looking over at Duke, I tell him, "Your dad may be a little crazy."

A little while later the front door opens, and I'm assaulted with the smell of fresh pizza. Luckily, I detect no hint of fish or fruit and my stomach growls right on cue, making me realize just how hungry I really am.

Duke rushes over toward the smell and I'm not sure if it's because he realizes it's his dad or if he thinks he's getting an extra treat.

"Hey, buddy, you look so clean," Jameson greets his dog right before I turn the corner and see him holding a pizza box in one hand.

Folding my arms across my chest, I say, "I told you I'm not hungry."

Right on cue my stomach growls again and Jameson gives me a pointed look, handing the pizza box to me. "Okay, then you can just eat that when you are."

I take it from him with a sigh. "Thanks. This doesn't count as payment, though."

"I know. It's because I know if I tried to ask you on a date you'd turn me down, so this was the closest option until I can convince you to say yes."

"I told you; I'm not looking for anything."

"That's why I didn't ask. Just figured you'd need to eat some-time." He smiles and it's so genuine, so sweet that I drop my shoulders, not realizing I had bunched them up near my ears.

"Thanks," I say softly.

"You're welcome. How much do I owe you for taking care of this vicious beast?"

I laugh lightly, looking down at the supposed vicious beast who's smiling as he sits with his back legs spread and it makes him look more human than he should.

"Well, considering he didn't bite me I guess I can give you a slight discount."

"Glad that didn't happen, I would feel pretty bad about the anchovy and pineapple pizza if he did."

I open up the box to check and see if he's serious, but breathe a sigh of relief when I realize it's just pepperoni.

Jameson smiles widely at me when I narrow my eyes at him, closing the box and setting it down. I tell him the total and he pays in cash, adding a generous tip that I try to refuse and give him change instead.

"Have you thought more about grooming my horses?" he asks on his way out the door.

I hesitate. I've looked into it, and I know I can do it. The question that's hindering me, is if it's a good idea to spend more time with Jameson. He doesn't seem to be letting up, and maybe I could just be friends with him. Maybe, it would be fine. He's nice. Persistent, but nice.

"I can try," I tell him.

"Great, now I have your number so we can set up a time for you to come to the ranch."

I almost ask how he got my number, but then remember I called him to get his dog. Something I clearly didn't think through all the way, but it's okay. Since we're going to be friends.

"Okay." I nod.

Jameson smiles, and his perfectly aligned, white teeth make his blue eyes shine with pride even more. He's clearly pleased he's worn me down enough that I agreed.

He opens the door, walking out with Duke and I think I'm actually going to have a moment where Jerry Lee doesn't try to completely ruin my life, but right before the door closes, he decides to announce, *"Hot guy, Jameson."*

"That's it, you're going to learn to survive in the forest, Jerry Lee!"

I swear I hear the deep timbre of a laugh from outside and I think about the best way to take up residence in a cave where I never have to see or speak to anyone ever again.

CHAPTER 12

Jameson

"SAW LILY IS BACK for the summer," Jo goads Parker while he's on dish duty tonight at the station.

I shake my head, knowing exactly how this is about to go down between them.

"Good for her," Parker grumbles.

"She looked really pretty. You think she has a boyfriend at her fancy college?"

"Wouldn't care if she did," he says, washing the dishes more aggressively than he needs to. We all know this is getting to him.

"Sure seems like you would care, doesn't it, Jameson?"

"Don't bring me into this," I announce.

"You'll probably see her quite a bit this summer if she works at Trish's again," Jo continues.

Parker continues to mumble under his breath, and I stop paying attention. We all know about Lily being the one that got away. They were high school sweethearts, and she chose to leave for college. He was pretty broken up about her for a while, and even got a reputation for being a bit of a playboy with how he acted afterwards.

"Speaking of pretty things over at Trish's, are you having any luck with the new girl?" Dave asks me, nudging my knee with his own.

"Don't call her a pretty thing. Her name's Sutton."

"So, it's going well then."

"What's with all of you wanting to gossip all the time?" I stand up, twisting to stretch my back.

"It's more entertaining than sitting here twiddling our thumbs," Dave retorts.

"Maybe to you, but I think I'd prefer if you did exactly that. It would save me from a headache."

The signal for a call goes off, and a rag is thrown at me, and I see it was Jo who threw it. I catch it before it falls onto the ground and toss it back to her.

"If you all are done screwing around, we have some lives to save," I taunt as we all get ready to go on the call.

We get to the small business office that's complaining about smoke, thinking there's a fire. Turns out it's just an issue with the fluorescent lights needing to be replaced. The manager of the building shows up and looks at us like we're the cause of the issue.

"What's going on? Why are you here?"

"We responded to a call about smoke in the building," I answer easily.

"This seems unnecessary, the building is fine. There's no fire," the manager snaps.

"There could have been, though," I reason.

"Well, there's not." The man, who couldn't be more than five foot seven and is wearing a shirt that doesn't even cover his gut, storms off and I look at the woman who made the call.

"He's great," she says sarcastically once he's out of earshot.

"You did the right thing by calling us," I tell her honestly.

Once we are back to the station, I tell my crew that I'm going to try to rest a bit. Really, I just want some space away from them for a few minutes.

Laying down on one of the hard cots, I take my phone out and see there's a text from the number I made sure to save after she called to tell me Duke was ready. I've shown an incredible amount of restraint not reaching out to her and seeing that she's texted me has a giant smile spreading across my face.

Sutton: I could come by tomorrow if you're not busy.

My stomach swoops when I think about her offering to come over but then remember it's because I asked her to groom my horse. My master plan to see her more suddenly feels like it's not good enough, but it's even worse when I have to reply saying no.

> Jameson: I'll still be on shift tomorrow. What about this weekend?

Sutton: Maybe. I'll check my schedule.

> Jameson: Any chance you could check your schedule for free time to hang out with me too?

Sutton: Nice try.

> Jameson: How was the pizza?

This time it takes her a little longer to respond. I think she's not going to, and I drop my phone face down on my chest right before it dings again.

Sutton: It was good.

Sutton: Thank you.

It may not be much, but for some reason her texts give me hope that maybe she's not totally shut off on the idea of us at least being friends. Even if that's all I get I'll take it happily with her.

"Jameson!" My name is called, and I groan, it's not like we're getting a call, this is purely station drama once again.

"Did you run away?" another voice yells.

"Not yet," I respond, putting my phone away and getting up to join everyone back in the main room.

As I head back down, I think about how this is one of the rare times that I'm counting down the hours until I can go home. There's a chance I could see Sutton for longer than a passing minute, and I haven't had something to look forward to in a long while.

AFTER I GET OFF SHIFT, I'm exhausted as usual, but I still make sure to check in with Ma as soon as I get home. Instead of finding her inside resting like she should be, she's out on the back deck taking care of some of the plants.

"Ma, what are you doing?" I ask, approaching her.

"Something I love. So if you tell me to stop I'm going to bury you with some of these flowers," she threatens, pointing her gardening gloves at me.

"It's not nice to threaten your one and only child, you know?"

"It's also not nice for my one and only child to try and take away my favorite activities."

"That's not what I'm doing. I'm looking out for you."

"So am I. Because if you ever tried to stop your future wife from doing something she enjoys she would already have you six feet under. I'm giving you a courtesy warning."

"Have I ever told you that you're vicious?" I laugh.

She joins me with her own laughter that quickly turns into a cough, and I rush to help her to the bench. Her coughing subsides and she waves me off. "I'm fine, you overreact."

I wish that's what it was, but I know she's downplaying it. I know we all want to believe she's not as sick as she is, and luckily most days she seems like she's not sick at all. But there's glimpses like this that bring us back to reality. The unknown of her diagnosis and treatment, the unknown of the disease as a whole.

"Can I go back to my gardening now?" she asks sarcastically.

"You don't need my permission." I gesture toward the flower boxes with an open hand, and she goes back to working on them.

I don't move from my spot on the bench, taking my phone out to act like I'm doing something on it.

"Go get some rest, you look exhausted," she tells me.

"I'm fine, if you're going to be out here then so am I."

"You're worse than an overbearing parent."

"I'm not a parent." I chuckle.

"You're not, so maybe you should do something about that and give me grandkids instead of hovering over me." She gives me a pointed look.

I shake my head, still messing around on my phone and end up pulling up the text thread with Sutton.

Jameson: How's your schedule looking?

"Are you texting a girl?" my mom asks suddenly. I look up at her, wondering if she has a superpower I've never been informed of.

"Who says I'm texting anyone?"

"So you are. Good, she can get you off my back for a little bit." She smiles over her shoulder at me.

"No woman will ever get me off your back, Ma. You come first."

She sighs just as my phone signals that I got a text.

Sutton: I'm free tomorrow.

Jameson: Perfect, come by any time.

Sutton: Can I bring my dog?

Jameson: Of course.

I send her my address and feel my mom sit next to me on the bench again. Her cool hand rests on my arm, pulling my attention to her.

"I'm worried about you," she says suddenly. I'm taken aback because if anyone should be worried between the two of us, it should be me when it comes to her.

"Why?"

"You saying that I come first. I love you, son, but when you find the right woman, she needs to be your priority."

"If that ever happened, you both could be my priority."

"You're such a sweet man." She takes my hand in hers, patting the top of it. "Someone must've done a good job raising you."

"Yeah. My ma did a pretty good job."

"She did. You should reward her by getting married and giving her grandchildren."

"Okay, we're done with this conversation." I shake my head.

"Good, I'm done out here. So, you go back home and get some rest while I hide away in the only place you'll allow me to be."

"Oh, stop." I pull her in for a half hug.

I assist her inside, where Duke greets me lazily after getting up from the dog bed I set up in my parent's house for when I'm working. He ends up following me back to my little house on the property, though I try to tell him I'm not going to be the most fun. He doesn't care, and it's evident when he plops down on the bed.

At least I'm in good company.

I didn't see my dad out on our walk home, which is for the best. I can really only handle him on days I didn't just get off shift. The exhaustion makes my fuse even shorter when it comes to him and our relationship.

As I lay down on my back, folding my arms across my chest, I'm planning to just take a short nap. My phone dings, and I glance at it to see another response from Sutton. Knowing I'm going to see her tomorrow makes it easier for me to relax.

Sutton: I'll be there around noon.

CHAPTER 13

Sutton

"I REALLY HOPE I don't regret this," I tell Bennet as we drive down the dirt road that supposedly leads to Jameson's property.

He sent his address and explained how to get to the barn, but I've had to talk myself out of canceling no less than five times since I woke up. I don't know how to groom a horse, and I don't know how it's going to be spending time with Jameson.

I drive past a large house, and I'm wondering if it's where he lives. I continue down the unpaved road until I reach the barn. There's a couple of horse trailers parked outside of it, so I park near them.

Bennet jumps out of the car after me, sticking to my side like he usually does as I walk inside. I find Jameson standing next to a gorgeous white horse with black spots and a striped mane.

"Hi," I greet, trying to hide the hesitation in my voice.

"Hey, I'm glad you're here," he says easily.

The soft tapping of another dog's feet on the concrete has me looking over to see Duke coming over to greet us as well. Him and Bennet sniff each other as I watch and wait to see how they'll react to each other. Luckily, they seem to be immediate friends.

"I think they like each other," Jameson says, pulling my attention to him.

I give him a close-lipped smile. "Yeah, so who's this?"

"This is Juniper. She's really sweet and is really good with getting her body clipped."

"Hi, Juniper," I greet, rubbing my hand on her nose. She's standing in cross ties, which my research just taught me.

"I'll be doing work around the barn in case you need any help. She's clean and shouldn't be a problem."

I'm acting a lot more confident than I'm feeling as I nod and say, "I shouldn't."

I try to remember everything I watched about grooming horses, and it's not much different than shaving down a large dog. Just add in a few hundred extra pounds. Before I end up chickening out and leaving, I set my bag down and get my tools out. I approach Juniper, letting her smell my hand like I would with any other animal before beginning.

While I'm running the clippers over the horse's soft fur, I think about talking to Jameson. I feel like I should try to make conversation with him in some way since we're both in here working. Maybe I could get to know him.

But that could lead to him wanting to get to know me and I don't know what I could share, because telling him why I'm here is off the table.

The weather is great, huh?

That sounds ridiculous, even in my own mind.

I continue to debate on if I should say anything, but nothing manages to come to mind. And Jameson checks in periodically.

"How're you doing?"

"Good."

Then he smiles and goes back to whatever he's doing. I hear him tossing things around when there's a thump, and I'm sure it's a hay bale.

I fight the urge to seek him out as I keep my entire focus on the large animal in front of me. I'm probably more meticulous than I need to be. I manage to get through grooming Juniper fairly easily. She does well standing for me, all while Bennet and Duke play through the hall of the barn. After I've finished shaving the extra fur off her, I'm running a brush through her soft mane and Jameson comes around the corner, leaning against the wall. Sweat is beading his brow, and his dark T-shirt is molded to his body.

"How's it going?" he asks.

"Good, I'm just about done, I think."

He steps forward, walking around and examining the horse. "She looks great."

"Thanks, I guess it's not too bad for my first time," I say proudly.

"Glad I can help you expand your resume." He starts undoing the ties and taking Juniper back to her stall. "Do you want a tour of the property?"

"No, I should head home. I'm sure Bennet is tired." I look over at the dogs who are currently wrestling and don't look tired at all.

"I think they're friends, which means you're really doing them a disservice, not letting them hang out."

"Was this your master plan all along?"

"I have no master plan, just a horse that needed grooming and you're the professional." He smiles innocently.

"Mhm, right. We really should be going."

"Jameson," a female voice calls out, and I furrow my brows at him because if he's married or lives with a woman then he's a piece of shit, and I've been right about keeping my distance from him.

"In here, Ma!" he calls out, and I don't even have time to wrap my head around the fact that he said "Ma."

I want to make a run for it. I shouldn't be here meeting his parents, but it's too late when the older woman appears in the entryway of the barn. She has a scarf around her head and is wearing sweatpants and a T-shirt that looks like it may have fit her previously, but she's now drowning in the fabric.

"I didn't know we had a guest. Hello, I'm Emily, Jameson's mother."

"Hi, I'm Sutton. It's so nice to meet you." I meet her for a handshake and her cool soft hands feel fragile in my own.

"Did you walk all the way down here?" Jameson asks the woman.

She waves her hand at him and rolls her eyes so only I can see, and I hide my light laughter. I may be nervous about meeting her, but I like her already.

"I had to come down and see my favorite child."

"Aw, you're not just going to sweet talk me."

"I wasn't talking about you; I was talking about Sandy." Emily walks up to another horse in the first stall, and feeds her a carrot she pulled out from her pocket.

I smile, looking down at my feet, enjoying their banter. No wonder Jameson always seems like a sweet ray of sunshine whenever he talks to me. How he isn't turned off by my refusals, and it doesn't seem to stop him from continuing to try. I can't help but think that has to do with the woman that raised him.

"Where's Dad?" Jameson asks, his tone of voice clearly devoid of the warmth it just had, and it's something I recognize all too well. I don't want to talk to anyone about the betrayal of my own family, but if I did then I would have a tone too.

"He's up at the house. He doesn't feel the need to babysit me like my own son does." She glares playfully at him. "Sutton, why haven't I seen you before now?"

"Oh, I just moved here not long ago. I'm only here to groom Juniper."

"Juniper needed to be groomed? Since when?" She turns toward Jameson whose eyes widen just barely as he looks at his mom.

"She was still fuzzy, the weather is getting warmer, I thought it would be a good idea for her to get her body clipped."

"Hm," she hums, and I feel like there's something here I'm not fully understanding.

"I really should head out," I announce.

"You don't have to, you could stay for dinner," Emily offers brightly.

I shake my head. "That's okay. Maybe another time. It was nice meeting you."

"I'll walk you to your car," Jameson offers.

"You don't need to do that." I gesture for Bennet to heel, which he does easily.

"I'm going to, even if I don't need to."

He does, walking the short distance to my car with me. I open the door to let Bennet jump in.

"Thank you. Let me know how much I owe you."

I honestly forgot about the money because I'm so flustered that all I'm focusing on is getting out of here.

"Oh, don't worry about it." I climb into my Jeep, but before I'm able to shut the door, Jameson holds it open.

"I can't let you do work for free."

"It's really okay, it was a practice run."

"Let me do something then. How about I take you to dinner."

I lift a single brow at him. "What's with you and food?"

He shrugs, leaning against my door. "I like food, don't you?"

I sigh, reaching for the door again. "I'll see you later, Jameson."

He backs up, letting me close it. "That wasn't a no."

I shake my head, closing the car door. He keeps his eyes on me, that soft smile on his lips as he watches me drive away. I keep looking at him in my rearview mirror, worried about how much longer I'll be able to keep saying no to him.

Or if I even should.

Jameson

"SHE'S PRETTY," Ma tells me once I come back into the barn.

"She is," I agree, because there's no use in denying it. Sutton's gorgeous and anyone with eyes would say the same thing.

"Are you seeing her?"

I chuckle. "I'm trying."

"Really?" She turns, suddenly very interested in this conversation with me, and I shake my head.

"She's not giving me the time of day, don't get too excited."

"I don't think that's true."

"I just tried to ask her out and she turned me down, Ma," I tell her lightly.

"Well maybe it doesn't have to do with you. Do you know why she moved here?"

Shaking my head. "She's pretty closed off."

"If anyone can make someone feel comfortable it's you." She smiles, and I know she means it.

"You have to say that, you're my mom."

"I'd still say it even if I wasn't. Now, you better be done pretending to work down here."

I bark out a laugh; I wasn't pretending, not really. I cleaned the stalls, fed the horses, organized the hay up in the hay loft, made grain bags to make feeding the horses easier.

"I am, but I'm going to work Jasper a bit."

She smiles. "Good. I can't wait to hear how you do at the rodeo."

Her comment takes me aback. "You aren't going to be there?"

"I'm going to try, but crowds can be a lot for me, you know that, honey."

I worry that she's not voicing the real concern which is the ones I have about the amount of walking it would be for her. Neither of us say it because I know she would just tell me to shush and not to worry about her.

"How about you stick around and watch now then?" I suggest, and she smiles widely, agreeing easily.

While Ma sits on a bench outside the arena, I lunge Jasper before getting on him and running some barrels. At one point, I think I even notice my dad standing and watching me, but once I'm done with the run, he isn't there anymore. Ma claps like I just put on a five-star performance.

"Call Sutton back over so she can watch you. If this doesn't make her fall in love with you, then you really do have your work cut out for you."

I laugh. "I don't think it's that simple."

"Well, it should be. I fell in love with your dad over something simple."

I know their story. He worked at a candy store where she would stop by with her friends after school every day. He was in college while he worked there, and she was a senior in high school. She would get the same selection every time she went.

It didn't take long for him to have her candy choices ready and waiting at the register for her.

Not unlike Sutton, she didn't agree to go out with him right away either, but after she finally did the rest is history.

I can only hope if Sutton does ever agree to give me a chance, that our story can be half as beautiful as theirs.

Without the tragedy of the illness hanging over us all.

The reminder is a slap in the face to my reality of why I'm back in the first place. It doesn't matter that she refuses to let us talk about how sick she is. It doesn't eliminate the fact that it's the truth.

"Run it again," Ma calls out, pulling me from my negative thoughts. I get Jasper back into position to run the barrels again, because I'll give Ma anything she wants while I still can.

Unfortunately, I know the one thing she wants more than anything else in the world is to see me fall in love, get married, and have kids. I just don't know if I'll be able to give her that in the time she has left.

ON MY DAYS OFF, I need to find things to do around the property. I know if I don't, I'll just find myself going into town and making an excuse to go to the fire station on the off chance I'll catch a glimpse of Sutton at the building next door.

Or I'll end up bringing Duke to be bathed, even if she says he doesn't need to be. Any chance I can see her, I want to grab a hold of.

Instead, I'm busying myself in every way I can. I start with the horses, feeding them, sneaking them treats. I clean out their stalls after turning them out into the pastures and then I work with Jasper. After that, I find different odd jobs to do, trying to make sure my mom doesn't notice because I know she'll yell at me if she does.

I'm working on one of the dead tractors we have, trying to see if I can get it to run again when I hear someone approaching me. Since they don't immediately start scolding me for working, I know who it is before I even look up.

When he doesn't say anything for several minutes, I decide to break the silence.

"Can I help you?"

He doesn't answer right away, and when I finally face him, he's standing in the opening of the shop with his arms folded. "What're you doing?"

"Trying to get this old thing to run again."

"I've tried, it won't."

"Then why's it still here?"

"Haven't gotten around to getting rid of it."

"If I can't get it to run, then I'll take care of it."

"Don't."

I narrow my eyes at his sharp tone. "Why can't I help?"

"You wanted to leave, but now that you're back you want to be helpful?"

I toss the tool in my hand down, standing up to face him. "Do you want me to apologize for getting out of here? For seeing what else is out there? Ma was never upset about it. She was happy for me. Why can't you be the same?"

He doesn't say anything, his jaw tics and I think he's going to storm away, but he doesn't.

"What is it? What is the reason you can't be happy that I tried to find a life outside of this town? Why can't you just be happy that I'm back?" I try again, attempting to get to the root of his resentment.

Instead of answering any of my questions, he grinds his teeth. "If you're just going to leave again, don't come back."

He walks away, and I drop my head back looking up at the ceiling, frustrated at the divide that we have. And even more frustrated because I don't think there's anything I can do about it.

CHAPTER 15

Sutton

IT'S the day of the rodeo; Bailey drove us the short distance to the fairgrounds and I'm a little surprised at how big it is. We find an open spot on the bleachers where we both can sit not long before the rodeo is supposed to start. I have no idea what to expect, and all Bailey has said is that the whole town turns up and it's a fun time.

There's also a festival, which I didn't expect, but I guess she wasn't kidding about this being the biggest event this town has.

It's the Amity Strawberry Festival, apparently.

"Is there a ton of strawberries or something?" I ask as we wait for everything to begin.

"There's really not as many as you would think."

"Why is it called that, then?"

She shrugs. "Sounds better than the Amity Nothing Festival."

I let out a short laugh while she chuckles. I don't think I've seen her genuinely laugh in any of our limited interactions. She seems nice but closed off. Except I do know she hates her next-door neighbor, Wes.

We haven't talked about him that much, but we saw him as we were leaving today. She made sure to tell me exactly how she feels about the tall, somewhat scary looking man that lives next door. Apparently, something happened when she moved in, and they're both the type to hold grudges. That fact has now led to a neighborly feud.

It makes me extremely glad that I'm not on Bailey's bad side, because she's someone I definitely want to have as a friend, not as an enemy.

There's an announcement crackling over the loudspeakers, cutting through the low hum of chatter and the distant smell of funnel cakes and hay. My heart gives a little jolt as the voice echoes through the stands. "Ladies and gentlemen, the rodeo is about to begin!"

Instantly, all my focus shifts to the arena in front of us. The noise fades, the crowd blurs, and my eyes lock onto the dirt ring as they announce the start of the barrel races and who's up first.

"Jameson Turner," the announcer bellows, and there's a noticeable shift in the crowd. "Making his return to the races after ten years."

My jaw drops because I wasn't expecting to see him here. The starting signal goes off, and Jameson is riding on a dark brown horse that runs out extremely fast. My eyes track the two of them as they run around the first barrel, he's so low to the ground on the turn I'm surprised he doesn't scrape the ground or fall off.

Then they're running to the next one and doing the same thing. The timer stops and the crowd erupts in cheers. Including Bailey and me, and I'm surprised to see her so animated as she claps for Jameson alongside the rest of the crowd.

I'm also surprised with how excited I am for him and how wide I'm smiling. I watch the area Jameson and the horse went through and watch him jump off, patting the horse on his head. He turns around and it's like he knows exactly where I am as his eyes lock on mine even from across the distance.

At first I think there's no way he actually sees me, he's just looking out at the crowd. But then that perfect smile appears on his face, the one that lights up in his eyes, and I'm annoyed with myself for recognizing it. I still can't bring myself to look away, so I raise my hand in a wave. I watch in fascination as he waves back at me.

"I think you caught his attention." Bailey nudges me softly.

"Yeah, I think I have for a little while, unfortunately."

"I've only ever heard good things about him. The town golden boy." Bailey shrugs. "There are worse guys to catch the attention of."

I shake my head, looking away from Jameson to face Bailey. "I'm sure a lot of women catch his attention, I'm not special."

"I wouldn't be so sure."

I hum, turning back toward the arena just as the next rider is announced. They're good, but not as fast as Jameson. My eyes continue to drift to where he is throughout the rodeo and every single time I look over at him, I find that he's already looking at me.

After the rodeo is finished, everyone takes their time getting up and finding their way out of the arena and over to the festival grounds. I don't seek Jameson out as Bailey and I leave. We walk the short distance to where the carnival rides and booths are set up in a large field.

There are pictures of strawberries all over, but when it comes to actual strawberries this place really is lacking them, which I find ironically funny. There are vendor booths set up in rows, selling various items and food.

Behind them there's a group of carnival games and in the largest part of the field, there are some rides including a tilt-o-whirl, a Ferris wheel, and a roller coaster that does not look safe. It's like a smaller version of a state fair. They could have named it something along those lines, but for some reason the Amity Strawberry Festival sticks,. Now I've made it my mission to find at least one single berry.

Bailey and I walk through the row of vendors, and while some have products with strawberries on them, none of the food carts have any. The closest thing I find is strawberry lemonade. As we're waiting in line, Bailey groans, turning to face me even more.

"What?" I question.

"Wes is here," she scoffs.

I look past her shoulder and catch sight of our extremely large neighbor pacing nearby. His head swivels every few seconds, scanning the crowd, the arena, the exits—anywhere but the people around him. He doesn't look like he even wants to be here. I'm not sure he's here for the rodeo at all.

"Do you think he's here with someone?" I ask her and she huffs out a half laugh.

"Doubt it. No one can handle more than five minutes of being in his presence."

"Hm." I wonder what his story is. I feel like the hate between them may be rooted in something else. Something that may explode in another way.

We get our food and sit on some benches to eat the barbecue sandwiches which are surprisingly good. The strawberry lemonade, though, is severely lacking in strawberry.

After we're finished, we wander toward the row of games. There's the usual line-up of tossing ones. Rings flying toward glass bottles, darts thudding into balloons. Nearby, a row of brightly painted booths features the water-gun races. The prizes are a colorful mess. Oversized stuffed animals, inflatable hammers, and even a sad-looking tank of goldfish.

Bailey and I are watching a couple of kids who are overly animated as they shoot the water guns toward the target. Their screams get louder as one of the kids starts to pull ahead of the others.

Someone steps up next to me, but I'm so entranced in the game that I hardly pay attention, even when the bell dings signaling the winner. The kid cheers loudly while the others take their defeat well, even though I'm sure they're sad about losing.

"Want to try it out?" a voice asks next to me, startling me and I jump.

I turn to see Jameson, looking down at me with that sparkle in his eye and giant smile on his lips. I'm not sure how he manages to look even more attractive right now than he has any other time I've seen him, but he does. Maybe it's because watching him race on that horse was hotter than I expected it to be. Now, here he is in a flannel with the sleeves rolled up to his elbows and jeans that hug him perfectly in all the right places. Don't even get me started on the brown cowboy hat on his head that should probably be illegal.

He's tall, large, and unreasonably handsome standing here next to me. All my hesitations about him seem to fade into the background right now because where I'm standing all I see are green flags.

"Try what out?" I ask, distracted by the sight of him in front of me; I hardly even remember where we are because all I see is him.

He nods his head slightly. "The game. Want to play me?"

"Oh, I don't know."

"Go ahead," Bailey suggests. "I'm going to head home, you enjoy."

I shake my head. "No, it's fine I'll come back with you."

"No, stay. Play a game or two," she encourages.

"Yeah, Sutton, stay and play a game or two," Jameson joins in.

"I'll talk to you later," Bailey waves, already walking backward toward the exit.

I open my mouth, but nothing comes out. I turn to Jameson again who looks extremely proud of himself that he has me in this position.

"Fine one game," I relent.

"If that's the case, then we need to make it good."

"What do you mean?"

"I mean that if I win, you have to go on at least one ride with me."

I grimace. "Please not the roller coaster, I don't trust it."

He laughs. "No roller coaster."

"What about if I win?"

"What do you want?"

I think for a second, looking around and it may be a dumb request, but dammit I'm determined. "I want you to find me a strawberry here."

"At the Amity Strawberry Festival? You should know, there's none around."

"Then you better win."

He barks out a laugh, it's deep and sends an unexpected shock between my thighs at how throaty it is. The man shouldn't have the power of a sexy laugh and look like he does.

"Go ahead," he instructs, and I do, managing to step ahead of him so I can stop being so distracted by every little thing he's doing right now that has my brain melting.

I don't need to become involved with him. Friends is fine, friends can play a game together. Friends can keep their hormones in check when the other looks the way he does.

Get it together, Sutton.

Jameson pays for both of us to play, even though I insist on paying for myself. He just gives me a look that has me rolling my eyes.

We take our positions behind our respective water guns, and the attendant starts counting down. Then we begin, both doing our best to aim our stream of water at the target. He's immediately ahead of me, finding the center right away, while it takes me a few seconds to get the angle right.

Once I do, it's too late and Jameson is already way ahead, so I attempt a distraction. Doing my best to maintain my own stream against the target, I lean over to shove at him to try and get his aim off.

"That's cheating," he scolds me, playfully.

"I think you're cheating since there's no way you're this good at this game."

"Don't be a sore loser," he taunts.

"I'm not going to lose."

I'm most definitely going to lose.

That's exactly what happens when the buzzer goes off, signaling Jameson as the winner. I groan in defeat, slowly turning to face him. He's silently gloating, a smug smile plastered on his face.

"Alright, what ride are we going on?" I relent.

"I'm not sure, I think we need to walk around a little bit so I can figure it out."

I narrow my eyes at him, but a deals a deal.

"Pick a prize," the worker says, drawing both of our attention to him.

"You pick," Jameson instructs.

"No, you're the winner."

"I'm already getting my prize; this one's for you."

I work to hide the blush creeping onto my cheeks, and pick a fuzzy looking teddy bear; the attendant hands it to me, and I hug it close to my chest. It's perfect to keep my arms occupied so I don't accidently do something stupid like try and touch Jameson because I can't control myself.

Especially while we walk toward the small selection of rides. He keeps his hands in his pockets, with a light look on his face and doesn't try to force conversation with me. I hug the stuffed bear tighter, as though it's going to protect me against what I'm feeling and the way I'm somehow softening for the man next to me.

There's some commotion in front of the tilt-o-whirl that draws both of our attention. There's a group of five or six teenage boys, and at first it seems like they are just messing around with each other, but they continue to push at one of the kids in particular and it becomes clear that this isn't just them playing around with some friends.

"Stop," the kid complains; he looks smaller than the rest of the group, but they continue to antagonize him.

"C'mon, Griffin, don't be a little bitch," one of the other boys' taunts.

"Stop it!" Griffin cries out again.

"Hold on," Jameson says gruffly before stalking over to the group while I stay rooted in the same spot.

He approaches the group, immediately drawing their attention. His back is to me, and I try not to appreciate how his strong shoulders look while he stands tall, so sure and confident. When I hear him actually confront them, I hold my breath, waiting to see what his plan is.

"There a problem here, gentlemen?" Jameson asks.

"Just messing around, sir," one of the bullies responds.

"What about you?" Jameson turns his attention to Griffin.

The boy looks down, appearing nervous about responding and I can't tell if he doesn't want to make things worse with the group, or if he really thinks they're his friends and that this would ruin it.

"Where are your parents?" Jameson asks.

No one answers him this time.

"Okay, well, how about you all head home, or I'm sure I could find out who your parents are and have them come get you."

"No, you don't need to do that," one of the kids says, sounding worried and they start backing away from Jameson. "We're going."

Griffin hangs back slightly, and I see him turn toward Jameson, a small smile pulling at his lips. I can't hear him, but it looks like he quietly says, "Thank you."

Jameson puts his fist out toward the kid, who bumps it with his own and I don't know why the simple action makes me melt. When this sexy firefighter turns back toward me, the softness in his gaze and that damn cowboy hat makes me feel weak in the knees.

Friends; that's all we can be. I need to keep reminding myself of this.

Every step he takes toward me has me feeling like that's less and less likely to happen. I can only hope he's as genuine of a person as he seems when I inevitably lose this battle with myself.

CHAPTER 16

Jameson

SUTTON'S DOING her absolute best to avoid eye contact with me. Holding onto the teddy bear I won for dear life and I'm pretty sure that I'm walking around with a perpetual smirk on my face because of it.

I take my time picking out the ride for us to go on. Pretending like I'm seriously weighing our options, even though I've known exactly which one I'd pick. I just wanted an excuse to be around her longer. I'm not ready for it to end. Because once she's done holding up her end of our little deal, that's it. She'll leave. Go home. And I'll be standing here alone, trying to convince myself it didn't mean more than it did.

This is the first time I've gotten to spend an extended amount of time with her since she came over to groom Juniper. Even then I tried not to hover because I knew she wouldn't want that. Right now, she's not complaining but she's also not saying anything, either.

"How about the Ferris wheel," I finally offer after the third time we've made a rotation around the small fairgrounds.

"That works."

We walk toward the ride, and there's a short line, but it moves quickly.

"You're going to need to leave the bear with me," the attendant tells Sutton.

"Guess you can't use him as a buffer between us," I joke.

"I wasn't going to do that."

"I don't think I believe that."

Sutton sets the stuffed toy down by the attendant's stand before we both sit on the small bench seat on the ride. The bar comes down across our laps and the attendant says, "Enjoy."

The ride starts to take us up, and Sutton is looking around, taking in the view as we get higher. I'm just looking at her.

Everything about her pulls me in. From her dark green eyes, to the perfect slope of her nose and her plush pink lips. But it's more than that. She's strong, funny, and enthralling. She's everything I've ever wanted in my life but never found. She's completely and utterly perfect.

"What're you staring at?" she finally asks, not looking at me.

"The only thing worth looking at up here."

I hear her sharp intake of breath as she turns to look at me and this view is even better than just her dimly lit profile against the setting sun. Her eyes flick down to my mouth, then back up to mine.

"Why do you keep doing that?" She sighs.

"Doing what?"

"Saying things like that."

"Like what? The truth?"

She opens and closes her mouth in the way she does when I've caught her off guard. I stretch my arm out around the back of the bench, not touching her. She does the most surprising thing, and scoots closer, ever so slightly so our sides are completely pressed together.

Sutton looks up at me, gaze bouncing between my eyes and my lips once again. "You make it really hard to justify being just your friend."

"You're the only one making that a rule." She presses into my side a little harder, and I feel myself leaning down slightly. "I'll take whatever you're willing to give me."

"I have nothing to give," she practically whispers, our faces only a couple inches apart.

"That's okay, because I'm here regardless."

Our foreheads are almost touching as we both lean toward each other. I feel her breath caressing my lips and we're closer than we've ever been. I think she's going to let me kiss her, and before it's even happened, I already know it's going to be the greatest kiss of my life.

Because it's her. It's Sutton.

Without thinking about it I bring my hand up to her cheek, cupping it, and running my thumb along her jaw, tilting her chin up just slightly, enough so our lips barely graze each other. It's not a kiss, not yet, but she hasn't stopped me. And I don't think she's going to.

"Alright, time to get off," the voice of the ride attendant breaks through the haze we've found ourselves in. I watch Sutton's eyes shoot up to mine right before she scoots away from me, seeming to realize exactly what was about to happen.

Her head is ducked as she stands up and beelines away from the ride. I remain seated a moment longer to glare at the attendant.

"Really? You couldn't have let us have one more time around?"

He shrugs. "Sorry, man."

I sigh, racing after Sutton because I know she's going to try and push me away again. I hope she doesn't, because she can deny it all she wants but we had a moment. And for that brief moment, I managed to break down one of the many walls she's built around herself.

"Sutton, hold on." I jog to catch up with her after snatching up the teddy bear she didn't remember to grab in her haste to get away from me.

It doesn't take long for me to catch up, stepping in front of her, effectively blocking her path as I hold the bear out to her. "You forgot this."

She freezes, panic written all over her face, probably already regretting what we came so close to doing. I don't want her to regret it. I don't want her to be afraid. She takes the stuffed bear hesitantly with a small, "thank you."

"How're you getting home?" I ask, because maybe if I pretend like the Ferris wheel didn't happen then she won't freak out as much.

"I came with Bailey because we're neighbors, so I was going to...*oh*." She seems to realize that Bailey left and that was her ride home.

"I can give you a ride if you need," I offer easily.

"No, no that's okay. I can call a ride-share or a taxi," she says, waving me off.

"Sutton." I give her a pointed look and put on a fake southern accent. "I know you're still getting used to this small-town life, but 'round here we don't have those fancy shubers or taxi cabs."

A laugh bubbles out of her, and I smile proudly at the fact that I was able to get it out of her.

"Seriously, though, let me give you a ride home."

She sucks her bottom lip between her teeth, nibbling on it slightly, and it only serves as a reminder of how close I was to knowing how those same lips would feel pressed against mine.

"Okay," she sighs quietly, and I call it another win for the night.

"Don't act like it's such a hardship," I tease. It earns me another small laugh and I feel like I should be collecting these, saving them up so I can savor them forever. If I have one goal in life, it's to make Sutton laugh at least once every single day because the sound of her laugh is the greatest thing I've ever heard. And to hear it every day forever would be a prize greater than anything I could ever win.

CHAPTER 17

Sutton

WE RIDE in a comfortable silence back to my house. Jameson has a nice truck, and of course even the way he drives is incredibly sexy. One handed, with it draped over the wheel at his wrist. His other arm is resting between us, and I stare at the veins that lead up to his hands which look like they're callused from hard work.

Sitting here, my eyes don't leave his arm, as though I'm trying to will him to move it over to me. "What would it feel like to have his hands on me? To have him reach over and rest his large hand on my thigh. Would he rub his thumb absentmindedly? Or grip me possessively?"

I have so many questions, but I shake my head knowing I'm likely not going to find out the answer to any of them. Mostly because I messed up the possibility of anything happening when I ran away after that almost kiss we had.

Dropping my head back against the seat, I close my eyes and revel in how much of an idiot I am. Now, even the possibility of friendship is out the window. I'm sure he'll avoid me for the foreseeable future after this awkward evening.

"You're thinking really loudly over there." Jameson's tone is full of humor. "Might as well tell me what it's about."

I roll my head to the side to look at him again. "If I'm thinking so loud then you should already know what it's about."

He smirks. "You would think. The problem, it's like your thoughts are screaming, but it's like this shrill high pitch noise that I'm not able to understand."

"Are you calling my voice shrill?" I gasp.

"No, of course not. Your voice is perfect. Your thinking voice on the other hand...."

I slap his arm lightly as he laughs, and then I feel the weight of his hand on my thigh, resting it there. Not in a possessive way. Not rubbing it up and down. It's just there, and it's even better than I thought it would be. It feels...*right.*

We get to my house too soon, and suddenly, my nerves are back. Especially when Jameson cuts the engine. Does he expect to be invited in? Does he think we're going to sleep together? I'm not prepared to sleep with him tonight. I shouldn't sleep with him anyway.

"Thank you for the ride, and this." I lift up the toy.

"I'll walk you to your door. Have to make sure you get in safe."

I look over to my house, all of twenty feet to my front door. "I think I'll be fine."

"It'll make me feel better," he insists.

I go to open my door, but he rushes out of his and finishes opening mine for me before I'm able to step out. I can't help the way my heart swoons at every little thing this man does. It may be cliché to be impressed by him opening the door, but it must be that way for a reason because it works.

We walk up to my door, and I hesitate before unlocking it, turning to face him. "See, safe and sound."

"Not until you're inside."

I sigh, turning toward the door, unlocking and opening it. I step just inside the threshold and look at him with a pointed look. "What about now?"

"Better. Goodnight, Sutton." He smiles that blinding smile that has me seconds away from grabbing his shirt and yanking him inside with me.

"Goodnight, Jameson," I say softly.

He lingers for a moment longer and I open my mouth to invite him inside, but he turns and walks back to his car instead. I watch him walk around the truck, giving me one last glance before climbing inside. He rolls down the passenger window, calling out, "Goodnight."

I wave, and he doesn't drive away. I shut the door, pressing my back to it, and slide down onto the floor where I'm immediately greeted by Bennet in my face.

"Am I making a mistake?" I ask him as he sits right next to me, his fluffy fur grazing my skin and soft eyes looking at me. I want to believe that he's telling me I'm crazy and I should go back to avoiding Jameson, but I know that's not the case. He likes Jameson, and I think I do too.

My head drops back, thumping against the wood so hard it almost sounds like a knock, but I know it's not. I sigh, and then there really is a knock. I furrow my brow, looking at Bennet, silently asking him who could be at the door.

Standing up, I turn to answer it, and my jaw drops when I see Jameson standing there. Before I'm able to ask what he's doing here, he closes the distance between us, cups my face, and drops our foreheads against each other.

My heart is racing, I feel like I can't breathe or move. I think I reach up to grab onto his flannel, but I also feel like I'm having an out of body experience at the anticipation or wondering if I'm hallucinating.

"I couldn't go home without knowing what it feels like," he rasps.

Somehow, I'm able to squeak out, "What?"

Instead of answering, he crashes his lips onto mine, and any other thought I have melts away. I grip his shirt even tighter, trying to pull him against me even more. He's so tall I have to lift up on my toes trying to deepen the kiss.

His hands slide to the back of my head, tangling in my hair as his tongue teases the seam of my lips and I open, letting him in easily. I feel like I'm about to float away and the only thing keeping me grounded is the fact that his hands are on me.

I hardly notice when I let out a soft moan as his tongue slides along mine. He swallows the sound, and I melt into him even more. We almost kissed earlier, but now I'm glad we didn't because I don't want to stop, and that may have been really awkward for everyone if we made out on the Ferris wheel. It would have been even more awkward if I'd climbed on his lap and ripped his clothes off, since I'm dangerously close to doing that right now.

My hands slide up his chest, wrapping around to the nape of his neck as our lips slide against each other, tongues teasing and I'm completely lost in him. I'm seconds away from dragging him inside and jumping him.

He lets out a low groan, and it makes my knees buckle. I feel like I may actually collapse, but the thing about Jameson is that I know he would catch me. I may just be getting to know him, but I know that no matter what, the man pressing up against me, currently making me stupid with his intoxicating kiss, would always catch me if I fall.

The problem is if I fall too far I don't know if anyone would be able to catch me. Not even him.

Pushing my fears away I continue to melt even deeper into this kiss while he ravages my mouth with his. He's soft and gentle, but with the way his teeth scrape my bottom lip I can sense that may not always be the case. And that only makes me crave him even more.

Before I'm able to push things any further, he's pulling back, and as soon as his lips leave mine I miss them. The thought has the panic surging again.

"Goodnight, Sutton," he rasps, rubbing his thumbs along my cheeks.

"Goodnight, Jameson," I breathe out.

He presses another quick kiss to my lips, and I fight the urge to chase his mouth for more. I don't. Instead, I watch him walk out my front door and back to his truck. Before he gets in, he turns back in my direction.

"Make sure you snuggle with that bear I won you." He smiles widely.

I roll my eyes. "You can take him with you to snuggle, I have Bennet."

"Then I guess you can cuddle both of them."

I shake my head with a huff. He climbs into his truck and waits for me to close the door before driving away. This time, I know he's not coming back for the night.

Too bad, because I find myself wishing he would as I get ready for the night. Especially when I get into bed, bringing the teddy bear with me. I think about what it may be like if it was him in my bed.

CHAPTER 18

Jameson

AFTER TWO DAYS of not hearing from Sutton I decide to reach out. I don't want to give her more time to freak out.

Jameson: I have a question that's been bothering me.

Sutton: No, I have not been thinking about you.

Jameson: That wasn't my question, but I'm glad to hear you have been.

Jameson: Have you named the bear I won you?

Sutton: Why would I name something I threw in the trash?

Jameson: *Shocked emoji* You wouldn't!

Sutton: Guess you'll never know.

Jameson: Sounds like I need to come over and check.

Sutton: Don't you have some fires to fight or
lives to save?

Jameson: Not yet, but I like that you know my
work schedule.

Sutton: I saw your truck parked at the station.

Jameson: Glad you're watching me.

Jameson: My vote for names are Sir Snuggles
or Captain Cuddles.

She doesn't respond, and I decide to give her some more time. I also debate if I should make an excuse to go over to the grooming salon to see her.

That thought is completely derailed when the signal goes off for a call, and we have to go.

"Turner, you coming?" I hear Dave ask.

"I think he's too busy pining," Parker retorts.

"You both are going to make me request a shift change," I threaten as they climb into the truck and Jo and I climb into the ambulance.

"You wouldn't," Jo scoffs.

"Probably not, but Parker's one to talk about pining."

"Dish it right back to him then, that'll shut him up."

"Maybe another time when we aren't going on a call."

We all drive to the car accident. Luckily, it's not too bad, just a driver that veered off into the ditch. No visible injuries, but we still look the young man over as protocol and offer to take him to the hospital. He initially declines, but then another car pulls up and an irate woman jumps out.

"Sweetie, are you okay?" She rushes over to where he's sitting on the edge of the ambulance.

"I'm fine, Mom," he grumbles.

"Fine? No, absolutely not you need to go to the hospital! You could have whiplash or internal bleeding! Who's in charge here?" She looks between everyone, then turns toward me, settling her narrowed gaze. "You."

"I'm not in charge," I inform her.

"Well, you have to take him to the hospital, don't you? That's what your job is? He's my baby and I need to know that he's okay. I want every test possible run on him. "

"Mom." The man who can't be less than thirty complains. "I'm fine. I just called you for a ride."

"Don't listen to him, he's clearly concussed. He needs to go," she tries again.

"I'm sorry, ma'am, but he's the patient. As an adult he has the right to refuse medical treatment if he wants and I have to honor his wishes."

"Even if he was dying on the side of the road?" she screeches.

"At that point, he would probably not be conscious and not

able to give me a verbal answer, at which point I would take him to the hospital."

She gasps. "How dare you speak that way about him!"

I furrow my brow and look toward my coworkers for any assistance because she's the one that brought up her son dying on the side of the road.

"Ma'am," Jo says, drawing the woman's attention away from me and to her, which I'm thankful for and will likely owe her after this. "I assure you; we have looked over your son and he's fine. We've offered to take him to the hospital, and he declined. We can't force him to go, but if you wish to take him then that's up to you."

The woman huffs and is clearly still unhappy about this, but she just shoots me a glare before stepping closer to her son.

"Thanks," I tell Jo quietly.

"You owe me."

I knew it.

WE GET BACK to the station, and as we are pulling into the bays, I notice Sutton leaving the salon. She's looking over at the station as she gets to her car. I think about going over there and trying to talk to her, trying again to ask her on a date after the kiss we had the other night.

I'm nothing if not persistent, but I also know I can't force her to want to go out with me. Even though it felt like she softened toward me that night. I wanted to take things further, and for a moment I thought maybe she did too.

But I'm a gentleman and Ma raised me right. So of course I wasn't going to push the first chance I got.

Without giving myself more time to debate, I hop out of the ambulance and jog over to Sutton before she has the chance to drive away.

"Hey," I say as casually as I can when I approach her Jeep.

"Hi," she responds softly.

"Did you make a decision?"

The look she gives me has me biting back a laugh at her confusion. "A decision about what?"

"You already forgot? Sutton, you wound me. I had a very important question for you earlier that you never answered."

She continues to look even more confused, and the way her lips purse makes me want to kiss the look right off her face. Now that I know what she feels like pressed against me, mouths molded together while our tongues tangle, it's almost impossible to focus on anything else. Especially when she's standing right in front of me because I want it to happen again.

"Must not have been that important since I can't remember what it was."

I press my hand to my chest and pretend to be injured. "Damn, next time you should actually hit me. It may hurt less than this."

That earns me a small chuckle she tries to cover up with a cough.

"Don't you need to be over there doing your job?" she asks seriously.

"They'll yell if they need me."

"Right, well I'm going home."

"Wait." I hold the top of her door. "Go out with me."

She sighs, looking down at our feet. "Jameson..."

I go weak at how she sounds saying my name. "Just bring Bennet over again. Duke misses him."

"I'm sure he does." She smirks. "I'll think about it."

"I'll take it. Have a good evening, Sutton."

"You, too." She climbs into her car, and I shut the door for her, watching as she drives away.

A hand clamps down on my shoulder, and I flinch in shock. "You got it bad, don't you?" Dave asks.

"Where did you even come from?"

"I'm like a ninja, always around and paying attention, but you don't always see me."

"Should I be concerned?"

He laughs, patting me on the shoulder again. "Probably not."

We walk back to the station, and I avoid my coworkers, especially Parker who I know will say something about me going over to Sutton. I busy myself making a quick dinner and eating so I can try to get a little bit of sleep, hoping we don't get another call for at least a couple of hours.

As I lay down, I look at my phone and see there's a text waiting for me. My heart races as I open it, and a smile spreads across my face. It's a picture of the teddy bear, notably on blankets and some pillows.

> Sutton: I guess I could call him Cuddles, but you only get to refer to him as Captain.

CHAPTER 19

Sutton

IT TAKES another several days of Jameson texting me at least once a day for me to give in to seeing him again. I only agree because I feel like I've managed to get my mind somewhat in order and I can handle seeing him in a completely platonic way, in a completely platonic setting.

Our dogs are hanging out and running around on his property, that's it.

I almost canceled because the weather looked questionable. I knew moving to Washington there would be a significant amount of rain, but in the summer, it doesn't seem to rain as much as it's supposed to in the winter. However, today it seems that may change and I'm on the verge of experiencing some classic Pacific Northwest rainfall.

The reason I don't cancel is because of the single text I see when I pick up my phone.

Jameson: I can't wait to see you.

I don't reply, instead I get dressed in a pair of jeans and a T-shirt debating if I should bring a hoodie as well but even if it rains it's not going to be cold enough, so I go without.

Bennet and I load up in my Jeep and drive over to Jameson's property. I guess it's really his parent's property, but he lives there so it counts as his to me.

I'm just as nervous driving along the unpaved ground as I was last time. Actually, maybe even more so. When I get to the barn, I park in the same spot I did before, but I'm instantly distracted by Jameson riding the same brown horse he rode at the rodeo. What he's doing right now looks leisurely compared to the racing.

Bennet jumps out of my car, immediately seeking out Duke who just exited the barn. I watch them act like old friends as they start to play.

"Hey," Jameson greets cheerfully, bringing the horse to a stop.

I step up to the railing of the arena, leaning against it. "What're you doing?"

"Working out Jasper. I can be done, though."

"No," I shout, and he stops from dismounting. "I want to watch."

"Like watching me ride a horse?" He smirks, and I roll my eyes. "Would you like to join me?"

"Uh, no."

"Come on, you can ride Juniper. She's sweet."

I scrunch my nose. "She may be until she bucks me off."

He barks out a loud laugh. "She wouldn't. I won't let her."

His words make my stomach swoop, and it feels like everything he says lately is making me feel this way. The fear continues to linger, but I focus on a distraction so I don't completely lose my mind.

"We'll see. Now, show me what I want to see," I taunt.

"Tell me what you want to see, and I'll show you anything."

I hide my smile behind my hand resting on the railing. He doesn't wait for my response before he starts riding around the arena. He does a couple slower laps, then goes a little faster before stopping on one end. The anticipation rises within me as I wait to see what he's going to do next.

Then he's off, just like at the rodeo, he's racing around the barrels so fast it makes my heart race. He turns, and again I worry about him falling off when he takes the turns. I don't even notice I'm holding my breath until he guides the horse to a stop, and I let out a sigh of relief.

"How was that? What you were wanting?" he asks with a wide smile that makes me weak. Add in the backwards cap on his head, and the way his shirt is gripping his biceps and it's a good thing there's so much space between us because I'm worried how I would react if I had the ability to touch him right now.

"Yeah, it'll do." I shrug, sliding my hands off the railing, and turn to go find our dogs, only to create some distance between us and get myself together.

I'm walking through the hallway of the barn when I hear the clicking of hooves on the cement, and see Jameson is tying the horse up to take off the saddle.

"What's his name?" I ask, daring to approach.

"Jasper, but he's not mine. I'm helping my mom with him while his real owner is at summer camp."

"That's nice of you. Does she know you're working him to the bone?" I joke.

He laughs, it's deep and throaty and sends a pang of electricity through me that has my legs feeling weak. Everything he does continues to pull me in.

"Of course she knows. That's why Ma asked me to help. He needs to stay in top shape for when Summer gets back."

Of course he's not only sweet. He's helpful and thoughtful for seemingly everyone. If the man in front of me could stop being so perfect, that would be extremely helpful.

He takes everything off Jasper, leading him into his stall and after brushing him down, gives him some extra food and a couple treats.

"Where'd our dogs go?" he asks lightly.

"Oh." I hesitate looking around because I'm just now realizing how distracted I was by him, and I never ended up finding the two canines I was looking out for. "I don't know."

"We can go look for them. Duke doesn't go far, I'm sure

they're close by," he reassures, leading me out of the barn. "You can see a bit more of the property while we look for them."

"This seems like a trap."

"You caught me, this was my plan all along." He winks, and I turn away to hide my smile.

We walk away from the main house and barn, further onto the property, and I'm starting to wonder if the dogs actually went to the house, and Jameson is just trying to get me alone. The thought should have my defenses rising, but all I can think is that I don't mind it at all.

That is until he asks the dreaded question.

"What brought you to Amity?"

I sigh. "A story you'd never even believe."

"Try me."

"Would you believe it was just because I wanted to?"

"Not at all." He chuckles.

"Why?"

"No one moves here. People leave here. This is the place you run from, not run to."

"Why are you still here then? Shouldn't you have run?"

He raises an eyebrow at me, clearly recognizing the deflection that this is. Luckily for me, he goes along with the diversion.

"I did." He tucks his hands into the pockets of his jeans. "I moved to Florida for a while, ten years to be exact. I just came back recently."

"Why Florida?" My immediate thought is that he's going to say a girl, and the thought has my hackles rising. I have no reason to be jealous of some other woman, yet that's exactly what I'm feeling before he's even had a chance to answer.

"It's the complete opposite of this place. I wanted to experience city life and warm weather. I wanted a change."

"And you enjoyed it?"

He nods. "I did."

"Why'd you come back?"

He hesitates, looking straight ahead and I feel like this is the first time I've seen him not have a hint of playfulness in his eyes. The lightness he always seems to carry dims at my question, and it reminds me of my reaction when he asked me.

Knowing we both have something that brought us here that we don't necessarily want to talk about makes me want to reach out and touch his arm. Reassure him that he doesn't need to tell me.

Before I'm able to do anything, the sky opens up and suddenly it's dumping rain. I squeal at the sudden flood falling on us. Jameson doesn't waste any time grabbing my hand without even thinking about it and pulling me behind him as we jog somewhere.

I hardly pay any attention to where we're going, more focused on not slipping and falling on the suddenly slick ground. He pulls me inside, and I look down at my drenched clothes, my hair is dripping onto the wood floor, and every piece of fabric is sticking to my skin.

"Let me get you a towel," he mumbles, rushing off. I look around and notice we're in a small house I didn't notice before.

It's simple with a couch that looks unbelievably comfortable, like I could simply sink into it. There's a TV and a large dog bed in the corner.

Jameson comes out with a towel, wrapping it around me instead of just draping it over my shoulders.

"Now I know this was a part of your plan," I tease him, and he smiles. The lightness is back in his features, and it makes me curious what he didn't want to tell me. But I would much rather see him look at me like this than how he was before.

"You caught me. I planned the rain. I'm really close with Zeus and he knows exactly when I need the weather changed."

I can't help the loud laugh I let out. "Is Zeus in charge of the weather?"

"To me he is."

I laugh even more, tightening the towel around me.

"I really like your laugh," he says, taking me off guard slightly. I look at him, and the way he's looking at me is full of something I can't quite place. Adoration, maybe. Whatever it is, I don't want him to stop.

I shift on my feet. "I like when you make me laugh."

"You're still cold. Do you want to borrow some clothes?" he offers, and I look him over before looking down at myself.

"I'm going to say something you may not have noticed, but we aren't even close to the same size."

"You're right, I haven't noticed that. Here I was thinking we could share closets with each other."

That earns him another laugh from me, I cover my mouth with my hand wrapped in the towel.

"Please, let me lend you something so we can dry your clothes. You can't go home soaking wet."

A surge of panic runs through me, mentioning being soaking wet. "Oh my God, we need to find the dogs; they can't be stuck out there in this." I'm about to bolt out of this house, but he stops me, stepping in front of me.

"Hey, it's okay. They're up at my parent's house, Ma texted to let me know."

I narrowed my eyes at him. "Was that before or after we were searching for them?"

He gives a wry look. "Possibly during. Though, I didn't see it until we came back here."

I want to give him shit for that, but I can't bring myself to do it. Instead, I accept the change of clothes he offers because the chill has now seeped into my bones, and I'm worried I'm about to start shaking like a little chihuahua.

He leaves me alone in the bathroom to change into his clothes that are drowning me, but the large T-shirt and boxers surround me in his clean, pine scent. So, I take an extra second to enjoy the feeling of it.

Once I come out, I see that he's also changed into a pair of sweatpants and a new T-shirt of his own. He's also not wearing that cap on his head, which is good because when he turns it backwards it makes me stupid. And don't even get me started on the cowboy hat he wears. Though, the sweatpants that are hanging low on his hips are doing the exact same thing.

"You're right." He shakes his head, looking at me with an undeniable heat in his gaze, though I don't know why.

"About what?"

"We aren't the same size, but it doesn't matter because you look damn good in my clothes."

I fight the blush creeping into my cheeks as he takes my wet clothes from me, turning to look around the house in an effort to distract myself.

"Do you want anything to drink?" he offers.

I plop down onto the couch, and it's as comfy as I thought it would be as I sink into the softness. "No thanks, I'm good."

"Okay, I'm going to get these in the dryer." He walks to where I assume the laundry room is, and I just glance around at the space, getting a glimpse of how Jameson lives. The sense of comfort that surrounds me here has nothing to do with the couch, and more about the space in general. It makes me want to run.

But unless I want to get soaked again and drive home in sopping wet clothes, then I'm stuck for the time being.

When he comes back into the living room, I can't help but ask, "Should we go get the dogs? I feel bad having your mom deal with Bennet."

He pulls his phone out of his pocket, and when he turns the screen toward me, I see the picture of my black and white fluffy dog curled up on a dog bed with Jameson's blue nose Pitbull snuggled up against him. It's like they're sharing the bed, with Duke using Bennet as a pillow.

My heart melts at the sight of the two of them together. Why can't it be that easy for humans to make friends? There's too much distrust and betrayal that comes with any relationship for us. A dog would never betray another dog or do something to ruin the other's trust. Dogs are the most loyal creatures there are, and the pure innocence of them only makes them even better.

If only I could let myself be like Bennet.

"That's so sweet, tell your mom thank you." I look up at Jameson who has that same look in his eyes every time he looks at me. The softness that sends a sense of calmness over me.

"I will," he assures. "I think we should wait out the storm a bit, hopefully your clothes will be dry by the time it lets up."

"Yeah, that's a good idea," I agree, feeling a slight awkward tension in the air at the reality of being here with him alone, wearing his clothes, somewhat stuck until the rain stops.

"What do you like to watch?" he asks, dropping down onto the couch next to me, but keeping enough distance between us so we aren't touching and something about the distance makes me want to close it.

I bring my legs up to hug them against my chest. "Anything is fine."

"Don't tell me that, I'll put on something extremely boring. Maybe a nature documentary, or sports." His tone is teasing.

I turn slightly toward him. "What makes you think I'd find either of those things boring? Maybe I love nature documentaries. I may be the biggest sports fan there is, you don't know."

"Oh yeah? What's your favorite sport?"

"The one with a ball."

"Which one?"

"All of them."

He laughs, it's so genuine I can't help but smile. "Only sports with balls, huh?"

"Of course, is there any other kind?"

"Yeah, hockey uses a puck."

I clamp my mouth shut because I didn't even consider hockey. "You got me there."

"Well, you're lucky because it's not in season right now." He sits back, relaxing onto the couch. "So, nature documentary it is."

I bite back my laugh, thinking he's not actually going to put one on, but he does. My stubbornness prevents me from saying anything about it. Even after ten minutes of neither of us saying anything and already being bored out of my mind.

"Wow, did you know that?" he asks, and I realize I was not listening to the show, so I shake my head.

"Nope, I didn't."

"Interesting." He nods like he's actually paying attention to the screen.

A laugh bubbles out of me. "Don't act like you're enjoying this."

"What do you mean? Of course I am."

I roll my eyes, settling deeper into the couch. I notice that somehow one of us has scooted closer to the other. I'm not sure who moved, whether it was both of us, or even when it happened, but our sides are practically touching. His arms are stretched out along the back of the couch while I remain with mine wrapped around my legs that are up by my chest.

The rain pounds the roof above us and the steady noise is all I can focus on because the longer I sit here, this close to him, the comfortable silence makes me want to reach out and touch him. It makes me want to feel what it may be like to kiss him again.

Would it feel the same as it did the other night? Would it pull every thought from my mind, and make him the only thing that matters in that moment? Would it be enough to break down my walls for me to give in and fall into him?

"Why're you looking at me like that?" he asks smoothly, and the slight upturn of his mouth has me focusing on his lips even more since he's still looking ahead at the TV.

I don't know what to say because I don't have a reason. There's no way I could say what I'm thinking. I can't tell him that I'm thinking about our kiss or that I want to do it again. The words won't come out, and that's when I consider throwing caution to the wind.

We're alone here, and nothing from outside these walls needs to matter. Not what I ran away from, not the reason he came back. Nothing needs to matter except the two of us.

In an act of boldness I've never had before, I close the small distance between us, swinging a leg over Jameson's lap, and he immediately grabs onto my hips.

"What're you doing?" he asks, surprised, but holding me in place like he knows I may try to run.

"Don't ask," I whisper, leaning down to press my lips against his.

CHAPTER 20

Jameson

I DON'T KNOW what's happening, or why it's happening, but Sutton is in my lap and she's kissing me. It takes me a second to catch up, but once I do I wrap my arms around her waist, pulling her tighter against me while kissing her back.

Her hands slide from my shoulders around the back of my neck as I deepen the kiss. She meets my tongue with her own letting out a small moan that has my dick thickening even more in my pants. Especially when she rolls her hips over mine, I know she can feel it by the small gasp she lets out.

I use that to my advantage, moving one hand to the back of her head, tangling my fingers in her damp hair while our mouths move against each other. I kiss along her jaw and neck, using my grip on her hair to give myself better access to run my lips along her soft skin. She rubs herself against me again, and I groan.

"Baby, if you keep that up, I'm going to end up really embarrassed," I grind out, but even as I say that, I help guide her movements against me. I can't feel her to know how wet she is, and I would give anything to shed the layers of clothes between us just so I can know. Even now I swear I can feel the heat of her against my cock.

"Keep what up? This?" she teases, rubbing herself even harder against me. I grip her even tighter, slamming her mouth onto mine in a vicious kiss that's completely untamed. Everything before this moment pales in comparison with the way we fight for dominance with our lips, tongues, and teeth.

"Fuck," I groan. "That feel good?"

"So good," she breathes into my mouth, taking it in a searing kiss.

I can't help but thrust up against her, my dick dying to get closer any way it can. The way she's swiveling her hips while she rubs herself only makes me think of what she would look like doing the same thing with my cock buried deep inside her.

"You going to make yourself come like this?" I rasp, gripping her hip even tighter to move her over my length.

"I-I don't...maybe—" She hesitates, and that causes me to completely take charge. She hasn't seen all the sides of me, but she's about to.

I hold her down on top of my lap where I know she can feel me, solid between her legs and she wiggles trying to get more friction. She tries to kiss me again, but I use my other hand to hold the hair at the base of her neck and stay just out of reach. She lets out the cutest little growl, and it makes me smirk.

"You going to get yourself off just by riding me like this, baby?" My voice is low, gravely and I recognize this is the second time I've called her that tonight, but she hasn't said anything and it feels too natural in this moment.

Sutton moans softly, dropping her forehead to mine and nods, squirming once again. I crash our mouths together once more, and help guide her movements against me while our tongues thrash against each other.

She feels so good rubbing herself against me like this. Everything about her is perfect, the way she moves, the way she feels, I want more but I don't dare push her too far.

"Show me what it looks like when you fall apart for me," I demand while I feel myself getting dangerously close to releasing myself. I do everything I can to hold back though because this moment is about her, not me.

"I want to feel you," she confesses softly between kisses, and my attempt to keep my release at bay is obliterated by that single sentence, because I want that too.

"You will," I tell her. What I don't tell her is that it won't be today. "But right now I need you to get there and come for me."

She moans louder, her movements becoming more erratic while we move together, fucking through our clothes and somehow it's the hottest moment I've ever experienced. I can only imagine how amazing it'll be if I get the chance to have her naked underneath me.

She gets closer to her peak, and I continue to hold mine back. But when her legs squeeze mine as her body tenses with a sharp whimper as she finds her release, the sound, the sight, the feeling, everything is too much and the orgasm I was barely holding back takes over. Groaning, I drop my head to her shoulder while she holds onto me tightly as hers racks through her.

We're both breathing heavily, but neither of us move. We're in this bubble, and as long as we don't move or speak we get to stay here. As the post orgasmic feeling fades, the fear creeps in that she's going to run again.

So does the feeling of needing to change my pants because she just made me come in them like a teenager. Which is why I resort to humor to try and lighten the mood, hoping she won't go running.

"You caused a little bit of a mess, are you going to help clean it up?" She pulls back slightly, looking at me, then down into my lap where her mouth tugs upward slightly. That simple look makes me relax slightly.

"You're a big boy, I think you can clean up yourself." She climbs off my lap slowly and I instantly miss the feeling of her on me. I have to fight the urge to grab her and put her right back where she belongs. Which is as close as possible to me.

I stand up, but before walking back toward my bedroom, I lean down, holding her chin and forcing her to look up at me. "Don't run."

Her gaze softens. "I won't."

I press a featherlight kiss to her lips, then go to my room, cleaning up something that should be embarrassing, but because of the look she gave me when she saw what happened I feel the opposite. I just hope that even once the rain stops she's not going to shut me out again.

CHAPTER 21

Sutton

I WOULDN'T SAY I ran away after the rain let up. But I didn't stay much longer, either. My mind is at war with itself because I can't bring myself to regret what happened. Although, I'm not sure it's a good idea for it to happen again, either.

Of course Jameson walked me up to the main house—his parents' house—so I could get Bennet, and then back to my car. It doesn't seem to matter how many times I tell him that he can go be free and do whatever I'm sure he'd rather be doing, but he insists he's right where he wants to be.

It only makes my mind swim with even more confusion, because I want to trust that he really is this genuine. I want to think this is just who he is, but I'm just waiting for a shoe to drop. Some deep dark secret that will come out at the worst time and ruin anything we may have.

Bennet doesn't jump into my car right away like he usually does. "Come on, hop in."

He sits down next to his new buddy, Duke, and I sigh.

"I think they like each other," Jameson states.

"You'll see your new friend again, okay?" I tell my dog, who still seems hesitant to leave. "Come on."

He huffs, but jumps into the car, and I shut the door behind him, opening mine and turning toward Jameson before climbing in.

"What about me? Will I get to see my new friend again?" He smiles, leaning closer to me.

"So we're just friends then?" I raise an eyebrow.

"If that's what it takes to ensure I get to see you again."

"We'll see." I shrug, getting into the driver's seat.

"You said you wouldn't run."

"And I'm not. I am going to drive, though." I reach for the door, but he shuts it for me. I roll down the window, because as weird as it may sound I look forward to hearing how he says my name when we part. "Goodbye, Jameson."

"Goodbye, Sutton."

I'M DISTRACTED at work the next day, replaying yesterday over and over in my mind. I've spiraled enough to regret it, and try to figure out when it can happen again. Luckily, Lily is here today, and if anyone has the ability to take you out of your own head, it's her.

She's high energy and hilarious. She also says things you'd never expect to hear, mostly because she doesn't stop talking for very long. Which I don't mind because it's kept me thoroughly entertained throughout my day. It's also kept me from losing my mind even more than I already have.

"So they met on a bondage dating app," she says, like that's an extremely normal thing to say when starting a new conversation. Though, maybe the last one hasn't ended. Truly, I'm not sure.

"Wait, who did?" I shake my head trying to catch up.

"My roommate freshman year, I just said that."

She may have, but I'm tuning out some of what she says. Or maybe she said it while I was washing or drying a dog and literally couldn't hear her.

"I didn't even know that kind of app existed."

"Me either, but it gets so much worse." She guides the dog she just bathed into the kennels to dry in there for a little. "So, we all go out for dinner and she said this guy, Steve, was going to meet up with her later. What she didn't say was that he was going to join us for dinner."

I hum, listening to her as she continues her extremely animated storytelling.

"This man in a suit walks up to our table and introduces himself as Thomas. I thought he was the manager because how he was dressed, but he sits down at our table, and I'm really fucking confused. I'm looking at Anna and our other friends wondering who this man is."

I think Anna is the roommate, but there's been so many names thrown at me from her stories that I'm losing track.

"Turns out his name is Thomas, but she thought it was Steve. I don't know how she screwed that up, but anyway she says he's joining us at this bar we're going to next."

I'm pretty sure she's not twenty-one, but even if I wanted to ask to clarify anything she doesn't pause long enough to give me the chance.

"We leave the restaurant and he goes to his car, and when Stevemas opened the door, his car was full of rubber ducks."

"What?" I screech.

"Yup, seat covers, steering wheel cover, floor mats, and just loose rubber ducks everywhere."

"Did he have a Jeep?" I know it's a thing that when you have a cool Jeep, people will leave rubber ducks on it. Mine has gotten a couple, but I would never go as far as to have seat covers and floor mats of them.

"Nope, it was a small car with just a fuckload of rubber ducks. Anyway, we all went to the bar and Anna ended up going home with Thomeve, but brought him back to our dorm so I had to spend the night in our other friend's room, which sucked because I had to sleep on the floor. The next morning I went back to our room, and when I opened the door there were condoms everywhere."

I grimace at the visual.

"Luckily he was gone, but she was still in bed, and I think he fucked her stupid, but they went to town. I couldn't help myself; I kicked her awake and said 'Damn, duck man really ducked you real good didn't he?'"

That does it for me and I laugh so loud I'm sure everyone at the fire station next door can hear me. I hold my stomach as though it can contain the sound that is bursting out of me. Lily looks at me, clearly amused, but I can't stop. Of course Jerry Lee feels the need to insert his two cents, *"Shut up, Vern."*

Because I'm already losing it, I end up laughing even harder. Tears prick at the corners of my eyes, and I try my best to pull myself together. Finally, I do enough to ask, "Did she end up seeing him again?"

"Nope, she hit it and quit it."

"Really? You'd think after such a solid ducking she would want to see him again."

"She may have been ducked out, but had a good time."

I may not know Anna, but I can say that thanks to her sacrifice, I also had a good time hearing this outrageous story. And it was the perfect distraction today, exactly what I needed. It's not until I get home after work that I let my mind take over once again as to why getting involved with Jameson would be a bad idea.

So, the text from him on my phone goes unanswered.

CHAPTER 22

Jameson

MA ISN'T HAVING a good day. After her appointment, which didn't go as well as we hoped, the mood is somber as we get back home. She tries to lighten it like she always does but I don't think anything can help right now. The disease is progressing faster than any of us thought and I can't bear to think about what that truly means.

"I think we could splurge for some ice cream, what do you think?" Her voice is just as bright as it always is, not a hint of sadness or fear.

"I think that's hardly a splurge, Ma. You have ice cream after dinner every day." She always has. It was basically a tradition as I was growing up. I'm not big on sweets, but I'll always have ice cream, especially her favorite, chocolate chip cookie dough.

"What if my splurge is having it twice?" She smiles.

I can't help but smile back and nod, agreeing. "Fine, but sit down and I'll bring it to you."

She huffs like she wants to argue, but no matter how hard she tries to hide how tired she is from me, it won't work. I can read the truth in her eyes, but I'm not going to call her on it. Instead of saying anything, she goes and sits in her chair while I go to the kitchen to get her a bowl of ice cream.

I don't think I can stand to eat any right now, but I'll give her whatever it is she wants. My dad ends up coming into the kitchen while I'm scooping the dessert. He didn't come with us because Ma insisted he didn't need to. He loves her, and I know he wants to be with her every step of the way, but being around me creates a tension in the air that's impossible to ignore. Ma knows it. My dad knows it. I know it.

I just want us to be civil, at least for Ma. He doesn't seem to agree with that. Especially with the way he's looking at me right now. I do my best to ignore his gaze, looking down as I scoop the second spoonful into the glass bowl.

"How'd it go?" his gruff voice asks quietly. I'm taken aback by the fact that he's asking me.

I sigh. "Not great. It's progressing faster than they would like and the treatment isn't as effective as they hoped."

His face remains blank, hiding any emotion he might be feeling just like he always does. I may know my parents love each other, but sometimes I wonder how I've come to that conclusion. They've never been overly affectionate. I would never walk into a room where they were dancing. We wouldn't come home to my dad scooping her up with a kiss because he missed her so much.

All the things I think I would want to do with my wife, if I ever get married. I would want her to know how loved and lucky I am to have her every single day of our lives.

On the other hand, I've never felt that way with anyone before and it's why I haven't gotten married. So maybe that doesn't exist for anyone, even if you are in love it is never as intense as I think it should be.

Except, I can't help but think about Sutton. The feelings I'm already having for her are stronger than I've ever felt for anyone, and I barely even know her. There's just something there, something about her. About us. I can feel it simmering under the surface and it's like the type of love I've thought about. The kind I wasn't sure existed may be real.

My dad still hasn't said anything, but him clearing his throat pulls me from my runaway thoughts. The ice cream I've scooped already starting to melt. I grab a spoon, and the bowl to take to Ma. I stop before leaving the kitchen, "She may not admit she's scared to me, but I can tell she feels more than she's letting on. Just like I know she would like to see us get along for her sake."

I don't give him a chance to respond before I'm joining my mom in the living room, handing her the bowl. She has a smile on her face, but her eyes are tired.

"Thank you, sweetie." Her eyebrows furrow when she takes in the one bowl. "Why don't you have one for yourself?"

"I'm not really hungry."

She narrows her eyes at me, taking a bite and I look down, huffing out a laugh at her glare. I don't expect my dad to enter the room, but Ma's expression changes from her lighthearted glare to a soft smile toward my dad.

Maybe that has been there before and I just haven't noticed or maybe it's something I've never really thought much about. Seeing the way she's looking at him and the concern in his eyes toward her makes me think that maybe I've just chosen not to pay attention to their kind of love.

"What if we all went to dinner at some point," my dad suggests out of the blue and I jolt at the surprise of his suggestion.

Ma on the other hand, is already beaming at the idea. "That would be so nice, we haven't all gone to dinner in...well since before you moved."

The reminder has my dad's posture stiffening and even though this is clearly his idea to do what I suggested, I can't help but think this may end up being a terrible idea.

"You can bring that sweet girl, Sutton," Ma says to me, and I grin at her name, but hate that I'm going to have to shoot the idea down.

"I don't think she would agree to come to dinner with us, Ma."

"Oh, you don't invite her, then. I will."

I chuckle. "You can try, she's more likely to say yes to you."

"Perfect, it's settled then. One condition." We both wait to see what her condition is about to be, though I know no matter what it is, I'm going to agree. "I get to pick the restaurant."

🦅

I END up at the grooming salon the next day when I drive by heading to the grocery store, and see Sutton's Jeep outside. It only takes me a second to decide to turn into the parking lot that sits between the fire station and the salon.

When I walk inside I'm immediately greeted by that bird barking at me, *"Hello."*

"Hello," I tell my fan club president.

"One second," the familiar voice calls out from further inside, and I regret not bringing Duke with me. But I really wasn't planning on stopping in here, and most people frown upon a dog at the grocery store. Plus he was sleeping on a bed next to the couch at my parent's house when I left.

As soon as Sutton steps out into the entry area and sees me, her face falls in shock. "What're you doing here?"

"You haven't replied to my last few texts."

She looks down to hide the way her face floods with color, but I catch it. I also know it doesn't help when the bird says, *"Hot guy, Jameson."*

"Jerry Lee, I'm opening a window for you," Sutton threatens and I smother a laugh.

"Since I knew this would get ignored like the rest, I decided to come in person to invite you to dinner."

She sighs. "Jameson, I've already told you—"

"I know." I almost remind her that she's turned me down, but also was the one to initiate our last encounter. The one that ended with her coming on my lap while I came in my pants like a teenager, but I have a feeling if I said anything about that she would kick me out. "I'm not inviting you for myself."

She gives me a curious look.

"My ma wants you to come with us."

"Why?" she snaps suddenly.

"She likes you."

"She hardly met me."

"Must just be a Turner thing to like you then." I smirk and she shakes her head and rolls her eyes.

"You're really persistent, you know that?"

"I know."

"Why does she want me to come with?"

"I already told you."

Sutton groans. "I don't think it's a good idea, I don't really do family stuff."

I note the grimace at the word family, and feel like there's more about that than she's letting on. However, I want her to come more than just because Ma wants her there. I feel like I'll need the distraction. I haven't been around my dad for an extended amount of time in years, and though he suggested this, I feel like the dinner will be anything but smooth.

"It's not for me," I tell her. "It's for my ma. She's sick," I choke on the last word, but do my best to hide it. "She wants you to come with."

"Oh," she sighs, looking down at her feet.

"So, will you come?"

She hesitates before nodding slightly. "But, only for your mom. Not for you."

"Good." I nod. "I wouldn't want it any other way."

As I leave I don't miss the way her gaze softens.

"I'll pick you up tomorrow at six."

I walk out before she has the chance to change her mind, and can't wipe the smile off my face. It may not be the date I thought I would get with her, but it's something. I can only hope this one dinner won't scare her away for good.

Even if it does, she's right about me being persistent and I won't be giving up any time soon.

CHAPTER 23

Sutton

"DON'T LOOK at me like that," I tell Bennet who's watching me get ready to go to dinner with Jameson and his parents. I don't know how I ended up in this position, but there's no way I can back out now.

Even if I've thought about it multiple times over the last several hours.

It's just a dinner, and it's not even for him. It's for his mom, who was really sweet when I met her. It makes me believe that maybe Jameson really is as good as he seems when he was raised by a woman like that.

Though he may be sweet, I saw a glimpse of another side to him the other day. The day I threw caution to the wind, let my mind turn off and just act on pure instinct, which at that moment was to feel good. It worked almost too well because every time I think about how it felt to be on his lap I'm tempted to relive the entire moment. The way his lips felt on mine, how I was so turned on I could practically cry as I rubbed against him. The low moan he let out when we both found our release without our skin even touching.

The feeling was already so strong, I can only imagine how strong it would be if we really got the chance to take things further.

Which is why we can't.

And why this dinner tonight doesn't count as a date. It won't lead to anything else other than making his mom happy, and maybe a few laughs.

What it will not do, is tempt me any closer to Jameson Turner.

Jameson's truck pulls up outside, and for another two seconds I debate telling him I changed my mind, or that I'm violently ill. Anything to get me out of this, but Bennet nudges my hand, something he often does to get pets on the top of his head, and I look down and see his big brown eyes looking at me. It's his silent encouragement. "Fine, I'll go," I tell him with a groan, grabbing my purse and walking out the front door.

I'm greeted by Jameson walking toward me, and I inwardly groan at how good he looks. The white button down is so simple, but hugs his frame in a way that should be obscene. The black slacks make my knees weak and I never thought I'd have such a visceral reaction to some *pants*.

Okay, aside from grey sweatpants I suppose, but those are obscene no matter who's wearing them.

"You look gorgeous," he tells me, and I scoff, looking down at my simple sundress, which compared to him seems underdressed.

"Thanks," I murmur, and as he takes my hand, my eyes shoot up to his. "You said this wasn't a date."

"It's not, my parents are in the car. Friends can't hold hands?"

I suck my bottom lip into my mouth as we walk toward his truck, and I want to argue that no, friends can't hold hands, but it feels too good. It's also short lived as we approach the car and I start to step toward the backseat.

"You're up front with me," he says.

I shake my head. "No, I'll ride in the back."

"The back is taken," his mom says from the now open window. "You're the guest, you get the front, sweetie."

Jameson faces me with a small grin. "I tried to tell her. Might as well get in the car, she's not going to change her mind."

I notice that an older man, I assume is Jameson's father, is also in the back seat, sitting next to his mother, but he doesn't say anything.

I relent as Jameson opens the passenger door for me, and I climb in, turning back toward his mom with a soft smile.

Jameson climbs in and his mom speaks up again, "This is nice, almost like we have our own chauffeur. I feel like a celebrity."

We both chuckle as Jameson starts to drive. I don't hear his dad make a noise, but when I glance back, I see their hands inter-twined together. I try not to make my smile too obvious because I don't want to seem weird smiling at these two strangers.

I realize I'm not sure where we're going and I'm about to ask when his mom speaks up instead.

"What're your intentions with my boy?" Her tone is teasing.

"Ma," Jameson scolds.

"Oh stop it, we're here to get to know the girl."

"That's not what you said." He looks up at her through the rearview mirror, and I cover my mouth to smother my laughter.

"Sutton, how'd you and my unruly son meet?"

"Unruly?" I sputter, unable to help myself.

"Yes, unruly because if he had any sense he would be settled down by now."

Jameson groans loudly, and rolls down his window, leaning toward it.

"What're you doing?" she asks.

"Just thinking about jumping out into traffic, Ma."

She reaches forward and slaps his arm lightly, and I bark out a loud laugh and quickly slap my hand over my mouth.

"See what I have to deal with?" Jameson raises an eyebrow in my direction quickly before looking back toward the road.

"I'd take this over my parents any day." I regret the words as soon as they're out of my mouth because I don't want that to lead to any questions. Luckily, everyone else in the car seems distracted enough that no one comments about what I said.

Jameson drives us out of town toward Aberdeen, which is the closest bigger city and the playful banter with his mom keeps up, though it seems to stay lighthearted. I'm pulled from my wandering thoughts when I feel his warm hand on my thigh.

I look over at him, and see the easy smile on his face, one hand steering, the other resting on me comfortably. He must feel me looking because he says, "Friends can do this."

Again, I don't argue, but I have to disagree with him. Friends definitely don't do this.

We get to the restaurant, and of course before I'm able to open my own door Jameson is there, opening it for me. I notice how his dad is doing the same for his mom, and though the man didn't say a single word on our drive over here, he helps her out of the lifted truck carefully. I'm staring, but it's so sweet and even before everything went down in my own family my parents were never like this with each other.

That probably explains why my dad cheated and why my mom didn't even care.

"Are you okay?" Jameson asks, his hand slipping into mine again. I look up at him, hoping he can't read me, but the way his blue eyes look at me with so much concern and care has my heart thumping even harder in my chest and I forget about the betrayal I was thinking about. Right now, all that matters is the way this man is looking at me.

"Yeah." I nod. The weirdest thing is that I don't yank my hand away from his. I tighten my grip and let him lead us inside.

He doesn't let go until he's pulling out my chair for me, and then sits next to me at the table. His dad does the same for his mom and I melt a little more watching them.

Once we're all sitting and looking at the menu, Jameson's mom speaks up again, "Sutton, sweetie, I hope you know I was just joking."

"Oh, it's okay, Mrs. Turner." I give her a smile.

"I know you only have good intentions with Jameson. I mean you're the only girl he's ever had us meet, and one day I hope to see him get married and—"

"Ma," Jameson cuts her off.

"We're just friends, Mrs. Turner, that's why I'm here."

"Ah, yes, *friends*." She winks at me and I bury myself in the menu pretending to decide what I'm going to order as if I don't order the same thing at almost every restaurant I go to.

Though, this place is a bit fancier than I'm used to so instead of the chicken tenders I would usually try to order I'm choosing some grilled chicken and vegetables.

"So how long have you all lived in Amity?" I ask to try and pull any attention from myself so no one asks me any questions.

"I'm from here, actually." I assume she's referring to Aberdeen, where we currently are. "Benjamin was here attending college when we met and decided we wanted to find somewhere small to settle down, found the beautiful property in Amity and the rest is history."

She looks over at her husband, and I'm just now realizing I didn't know his name until right now. His gaze softens toward his wife and I smile.

"And all we wanted was for Jameson here to take over the ranch, but he wanted to run off to the tropics instead." Benjamin's face hardens again as he faces his son, his gruff voice only makes him sound resentful.

My spine stiffens at his tone and I feel Jameson tense next to me. Without thinking I place my hand on his thigh, attempting to comfort him.

"Benjamin," Jameson's mom scolds softly.

"And now I'm back," Jameson says through gritted teeth.

"Which we're both so happy about." She reaches her hand across the table with a wide smile.

Benjamin huffs and Jameson clenches his jaw.

"I'm happy about it, too." The words escape my mouth before I'm able to stop them, I just want to do anything to help ease the tension that has come over the table.

His eyes swing over to me in shock. I give him a soft smile and squeeze his thigh. He seems to relax slightly, his hand covering mine. "Me, too."

CHAPTER 24

Jameson

I WANTED dinner to go smooth, and I thought maybe my dad and I could get along for my mom's sake. Sutton is with us and fits in so well with my mom. Then, of course my dad couldn't hold back his comment even though this dinner was his idea.

The only thing that kept me stable was Sutton's hand on my leg. Knowing she was right there with me. Luckily, Ma was able to draw the awkward tension away from the territory it ventured into.

The rest of dinner goes well, my dad stays mostly silent as he usually does. I subtly pull Sutton a little closer to me, and whisper a soft, "thank you," into her ear.

Despite my parent's protest, I pay for dinner, and refuse to let either of them argue with me about it. Sutton too, but she continues to insist it's not a date. Of course it's not, I would never bring my parents on a first date. Or second, whichever this would count for us.

On the drive back to Sutton's house, I notice Ma dozing off in the backseat, her head resting on my dad's shoulder. Music plays softly throughout the cab while no one speaks. Sutton is looking out the passenger window with her head resting on her hand. I almost think she's fallen asleep, until I park outside of her house and she sits up, looking over at me, her mouth pulled up in the smallest smile.

"Thank you," she says quietly.

"I'll walk you to your door." I'm already climbing out and walking over to help her out.

I walk her the short distance to her front door, and when we get there she turns to face me. I stand so she's hidden from view of my parents because I swear my mom has some sort of sixth sense. Even if she fell asleep, she's probably awake now and staring at us, just to make sure she doesn't miss the chance to give me a hard time.

"Thank you for coming with me," I tell her sincerely.

"It was...fun." I hear her hesitation and chuckle.

"You don't have to lie, it was awkward and that's okay."

She shakes her head. "No, not awkward. Your mom is amazing, your dad seems...nice."

"He and I have our issues; it's really okay."

"I know what that's like. Thanks for tonight."

I reach down to lightly graze her fingers with mine, not quite holding her hand, I use my free one to cup her face, running my thumb along her bottom lip. "I want you to know that I want to kiss you so badly right now. But I'm not going to when I know my mom is watching us like a hawk."

Sutton chuckles. "Good, because this isn't a date and friends wouldn't kiss each other."

"Right," I agree with a wink, knowing we've done more than that. "Goodnight Sutton."

"Goodnight, Jameson," she whispers.

Unable to help myself, I press a chaste kiss to her forehead, before letting her go and walking backwards toward my truck. I make sure she's inside before I climb in.

"I like her," Ma's sleepy voice says from behind me.

"Me too."

Unsurprisingly, my dad doesn't say anything which is fine by me. I just turn up the music to fill the air while I drive us home.

My next shift at the fire station is uneventful as far as calls go. We play some basketball and I keep my eye out looking for Sutton's Jeep to pull up to the building next door. I don't see her, and I'm tempted to text her, but refrain. Just barely. Especially on the second day when I'm only a couple of hours from getting off.

"Yo, we got a call from your girlfriend," Parker tells me as I'm lying on my cot unable to sleep.

I shoot up quickly, immediately panicking that Sutton is hurt.

I'm rushing downstairs toward the truck that everyone else is already in.

"Damn, I've never seen you this excited to see Margaret." Jo chuckles.

"What?"

"Your girlfriend, Margaret, the woman who only calls in while you're on shift," Dave speaks like I should've immediately known who they were talking about.

"I'm getting you all back, just remember this," I threaten as we drive the short distance to the call I already know is a false alarm.

Margaret is a woman in her sixties who's lived in the same house for as long as I can remember, and after her husband died fifteen years ago she started making false calls for attention. My attention, more specifically. I'm not sure if she did this while I was gone, but somehow she's learned I'm back and is starting them up again.

"Careful, Parker, I think you might end up being her new favorite," I tell him.

He doesn't say anything snarky back for once, and I glance over to where he's sitting, noticing him just staring outside. I furrow my brow; it's odd for him and I wonder if something's wrong.

We get to the destination and immediately a woman runs out in a long flowing robe, not looking the least bit distressed. In fact, the smile that takes over her face the second I step out of the truck already has my coworkers laughing behind me.

"Oh Jameson, I didn't know you were back. I'm so happy to see you."

"Hello, Margaret," I greet as pleasantly as I can. "What seems to be the problem?"

"It's Fluffy, she's stuck." She doesn't sound distressed about Fluffy.

Jo approaches her and says, "And Fluffy is your…"

"My cat," she snaps at Jo before looking at me, batting her eyelashes.

"Where is she stuck, ma'am?" I try to remain professional and respectful.

"Behind my water heater." *I think she's gotten closer to me.*

"Lead the way." I raise my arm gesturing toward her house, and I catch the way her eyes eat up my exposed arm. I fight the shiver, and not in a good way like when Sutton checks me out. The way Margaret is looking at me makes me feel like a piece of meat in front of a lion.

She walks in front of me, and I dare a glance back at my coworkers who are all stifling their laughter and I silently lift my middle finger to them, which only makes Parker bark out a loud laugh that has Margaret sending daggers in his direction.

So much for hoping he can steal some of the attention off me, I guess.

The entire time we're working on getting Fluffy out from

behind the tall water heater, I feel Margaret's eyes on me. There's even a time she runs her hand up my back, and I flinch, but she doesn't seem to care.

Jo ends up being the one to grab the cat, who's aptly named, and hands her back to her owner.

"Thank you so much, Jameson. You saved her life."

"Nah, my team did all the work. Glad we could help." I nod in her direction, and we all move to leave.

Margaret stays close by, offering coffee or snacks, which I decline for everyone and manage to make it out mostly unscathed.

Back in the truck I let a whole body shiver run through me, with a dramatic noise that has everyone cackling. "Why am I the one that has to be objectified?"

"Because you're the town favorite, pretty boy." Dave slaps my shoulder.

I groan, driving us away and thinking about the only woman who I want the attention of. When we get back I still don't see her Jeep next door. I check my phone, there's nothing from her either. Even though I don't want it to affect my mood, I can't seem to help it. While everyone else busies themselves, I separate myself to distract my mind by working out, vowing not to think about Sutton. I'll give her the space she wants, and she'll reach out when she's ready.

I know she will.

CHAPTER 25

Sutton

I WAKE up to the loud sound of an engine revving outside. I groan, burying my face into my pillow, I don't know what time it is, but I'm sure it's too early for whatever idiot decided to wake up the entire street.

I'm about to get up and see what's going on when it happens again, but someone clearly beats me to it when I hear a feminine voice yelling outside. I should mind my business, but that's never been my strong suit, so I get up and go to the front window to see what's going on.

The entire commotion is across the street, and I'm straining to see because my eyes are still waking up and attempting to focus. I'm pretty sure I see Bailey standing next to the driver's side of her neighbor's dark sports car while she's yelling at him.

I can't see or hear him because the car is still rumbling loud enough to muffle most of their conversation. It's hardly a conversation since it doesn't look like Bailey is letting him say anything. She's standing tall next to the low car which only makes her seem taller, and finally she throws her arms up in the air. Wes revs the engine again before peeling out of his driveway. I watch as Bailey flips him off while he leaves before storming back to her own house.

I step back from the window, really wondering what the deal is with them because it feels like a little more than just Wes driving an obnoxiously loud car. When I look at the clock I see it's seven in the morning, which is way before I'm usually awake, but I don't think I can go back to sleep.

Bennet is still asleep on his back with his legs in the air as I go back to my bedroom. I'm jealous that he's able to sleep through that, but since I'm awake now, I'm going to make it his problem too.

"Get up, Benny boy. We're going for a walk," I tell him as I get changed. I swear he ignores me on purpose, not moving as I pull on some leggings and a loose T-shirt.

"Come on," I try again, nudging him with my foot. He turns his head and his floppy snout makes it look like he's grimacing. "It's good for us, and maybe we can get a treat."

That last five letter word is what gets him up like I knew it would. *Sucker.*

On our walk, I make a mental list of all the things I should get done today, other than wait for my couch to be delivered since it's my day off. I really should go grocery shopping, and maybe even brave a home good store to get some decorations. Maybe I should reach out to Jameson....

I shake my head at the last thought. I haven't talked to him since we went to dinner, and I'm worried about how much I've been thinking about him. Every time I'm close to him it's like another piece of my wall breaks down. I'm worried that when it's gone, I'll fall hard and that can only lead to heartbreak.

"Sutton," a voice calls out, pulling me from my thoughts, and I'm thankful for it because they were headed into dangerous territory.

I look up to see it's Bailey walking toward me. Somehow, I've managed to make it back onto our street without even noticing.

"Hey," I greet with a smile, not daring to bring up what happened earlier.

"Who's this?" she asks, referring to my dog.

"Oh, this is Bennet. He's friendly."

She gives him a closed lip smile, and reaches her hand out tentatively. He sniffs her, and nudges her fingers slightly, which leads her to pet him softly. "Sorry if you heard that this morning."

"Oh." I wave my hand, acting like it's not a big deal. "I was already awake."

She gives me a look like she knows I'm lying. "Well, still. He's a fucking obnoxious asshole and doesn't care about anyone other than himself."

"Do you know him well?"

She scoffs. "No, I mean not really. We've been neighbors for a couple of years so I know that he's a selfish dick. And he *clearly* doesn't know what respect is."

"Hm," I hum, wanting to know more information, but she clearly isn't going to give it up.

"Anyway, feel free to file a noise complaint on him. Maybe if he gets enough of them, something will actually be done."

I chuckle softly. "Okay." I won't be doing that, but she's fired up and I'm not about to argue with her about it either.

"Alright, well I have to head to work, but have a good day."

"You, too," I call out, walking the short distance back home with Bennet.

Once inside, I place my hands on my hips and look around. I guess I have a day of distraction ahead of me.

WHEN I WAS TOLD my couch was going to be delivered, I didn't realize it was going to be a whole ass couch I'd have to get through the door and set up by myself. For some reason I figured it would be in pieces, and I would have to put it together.

Apparently, I was wrong. As much as I'm a strong independent woman, having a man around would be really helpful in these situations. Too bad Bennet doesn't count.

I let out a sigh, placing my hands on my hips and looking across the street. I could always ask Bailey, or maybe even Wes. Though I've never really spoken to him and he seems so intense all the time, so I'm not sure how that would go over. Especially with how the day started with him.

There's also Jameson.

I'm not sure if he's on shift right now, but if he's free then I know he would run over here if I called.

But I don't know if I should.

After what happened at his house, I feel like I'm tip-toeing in dangerous territory with him. I know that at some point we won't be able to come back from it if it goes much further. I should just continue to distance myself even more.

The thought causes a pang in my gut I choose to ignore.

"I can do this," I declare to no one, right before I start to pull the couch into my house.

It's way heavier than I expected it to be and I'm straining as I try to pull it inside. I pause, already breathing heavily as I stare at the piece of furniture half inside the threshold. I climb over it to the other side and see if pushing it is easier.

My feet slide on the concrete as I push and I don't think this is much better. I end up sliding onto the ground completely and groan. "Dammit."

I mentally go over my options again, waiting for Bailey or Wes to be home and asking if one of them could help me...calling Jameson. *No. I can do this.* Standing up, I try pushing, again, and manage to get it past the front door before I have to take a break, flopping down on the couch that's now blocking the front door and I can't bring myself to even care.

I could leave it like this. It'll be fine, right?

At least it's comfortable. That should make this all worth it.

Bennet ends up climbing onto the couch with me and on top of my body, practically crushing me.

"Bennet, I can't breathe," I croak, his weight and fur are suffocating me and he doesn't even seem to care. "Are you trying to take me out and have the place to yourself?"

He rests his head onto my face, and I turn away so his drool doesn't get in my mouth. "Get off," I demand, trying to push him off.

He grumbles and doesn't move, but I manage to roll myself out from underneath him and drop onto the floor. I look at him, still laying on the couch, completely unbothered and narrow my eyes. "You're a problem."

He doesn't move, and I know there's no way I'm going to get anywhere with this couch and the added hundred and fifty pounds of fluff that are now on it. I climb over once again to get in position to push. "Bennet, off. You can take it over later."

At first he doesn't listen, and I have to give him some pats on his butt to get him to jump off. Once he finally does, I get back to pushing it into the living room. When I go to turn it, it's a little too soon and I end up pushing it into the wall. I cringe, hoping I didn't do any damage and somehow manage to get it turned and into the spot I wanted it.

My arms may feel like Jello, but I'm proud of myself, as I stand there, taking it all in. When I turn to look at the wall, my pride drops because there's a big gouge in the wall where the couch hit it, and I throw my head back on a groan.

Could I figure out how to fix this myself? Yes. Am I done being an independent woman for the day? Kind of.

I chew on my bottom lip, debating on what I should do. Bennet jumps up on the couch again, and I narrow my eyes at him. "You enjoy my hard work then, my friend."

Pulling my phone out, I admit defeat and ask for help.

> Sutton: Any chance you know a thing or two about fixing a wall?

> Jameson: If you wanted to see me you just needed to say that.

I look over at Bennet. "See what you did," I blame him, because it makes me feel a bit better. Of course he doesn't respond to me, more than content to be laying on the couch.

To be fair, I know the only one to blame here is myself, because if I'm being honest maybe it is an excuse to see Jameson, but I'm not going to admit that.

CHAPTER 26

Jameson

I'M EXHAUSTED after my shift, but Sutton texted asking for help, so sleep can wait. After a quick run to the hardware store to get what I need to help with her wall, I head to her house. Luckily, there's not a lot of damage I can see from the picture she sent me and what there is could wait, but I'm not about to tell her that. I said I would let her reach out to me and this feels like an olive branch that I'm going to hang onto for dear life.

I'm greeted by both Sutton and Bennet when she opens the door. I can sense her nerves from where I'm standing even though she gives me a small smile; she doesn't say anything when she opens the door wider letting me in.

"The damage is over here." She leads me to the spot where a small dent is. It really doesn't look bad at all and it won't take me long to fix, but I plan on stretching it out.

"Thank you for doing this for me," she says while I'm unloading the supplies I brought.

I turn toward her slightly. "Anytime you need me, I'll be here."

Her breath catches, and she immediately looks around, clearly trying to find a distraction and I let her, for now.

"Do you want something to drink?" she offers from further away than she was before.

"No, thanks."

I work slowly to fix the damage, the only thing missing is paint to cover it since I didn't know the color I would need. Once I'm done, I know I can't draw this out anymore, and I turn looking for Sutton but she's already right by me.

"All done, just needs some paint," I tell her, standing up so I have to look down at her.

"Thank you," she says, softly.

"Anytime," I answer, just as softly. We're closer than we need to be, our chests only inches from each others.

I expect her to step away, but she doesn't. She's looking up at me and her wide eyes draw me in like they always do. I'm taken back to every time I've gotten the chance to touch her. And the way my fingers itch to do it again.

I would give anything for her to let me in, to give me more of herself. To break down the walls and just let me show her how things could be between us.

If she would just take a chance.

Right now, I'm not seeing the walls behind her eyes. The way she's looking at me seems like she's open to letting me in, so I close the distance between us, turning so her back is against the wall.

"What're you doing?" she practically whispers.

"What do you want me to do?"

"I don't," she shakes her head slightly, "I don't know."

I slide a hand up the side of her leg, only feeling the soft fabric of her leggings covering her skin. I move up to her hip, gripping it, while the tip of one of my fingers grazes her waistband just barely touching her skin there.

"You don't?" I run my finger gently along her skin.

Sutton lifts her hands so she's gripping my forearms, but she doesn't push me away. Our faces get closer as I lean down without even thinking about it, continuing to touch her gently.

"No," she breathes, her eyes hooded and grip tightening on my arms.

"Do you want me to stop?"

She lets out a small whimper, "No."

"Do you want me to keep going?" I drop my forehead to hers, feeling her soft breaths against my lips, only tempting me to close the rest of the distance between us. To feel her plush lips on mine once again. My hand slides up under her shirt, pressing my hand against the bare skin of her back. She arches into me, and I crowd her against the wall, pushing her fully against it while bringing my other hand up to run my thumb along her jaw, then over her bottom lip.

"Sutton."

"Hm," she hums.

"If you want me to keep going, you need to tell me."

She hesitates and I can tell she doesn't want to say the words, but I need to hear them. I need to know that she's not going to regret this as soon as it's over. I need to know that she's feeling this pull just like I am.

I lean forward a little more, our lips barely grazing, but I don't close the distance.

"Say it, Sutton. Tell me what you want." I press my hand on her back more firmly, pushing our bodies completely flush. I'm sure she can feel the hardening length in my jeans, if her little gasp is anything to go off of.

"Jameson," she breathes against my mouth, her hands pressing against my pecs almost like she's wanting to push me away. But the next two words that leave her perfect mouth may be the two greatest words I've heard, especially when they come from her. "Kiss me."

Without a single second of hesitation, I do what she says, closing the small distance between our mouths. I love the way as soon as we're connected I can feel her soften for me. It's like everything she's holding in melts away in this moment and whatever it is that brought her here, whatever is making her walls so high, disappears for just a moment. This moment. With me.

Every time we've touched, I feel like the walls she builds back up are a little shorter than they were before. Right now the way she opens for me when I deepen the kiss has me hoping she'll give me more, but I'll take whatever she's willing to. I'll greedily take anything and everything even if it's just pieces at a time.

I want her, and I'm not going anywhere.

One of my hands slides up the back of her neck, tangling in her hair, pulling slightly to angle her head back while our kiss turns even more heated. She moans as her fingers dig into my back trying to bring us impossibly closer.

Using my grip on her head, I break our mouths apart and move to kiss along her jaw and down her neck while she gasps and her nails scratch me lightly. I graze my teeth along her throat and she gasps out my name. The sweet sound has me rock hard for her, and my hips jut forward involuntarily at the sound. Dying to feel her, to get a taste of her, anything she'll give me.

Sutton moves her hands up my back, pushing my shirt up and I reluctantly remove my mouth from her skin. Reaching back with one hand, I pull my shirt off over my head and don't miss the way she stares at me. For a moment I worry that I moved too fast. That she's going to kick me out. Kissing is one thing, taking clothes off is another.

No woman has ever made me feel more like an unsure teenager than the one standing in front of me, eyes locked on my chest, while hers rises and falls quickly with rapid breaths. I reach toward her, knowing she'll either shoot me down and kick me out. Or she'll want to continue what we've started.

And fuck, I hope she wants this to continue as much as I do.

My worry fades instantly when our mouths crash together in another feverish kiss, tongues lapping at each other, and I know at this moment there's no way I could stop. I run my fingers along the waistband of her soft leggings, sliding into them, teasing her over the wet fabric covering her core.

"Do you want me to touch you?" I rasp against her mouth.

She nods, and normally I'd want her to use her words, but right now I'm so desperate a nod will have to do. But I know I'll have her begging for more.

Moving her panties to the side, I run a finger through her wetness, grazing her clit causing her hips to buck with a sharp gasp. She grabs the back of my neck, yanking me down to her, mouths fused while I push a finger into her wet heat. The low groan I let out at the first real feel of her is primal and lights a fire within me. One that's only ignited and fueled by her.

Sutton hums against my lips, moving her hips and trying to rub herself harder against my hand while I push in even further, my palm rubbing against her clit. Everything about her feels even more perfect than I imagined and I don't know how that's possible.

It's not enough, I have a feeling nothing with her will ever be. I'm going to want more, and more and more.

I remove my hand from her pants, and start to kiss down her body. I kneel, looking up at her wide eyes, heaving chest, and flushed skin as I peel her leggings down, slowly. She watches me, and I'm just waiting for the moment she tells me to stop. For the moment when she realizes she's letting me in, even just barely and stops it before it can go further.

But she doesn't.

Instead, she lifts one leg at a time for me until she's bare in front of me. The sight is the best thing I've ever seen in my life. I look up, gaze locked on hers. "Once I get a taste of you, I don't think I'm going to be able to stop myself."

She smirks before boldly swinging her leg over my shoulder, opening herself up to me even more, and I bite back a groan at how wet and perfect her pussy is right in front of me. My mouth waters at the sight. I take it back, I'm not going to be able to stop even before I've had a taste.

Her hand slides into my short hair on the top of my head, gripping the strands. "Then you better get started."

Without a single second to question her or myself, I dive forward, licking her entire seam before sucking her clit into my mouth roughly. She squeals, pulling my hair so hard there's a twinge of pain, but I don't stop. I continue to lick and suck every delicious inch of this perfect pussy. I groan against her, and I know she feels the vibration because she moans, and when I look up her head has dropped back against the wall.

"You're perfect," I tell her before pushing a finger into her heat once again while sucking her clit into my mouth. I flick with my tongue rapidly in a way that has her gasping, grabbing at my head and bucking her hips against me.

When she tightens around my finger, I know she's close. I push another finger in, and curl them while continuing to work her with my mouth. I groan against her again and that sets her off with a cry so beautiful as she comes. I don't stop until she's pulling me off and up to her mouth again, licking my lips before kissing me even more fiercely than before.

"I'm not done with you yet," I tell her right before grabbing the backs of her thighs, lifting her up. She wraps her legs around my waist, and I have one goal—to get her to a bed. That isn't going to be the only time she comes for me today. Not even close.

CHAPTER 27

Sutton

SOME DISTANT PART of my mind recognizes I shouldn't be doing this. I know I'm already too far gone for this man, but there's no way I'm stopping it either. His words, that mouth. Oh God, that mouth. It should be wrong to be that good looking and that skilled. Maybe his dick will be small because the universe has to have something wrong with him.

Though, I've felt it through our clothes and it definitely did not feel small.

Maybe he's a one pump chump. Either way, I'm about to find out because I'm so desperate to feel him inside me. I think I may actually combust if I don't find out what it feels like to have him over me, filling me, groaning with pleasure.

I kiss him even harder at the thought, right before I'm dropped onto my back. I squeal until I realize I've landed on my bed. The gorgeous shirtless man currently kneeling on the edge pushes his rough, callused hands up my stomach, taking my shirt with them. Normally I would be self conscious having a man touch me in my most vulnerable area, but with him I don't mind it.

The way he's looking at me with pure desire, whispering praises while looking like he wants to eat me alive. He sheds me of my shirt and bra, but he's still too clothed for me. His muscled chest isn't cut like a bodybuilder, he has a scattering of chest hair that's soft as I reach out to run my fingers along his skin to feel him.

He's hardened by work, not just the gym. He's the hottest man I've ever laid my eyes on and he wants me. I reach for his waistband, popping the button and unzipping them. He backs up before I'm able to go further and I want to protest, but he's pushing them all the way off, but leaving his black boxer briefs on.

I raise an eyebrow at him, as he climbs over me, balancing himself on his forearms next to my head, his confined erection poking into my stomach, and I squirm, wanting it lower. I expect him to kiss me again, but he doesn't. He lingers, just barely out of reach. I run my hands along his chest, up to his neck, looping them there, arching up into him just slightly.

"I thought you said you wouldn't stop," I say softly.

"I did, but I'm giving you one last chance."

Our lips graze, just barely. "If you're going to fuck me, don't be sweet and gentle about it."

The side of his mouth quirks up. "Yes, ma'am."

He dips down like he's going to kiss me and his tongue flicks my bottom lip so softly I'm sure I imagined it. Before I even realize what's happening he grabs my hips and flips me onto my stomach. His weight descends on my back, pushing me into the mattress and I'm only able to lift my head as his lips graze my ear.

"Stay just like this," he commands darkly, and my core clenches at the demanding tone of his voice. It's so different from how he usually is. The sweet, smiling, small town golden boy is not the man currently behind me.

This man is one that promises pleasure, one that's sure to make my body sing and program me to crave more from him and only him. So I listen to him and don't move, even as I feel him lift off me. The cool air hits my skin and I fight the shiver that wants to run through me. I feel so exposed like this.

The room is silent except for my rapid breaths and the pounding of my heartbeat in my ears. I still hear the second Jameson's underwear hits the floor, and the groan he lets out.

I sway my hips slightly, the friction from the soft blanket underneath me feels good. "Is there a problem?"

"I don't have a condom." He sighs.

I freeze, looking at him over my shoulder and I go weak at what I see. The naked man standing at the foot of my bed, his large hand wrapped around the impressive length jutting from his body, squeezing it while the look on his face is tortured, but soft as he looks at me. I know if I tell him this ends now, he'll accept it. It doesn't matter what he's said in the heat of the moment, I can see how much he truly cares.

"I'm on birth control," I squeak out. "I've never been with anyone bare."

"Me either," he rushes out. "We don't have to."

"I want to."

He raises an eyebrow at me, like he wasn't expecting me to say that. I know I probably shouldn't. It's irresponsible, but I'm too wet, too out of my mind, and too completely out of control for the man in front of me to let this end right now.

His eyes search mine for any hesitation, but I won't let there be any. And when he climbs on the bed again, he pushes my body down with his, I feel his cock dig into my back, and I arch up against him.

He runs his lips along my shoulder gently, up my neck to my ear. "Tell me if it's too much."

I turn my head, our lips less than an inch apart. "I can take it."

He leans forward like he's going to kiss me, but instead his hand tangles in my hair, and pushes my head down onto the mattress, as he angles himself at my entrance, teasing the tip through my wetness, coating himself before pushing in, just barely.

I gasp at the sudden stretch, already feeling like it may be too much; he's even bigger than he seems as he's pushing inside me.

"Yeah, you can," he groans, pushing in fully and I cry out, the pain mixed with pleasure is so consuming my legs shake, and he stays there for a second, letting me adjust to his size. When I start to move against him, he listens. Removing his hand from my hair, moving back slightly, bringing my hips with him as I balance myself on weak knees.

He leans over me, kissing my shoulder softly. "I want you to remember how much I respect you, because with the way I'm about to fuck you I think you may forget."

Turns out he wasn't kidding because before I'm able to say anything in response he's pulling back almost completely before slamming forward again. He's holding my hips so hard I'm sure I'm going to have bruises and I'm going to look at them as badges of honor. Something left behind by the man that's so sweet, and only ever treated me with respect, but is now fucking me like his life depends on it.

His moans mix with mine as he slams into me over and over, each time hitting that perfect spot inside me that has me seeing stars. He pulls me back, my back flush with his front, one arm banded across my chest and the other around my stomach as he fucks up into me. I drop my head back against his shoulder. He's hitting spots I didn't even know existed in my own body, and I'm racing toward the edge of release so fast I feel like I can't breathe.

The hand that's on my stomach, dips down almost to where we're connected as he rubs tight circles on my clit and I cry out, both trying to rub myself harder on his hand, and fuck myself on him.

"You're close aren't you, baby? Going to show me again how pretty you are when you come for me? Going to squeeze my dick even more in this sweet pussy?"

"Jameson, *fuck,*" I cry, grabbing his forearm, digging my nails into his skin as his words and the feeling of him overwhelm me completely. My orgasm slams into me, I'm grasping for anything to hold onto as my entire body shakes with pleasure.

He holds me still, while he fills me so completely and lets me ride out my release. Once I come down, he's lifting me off him and turning me around to face him. I look down at his erection, shining with my release, the tip dripping, but it looks painfully hard, red, and angry and I know he hasn't finished.

Before I'm able to comment on it, he's lifting me up so I'm straddling his lap, and pushing inside me once again. We gasp against each other's mouths, and I'm already so sensitive, the stretch doesn't hurt like it did before, but his pelvis grazing my clit has me whimpering.

"I got to feel it, but didn't see this pretty face when it happened, so I'm going to need you to give me another one."

I shake my head. "Jameson, there's no way."

"Yeah, you can," he insists, right before making it his singular mission to make me come more times in a row than I ever have.

He's fucking up into me, guiding my hips to rub against his pelvis while his mouth moves against mine, tongue invading my mouth. The orgasm I was sure wouldn't come is dancing just out of reach. I'm moaning, pleasure and frustration battling within me at the way he's making me feel.

"Come on, baby. I'm close. I need you to give me one more."

"I told you, I can't," I insist.

He grabs me with an arm around my back and slams me onto the bed, without leaving my body. He's over me, his body weight pressing into me as he fucks me even harder, the new angle hitting exactly where I need for the release that's been just out of reach to take over.

I'm lost in the sensation once again, and this time he groans above me, pushing in as far as he can go, swelling as he comes which only prolongs my own orgasm as he fills me. The room goes quiet as we come down, reality setting in slowly. I wait for the regret to hit, but it doesn't.

Jameson moves off of me and I bite back the whimper at the loss of him from my body. He doesn't say anything as he pulls on his briefs and walks out of the room. My mouth drops open in shock. I expected a little more from him than to just...leave.

I guess everything I was worried about was right. It was all an act with him. The sweet guy, acting like he cared, wasn't real. I'll give it to him, he's good. He had me practically fooled. The pang of disappointment is impossible to ignore. The chill on my skin makes goosebumps appear and I pull the blanket over myself as I attempt to stand up. My legs are weak, and it takes me a second before I feel steady enough to actually stand.

I'm about to try and find some clothes, shame starting to wash over me, when Jameson appears again, eyebrows furrowed. "What're you doing?"

"Getting dressed," I say as calmly as possible.

"Get back on the bed; I'm going to take care of you."

I notice in his hand he has a washcloth and my jaw drops slightly. "Jameson, I really can't handle anymore orgasms."

He barks out a laugh. "You can, if I say you can, but no, baby, I'm talking about aftercare."

I want to question him, but instead, I end up getting back on the bed, and Jameson does exactly what he said he's going to. He takes care of me. Cleaning between my legs so gently, bringing me water, and helping me into new clothes. Just when I think he's done and is going to leave, he climbs into my bed with me.

I turn back toward him, ready to argue, and he can see it on my face because he yanks me into him, my back pressed to his chest. "Don't even try to argue with me, Sutton. Just lay with me for a minute."

I bite back my smile even though he can't see it as I let myself relax into him. I don't expect to fall asleep, but surrounded by his warmth and completely sated, I can't stop my eyelids from falling shut.

I feel like I barely dozed off when the noise of a phone going off has me shooting up. I realize Jameson is still here and it's his phone. He grabs it quickly, answering, his voice groggy which tells me he fell asleep slightly too.

"Hello?" He's quiet for a second, but immediately gets up and starts getting dressed. "I'll be right there."

I tighten the blankets around myself, feeling vulnerable. Maybe this is an excuse to leave, which is fine he doesn't owe me anything. He hangs up, pulls his shirt on, then cages me in with his arms on either side of my body, crowding me against the bed.

"It's a recall, I have to go, but I don't want you to think it's because I want to."

"Recall?" I squeak.

"They need some extra help, but I can come back."

I shake my head. "No, no that's okay. I'll see you around."

I don't want to show the fear that's caused inside me at whatever he's being called in for needing extra people. It must be something pretty bad. But I'm not going to show it. It's better if he goes now, gives me time to get my head back on straight.

"I'll see you soon," he insists, barely grazing his lips against mine. "And I'll let you know when I'm back safe."

CHAPTER 28

Jameson

WE DON'T TECHNICALLY RUN a horse therapy ranch, it's something Ma has always been passionate about. Anything related to equine and mental health, really. She's worked with kids and adults with disabilities, those suffering with mental illness, and people who have had an interest and love for horses.

It's something she's made clear she wants to continue no matter what happens to her. Even though I try not to think about her not being here, that's something that I vowed to continue regardless. Not many people know the benefits to equine therapy, but recently I met Wes, an army veteran, and while he hasn't admitted to it, I think he has some pretty severe PTSD. He doesn't talk much at all, but has come here a couple of times to learn about the horses.

Juniper has taken a liking to him it seems and while he hasn't gotten on any of the horses yet, he comes here for about thirty minutes, gives her some treats, pets and brushes her before leaving with a gruff goodbye.

I don't ever push. I know if he wanted to talk about anything he would, and I'm not a therapist or here to act as one. The horses are, and I just monitor or answer any questions.

"See ya next week," he says on his way out of the barn, which is more than he usually says.

"All good, see ya then."

I wasn't going to rush him, but there's something I'm hoping to do today. Once I make sure everything is settled with the horses, I check on the goats and pigs before calling Duke over and he bounds toward me with his tongue flopping out of his mouth.

"C'mon, bud. We have someone we have to go see." I lead him toward my truck, making sure to grab his harness from the main house on the way.

We park by the fire station, and I notice that Parker's car is here, which is weird because he's not on shift right now, or at least he shouldn't be. I get Duke out, tucking the flowers and note I brought with us into his harness, and notice movement in the car. I walk up, knocking on the driver's side window.

Parker jumps slightly, then rolls the window down. "What's up?"

"What're you doing?"

He looks around, hesitating, clearly not sure what to say and I just look at him waiting for an answer.

"I came by to get something I forgot."

"Right. You weren't going to go try and talk to a certain someone at the groomers?"

"No..."

"Come on." I nod my head toward the building, knowing he's going to follow.

I let Duke in, and he trots inside happily, but I don't miss the bark greeting from the bird. I don't step inside yet, even when I hear Sutton's voice, "Just a second."

My heart immediately pounds at the sound, remembering everything from the other night. The way that same voice sounded as she came for me. How beautiful she looked as she fell apart. I figured she wouldn't reach out to me, even after I told her I was back home safe after the call. It was late, but she didn't respond. I don't take offense to it. I know she wants me, I just need her to let herself accept it.

"Duke, what're you doing here? Where's your dad?" Sutton asks, and I take the opportunity to walk inside with a wide smile on my face that grows when I see her. Every time my eyes drink her in I get lost in her beauty. She can bring me to my knees instantly and I don't think she even knows it.

"What're you doing here?" another feminine voice asks, and that's when I notice the younger woman behind Sutton.

"Just backing up my boy. Aren't you happy to see me, Lil?" Parker answers.

"Is someone talking? All I hear is a buzzing like the world's largest and most annoying bug." Lily looks around, refusing to make eye contact with Parker.

"What is this?" Sutton asks, bending down to take out the flowers and note I tucked into Duke's harness. Lily looks over her shoulder at the note, and I catch the tiny smile on Sutton's perfect lips.

"Damn, cowboy, you've got it bad, don't you?" Lily announces and I stand proud because yeah, I do and I don't care who knows it. I've never understood men being ashamed for how much they want a woman. "Could you teach that one a thing or two? Because sending a 'you up' text is not the move."

I turn toward my coworker. "You didn't."

He looks away guiltily, and I shake my head. We're trying to train him, but there's only so much you can do for a twenty year old guy, he'll learn eventually. It seems like Lily isn't the type to shy away from teaching him either.

"Thank you, Duke. This was very sweet of you." Sutton bends down to squish my dog's face.

"Hey, he's just the messenger."

"He's also cuter." She smirks up at me.

"Oh shit." Lily chuckles.

"Tough luck, man." Parker claps me on my shoulder.

"I really enjoy having an audience for this," I joke.

"Thank you for the flowers," Sutton tells me softly while I'm pretty sure Parker and Lily are in the middle of a stare off.

"I'll make sure a vase is always full of them in your house if you let me," I tell her honestly and I don't miss the way her cheeks fill with color. "Bring Bennet by sometime soon, Duke and I miss you both."

She nods slightly. "Okay."

"Let's leave the pretty girls alone to get back to their jobs." I start to guide Parker and Duke out the door.

Once we're outside and almost to our cars Parker says proudly, "She wants me."

I scoff, "Yeah, I'm sure she does, buddy."

Duke and I hop into my truck, and I just hope that Sutton won't find an excuse to shut down again.

When I get back home, I check on Ma with Duke happily by my side.

"There's my boy," Ma greets, and I know better than to think she's talking to me. It's confirmed when she bends slightly to pet my dog and I just shake my head.

As she starts to stand up, I notice how unsteady she is, and I move quickly to help her. Just like she always does, she shakes me off, insisting she's fine. I want to believe her, I want to pretend that she's fine and that the cancer isn't taking over her body. I want to believe the treatment is doing what it's supposed to and she's getting better.

But it's not the truth, and we know it, even though we don't talk about it. Ma comforts me more than I comfort her, even if it's not completely obvious. She accepts her reality, while I'm continuing to live in some variation of denial. The variation where she's okay and going to get through this even though everything is saying otherwise.

"I'm fine, don't you have a girl to dote on?" she teases.

"Just did. Duke brought her some flowers."

"That's so sweet of you. I knew I raised you right," she tells the dog and I chuckle.

"What about me?"

"You were my first son, my trial run so I did what I could."

"Well, thanks." I shake my head. "Do you need anything?"

"Would you mind seeing if your father actually wants to eat dinner tonight?"

I give her a questioning look because as far as I know they eat together every night, and I feel like this is one of her ploys to get us to talk to each other.

"Sure, do you need help with getting it ready? Or want me to join you?"

"Nope, you take your girl out, or invite her over and cook her a nice meal."

I shake my head. "You're pushy, you know that?"

"You come by it honestly."

"But really, do you need anything from me?"

"Jameson." She gives me a pointed look. I raise my hands up, backing away slowly while Duke stares at me from his spot by Ma's feet.

"I'm going. Duke, are you joining me or staying here?" He looks at me, then Ma, before finally deciding to follow me.

"Find your father and ask him, please," she calls after me and I almost forgot she asked me to do that. Even though I would rather continue to ignore him, I'll do anything she asks. I'm also curious if he really hasn't been eating with her. Growing up, family dinners were important to both of them. No matter how busy of a day my dad had, he would always make it back for dinner.

But then I left. Sometimes I join them, but Ma is so focused on me doing my own thing, but now I wonder if it's because she doesn't want to see my dad not joining her for their nightly tradition anymore.

Duke and I hop in my truck again, and I look out for my dad as I drive through the property back to my place. I end up seeing him by the cattle, seeming to struggle lifting the feed bucket, but he covers it well. He's a proud man, always has been, and just like Ma, he refuses to ask for help even when they so clearly need it.

I meet him at the fence, while Duke chooses to hang back in the cab already seeming to settle in for a nap.

"You need any help?" I offer, knowing he won't accept it.

"No," he grunts, tossing the feed to the animals.

"Ma wanted me to ask if you're actually going to join her for dinner." I don't do a very good job hiding the disdain in my voice.

"Mhmm," he gives a non answer.

"I remember when you used to make sure to be home for dinner every night. That change? You just let Ma eat the meal she cooked all by herself?" The anger increases; I'm growing tired of dancing around him and his mood. He can be pissed at me for leaving, he can think it's the worst thing I've ever done, leaving this town to try and do something more with my life.

But I came back.

I'd have come back in a second if either of them asked, if either of them needed me, but he never did.

"I don't see you joining her either," he retorts.

"She won't let me," I scoff. "You think I'm awful for leaving, and that I did it to hurt you both, but Ma wants me to do more with my life. Ma doesn't want me to hang around here all the time. You know what she does want? You. She wants you to be around, to support her as her husband. Most of all she wants us to get along for her sake, but you can't even pretend to do that."

I don't let him respond before I'm stomping back to my truck, letting him sit on what I just told him. It would be ridiculous to think anything I said actually gets through his head, but maybe it will. And maybe he'll pull his head out of his ass before it's too late.

CHAPTER 29

Sutton

I'M LYING awake in bed, the very same bed where Jameson made me see stars in a way I never have before. I haven't dared wash the sheets yet, so they still smell like him. Even though it's late, I pull out my phone before I can think too much about it and text him.

> Sutton: I've never ridden a horse before.

I don't expect him to respond, but he does almost instantly.

> Jameson: Lucky for you I have several in case you want to change that.

> Sutton: Why are you awake?

> Jameson: Why are you?

> Sutton: Because I was really thinking about how I've never ridden a horse, duh.

> Jameson: How weird, I was really thinking about how you've never ridden a horse either, great minds, huh?

Sutton: Or creepy?

Jameson: I'm on shift, barely sleep when I'm here.

Jameson: So, probably creepy since I'm basically a zombie.

Sutton: I don't think I'd want a zombie saving my life in an emergency. I actually think their goal is the opposite.

Jameson: I'm one of the good ones. I'd always save your life, zombie or not.

Sutton: How sweet.

Jameson: That's my middle name, how'd you know?

Sutton: Guess I can be creepy too.

Jameson: I don't get off shift until Thursday, but if you want to come over I'll give you a riding lesson.

Sutton: …

Jameson: On a horse, jeez, get your mind out of the gutter, Sutton.

I laugh, and it's so loud in my quiet bedroom, I bite my bottom lip to try and stifle it, even though no one's around to hear me.

Sutton: We'll see, maybe I'll take you up on that offer, cowboy.

Jameson: Let's not start that. I much prefer fireboy.

I bark out another laugh, and Bennet looks up at me, like he's mad at me for disturbing his sleep.

"Sorry."

He huffs, resting his head back down at the foot of my bed.

Sutton: You have to earn that title, I haven't seen you take on any fires.

Jameson: You also haven't seen me wrangle any cows.

Sutton: Fair point. Goodnight, Jameson.

Jameson: Goodnight, Sutton.

I swear I can hear his voice as he says it, something about the way he says my name when we say goodbye, it's become our thing and it gives me the same reaction every time. The deep timbre of his voice settles between my thighs. The way his eyes stare into mine like I'm all he sees.

The way he cares for my body, bringing it so much pleasure. The way he takes control, and isn't soft with me, but can be when he needs to. He's perfect. Too perfect it's scary.

I settle deeper into my bed while I try to talk myself out of whatever is going on but all I can seem to do is replay our night together over and over until I can't help but to slip my hand into my shorts, trying to recreate his touch.

His voice plays in my mind, his every move is burned into my brain, but my own hand does not do it justice and the orgasm I give myself is nothing like the one he gave me. I'm frustrated, but end up drifting to sleep knowing deep down I won't be able to stay away.

"Do you think God actually wants his followers to be virgins? I mean, if there even is a God...wait, are you religious?" Lily races through her thoughts like she usually does.

"No, I'm not." I chuckle. "And I don't think if he or she is real that they want everyone to be a virgin because they need to produce more followers."

"Good point." She points finger guns at me.

"What brought this up?" It's a dangerous question when it comes to Lily because sometimes there's a reason, and sometimes it takes me down a rabbit hole of her mind, which is more complicated than figuring out an illusion at Disneyland.

"I heard something about the Pope and it made me think about how he's probably a virgin, right? Because they have to start out as a priest and then get to be a cardinal or something, right?"

"Sure." I shrug, really not sure about any of this.

"Right, so they go their entire lives without boning and then I thought about...well can they masturbate? But I don't think they can watch porn, so do they even know what a naked woman looks like? What would they fantasize about if they don't? Do they just go their entire lives without coming because that sounds unhealthy."

I don't know whether to be horrified or laugh. Especially when she continues.

"Seriously, decades of pent up ejaculate just there? That has to cause some sort of blockage or something."

I burst out laughing. "Did you just say ejaculate?"

"Is there a word you'd prefer? Jizz? Splooge? Baby batter?"

I double over, holding my stomach in laughter, unable to stop. Jerry Lee takes advantage of the moment, and starts squawking out a new word in between barks, *"Jizz."*

During the chaos, Trish walks in at the exact moment Jerry Lee screams out, *"jizz!"* And she gives the bird a questioning look.

"Who taught my bird the new word?" she asks lightly.

"That would be me. Sutton didn't like the word ejaculate so I gave her other options, and Jerry Lee picked his favorite, apparently."

"I don't think I even want to know." Trish shakes her head.

"Oh, I'll tell you, Auntie." Lily bounces after her, already back on her tangent once again. I shake my head, getting back to sweeping up the dog fur around my station from my last client.

I look out the window that faces the fire station and notice the truck getting pulled out, and Jameson stepping out from the driver's seat. My eyes stay locked on him as he moves around doing whatever he needs to with the truck.

The other guy that came here, Parker, comes outside and they start talking and Parker pushes on Jameson's shoulder while they laugh. I'm so focused on watching them I don't notice Trish until she speaks from behind me and I jump, pretending like I wasn't just gawking out the window.

"Told you there was a good view," she says.

"Huh, what?" I finish sweeping up the fur on the ground, not looking at her so she doesn't see the blush that's surely covering my face.

"The view. It may not be your typical one, but it's pretty great."

"It's fine." I work to make sure my cheeks return to their normal color before I dare face her. When I do, she's smiling at me like she knows everything I won't say out loud.

"How're you liking it here? I haven't gotten to check in much with you, but you seem to be handling Lily pretty well, which is not always the easiest."

"I heard that," Lily calls out from the other room.

"Then you know it's true," Trish calls back. "Anyway, you've been busy which is great."

"Yeah, most everyone has been nice, and I do really like it here. Lily is...entertaining."

"Heard that, too!"

"That's a nice way of putting it," Trish says quietly just between us. "I've heard someone has been extra nice to you."

"Who?"

She raises an eyebrow.

"Jameson has been welcoming, but how do you know?"

"Hot guy, Jameson."

Thank you, Jerry Lee.

"Welcome to living in a small town,. She winks. "And Jerry Lee. Are you done for the day?"

"Yeah, just cleaning up, unless you need me to do anything else."

"Nope, you go enjoy the rest of your day, and maybe spend some time with a certain someone."

"He's on shift." I chuckle.

"Oh is he?" She starts humming as she walks away and I want to explain, but realize there's nothing to explain. I'm sure anything I say will just get twisted and shoved into the gossip mill around here anyway. Seems to be the case for a small town, if Trish is actually hearing things.

Though, I guess she probably just heard from Lily since she seems to share stories about anything and anyone all the time. I mean, how else would I have learned about her friend having a nice ducking time with bondage duck man, and her thoughts on popes masturbating.

CHAPTER 30

Jameson

SUTTON SAID she would come over for a horse riding lesson, so after I get home from work, I take a nap. I can't help but think that this is just an excuse she can use to keep that little wall up between us. Which is fine by me, I'll take any reason to see her and be happy about it.

Duke perks up at the sound of tires outside and I go out to greet her, with him following happily, probably hoping his friend came along. We get outside and Sutton is already exiting her Jeep and letting Bennet out of the back. The dogs greet each other happily as I approach her.

"I'm glad you came." I wrap my arm around her back to pull her in for a hug. I can tell it catches her off guard, but the need to touch her was just too strong to resist and she doesn't fight the action. She wraps an arm around me as well, returning the quick embrace.

"Hoping I don't regret it," she teases.

"You think I would let anything happen to you?" I pull back, worried she doesn't trust me.

"No, weirdly I don't think you would. You seem like the kind of guy to take off your shirt, and lay it on a puddle so I don't have to get my shoes wet."

I nod, easily. "You're right, I would do that without hesitation for you. And so much more."

Her gaze softens up at me, but she looks away quickly. "So what horse am I going to make friends with today?"

"You get to ride the sweetest mare we have," I explain as we walk toward the barn. Bennet and Duke are already ahead of us, running around and playing with each other.

"Yeah? Who is she?"

"Her name is Sandy, she was Ma's old riding lesson horse when she would teach."

"I didn't realize that's what she did." I catch Sutton's subtle smile.

"You never asked, but I'll tell you anything you want to know. Ma's passion has always been helping people with horses. She would teach anyone. She loved helping with kids, disabled adults and children, people with mental health concerns. If they need help, Ma has always said horses can help them."

"She's amazing."

I nod. "She really is."

"Is she going to be okay?" Her voice is quiet as she hesitates to voice the question that has my heart pinching in my chest.

I answer the only way I know how because I can't fathom thinking about the worst case, even if it's the reality. But I'm not going to lie, either. "I don't know."

Her hand slides into mine easily and the shot of electricity between us is so prominent as our fingers slide together. "I'm sorry." I grip her hand tightly, loving how they fit together and how she grounds me.

"It's okay. She's here and loves to cause me distress and embarrassment."

Sutton chuckles. "She does seem really good at that."

"You haven't even seen the worst of it." I don't let go of her hand, and she doesn't try to let go of mine either.

"I haven't?"

"Not at all, she hasn't brought out the baby pictures for you yet."

"Oh, is that what she does with all the women you bring around?"

I rear back slightly, pausing in my steps, and she does the same.

"Ma was serious at dinner. I've never brought any girl around, just you."

She shakes her head. "Really? No I'm sure you did in high school or just at some point you've brought a girl home."

I shrug, "I mean I'm not going to get into the dirty details of everything I did as a teenager, but I've never brought a girl to meet Ma before."

Her mouth gapes before shutting it, her eyes bouncing across my face like she's trying to detect the lie, but she won't find it. We continue walking again, and I can tell she's thinking extremely hard.

"What about prom or homecoming or anything like that?" she finally asks.

"Went stag. No one was going to tie me down," I joke.

"Oh, there's your flaw. You're afraid of commitment."

I chuckle. "Not afraid of it, but even if I was then it would seem like we're a good pair, huh?"

"I'm not afraid either, just...reserved."

"And why's that?"

She hesitates. "Because the people closest to me tend to do things to hurt me."

"Is that why you moved here? Did something happen?" My hackles rise thinking of someone hurting Sutton.

She's quiet and I feel her start to pull her hand away from mine, but I hold on tighter. We're at the barn, so I divert the conversation away from a subject she clearly doesn't want to talk about and ease the tension she's holding.

"If you don't want to tell me, feel free to tell Sandy, she's a great listener. Even better than a human therapist."

"How do I know she won't spill all my secrets once I'm not around?"

"You caught me, she's really my little spy." I grab Sandy's halter off the front of her stall before opening the door to put it on her.

"I knew you had some ulterior motives. No one's as perfect as you seem."

I scoff, guiding Sandy out to put her in the cross ties and get her tacked up for riding. "I'm not perfect."

"Could've fooled me."

I show Sutton how to tack up the horse and she stands off to the side watching as I do the actions I've done hundreds if not thousands of times in my life while preparing a horse for a ride. When I'm done and Sandy is ready, I switch out the halter for a bridle with a bit and guide her out to the arena.

Sutton follows, and I can feel her hesitation, but I would never put her in any danger and the only problem she's going to have with Sandy is getting her to move, not getting her to stop. I shut the gate to the arena, and Sandy stands, just waiting for her rider.

"Do you want me to walk her around for you or just walk next to you?"

"Walk her around for me to start."

I nod. "Okay, let me help you up." I could have brought her over to the mounting block, but wanted an excuse to get my hands on her again.

She takes a couple tentative steps toward me, and when she's close enough, I hold her hips to guide her to stand in the best spot next to Sandy. Before anything else, I take my brown cowboy hat off and place it on her. "Now you're ready," I tell her with a smile.

"Hold onto her mane, right here." I take her hand in mine and move it up to the base of Sandy's mane to hold it there. "And this hand holds onto the saddle." I step up behind her, our bodies almost completely flush, sliding my hands down her arms, over her sides, and settling them on her hips. I speak directly into her ear, "I'm going to lift you up and you're going to swing your leg over. I got you."

Sutton nods subtly, and I take that as my cue to lift her while she pulls herself up and swings her leg easily before settling in the saddle. "How do I look?"

Like mine.

"Like you were born to be in a saddle. Comfortable?"

She adjusts slightly, holding onto the horn to help keep her balance. "Yeah, please don't make her run."

"Trust me, Sandy wants to run just as much as you want her to, if not less."

I pony her around the arena slowly, and I can tell she gets

more and more comfortable as time goes on when Sandy doesn't do anything crazy. After a few minutes she even asks to hold the reins. I hand them to her, staying close by as she guides Sandy around the arena herself.

"So when am I going to learn how to barrel race like you?" she jokes.

"Maybe try trotting her around before we step it up to barrels," I tease, knowing Sandy wouldn't trot even if she asked and that working up to barrel racing takes more than a day.

"No, I'm good with this pace for now."

And I'm good with whatever pace she wants.

CHAPTER 31

Sutton

AFTER RIDING Sandy for a little while, I don't feel worried about her taking off underneath me anymore. I can tell how sore my thighs are going to be from squeezing so tightly and working muscles that have rarely worked. I get off the horse with Jameson's help, the warmth of his hands burns through my clothes as he helps me down. I go to remove his hat from my head, but he stops me.

"Keep it on for now." He winks, taking Sandy's reins and guiding her out of the arena.

"You know, I've heard something before about a cowboy and his hat." I follow him into the barn.

"Yeah? What's that?" I hear the humor in his tone.

"You know." I shrug.

"No, I think you need to enlighten me." He looks back at me with a grin.

"It's like a claiming thing or something," I look around for the dogs, regretting saying anything.

"Or something." Jameson chuckles while getting the saddle and everything off Sandy. He walks her over to another spot and takes the rope attached to her halter, looping it through a metal ring and then tying a knot that looks extremely elaborate.

"You really are a cowboy, aren't you?"

"Hardly," he breathes, humorously.

"The hat, the horses, the rope. All signs point to a classic cowboy to me."

He looks at the rope he just tied, then up to me. "That's nothing."

I raise an eyebrow at him.

He moves closer, crowding me against the stall door. I look up into his eyes, the blue has darkened the same way they did when he was at my house. The day he touched me. The day I'll never be able to forget because of how good he made me feel. And with the way he's against me right now, my body responds immediately. My heart rate quickens and my thighs squeeze together, especially when my back hits the stall and Jameson leans toward me with his hands pressed against the wood.

"I could use some of this rope on you, make sure you couldn't run away from me again."

I suck in a quick breath. My body *really* likes the sound of that. "W-Why?" I manage to squeak out the single word. It's the only word I'm able to say, even though the word I should be saying is, "*yes.*"

"I could tie you up, and leave you here for hours. Edging you for as long as I want until you don't think you could take any more. Then I would keep going and only let you come when I think you're desperate enough to deserve it."

I'm unable to hide my gasp and the way I arch into him. I saw a glimpse of this other side of Jameson. The sweet man that would help anyone in need also has a dirty side to him, and it's that side that has me ready to drop down to my knees right here, right now.

In fact, that's exactly what I do.

Keeping my eyes locked on his, I slide down to my knees, not caring about the dirt on the hard ground because he's looking at me with so much heat, like I'm the only thing he sees, and it fuels me even more.

He adjusts his hat on my head, tilting it back a bit so he can see my face. "What're you doing?"

"Do you want me to tell you and ruin it? Or do you want me to show you?" I run my hands up his thighs to his belt, holding them there while I wait.

Jameson reaches down, gripping my chin, and rubbing his thumb along my bottom lip. "Go ahead, then. But the hat stays on."

I'm not sure what it is about that seemingly innocent sentence that has me clenching my thighs together, but he always knows just what to say to me. I work his belt open, keeping my eyes locked on his while he watches me.

He lets go of my chin, fists clenching at his side as I undo his pants and start to pull them down. I work slowly even though I'm dying to touch him.

"What if someone comes in here and catches us?" I ask, trying not to let him hear how shaky my voice is.

"That may be pretty awkward; hope it doesn't happen." He smirks and I hesitate with my hands on the waistband of his boxers, his dick tenting the fabric and my mouth waters at the thought of him, but getting caught has me worried.

Jameson notices, because of course he does, and he puts his hands over mine. "We're fine, but if you want to stop you can."

I shake my head adamantly. I don't want to stop. I don't want to think of any negative consequences, and I don't want to hesitate. I just want him. So I pull on the stretchy fabric enough to have his rock hard cock bob in front of me. He's thick, and hard, and it's all because of me.

Wrapping my hand around his length, I pump my fist once, squeezing the tip slightly and he groans. Adjusting the hat on my head again, I look up at him and see the fire blazing in his eyes as he watches with rapt attention. He doesn't rush me, or push me for anything I don't want to do. He just looks at me like I'm the only thing in the world he wants.

And I feel the same.

I lean forward, running my tongue along the slit and tasting the salty precum there. Jameson moans even louder, and I see the strain in his arms as he holds himself back and it makes me want to push him further so he'll completely lose control.

I like the soft, sweet Jameson. But the dirty Jameson who can control my body in ways I didn't think were possible is who I want right now. With that thought, I wrap my mouth around the head of him, sucking him in as far as I can the first try. Which isn't very far because the man is huge.

"Fuck, Sutton," he groans and I smile around him, letting out a soft hum that has him jolting forward, further into my mouth from the vibration. I love the way he sounds saying my name, and moaning it is even better.

I pull back so just the tip is in my mouth before sucking him in again, keeping my hand wrapped around the part of him that I can't fit yet. But I'm determined. I want to make him so crazy he has no option but to completely lose himself.

Flicking my tongue along the sensitive part under the tip, I pull away looking up at him. "Use me. I want it." I open my mouth wide with my tongue out waiting for him.

"How are you so perfect?" he whispers. I want to argue that I'm not, but I'm also not wanting to ruin this moment. Not as he pushes forward, sinking into my mouth, and pushing in far enough I have to breathe through my nose not to gag around him.

His hand drops to the top of my head, where his hat still rests as he thrusts into my mouth. I hold onto his thighs, letting him use me for his pleasure, doing exactly what I asked him to do. And use me he does. His thrusts increase their pace, and I just hold on as he fucks my mouth moaning around him.

"Baby, I'm close," he groans, slowing down and giving me the chance to stop, but I don't want to stop. I don't think I ever want him to stop. "Do you want me to come down your pretty little throat or do you want to be marked as mine?"

The way he growls the last word has me moaning, my thighs tightening trying to find enough pressure to relieve the ache there. I want whatever he's willing to give me, but I end up pulling back, whimpering at the loss of him in my mouth. I look up with tears streaming down my face, my rough voice answering, "Mark me as yours."

The words seem to have the same effect on him because as soon as I pump my fist over him twice more, he's coming with a loud groan, and I open my mouth as the salty liquid coats my skin.

It should be demeaning and gross. I shouldn't be even more turned on knowing his ejaculate is covering my face.

Dammit, Lily.

Jameson immediately reaches behind his neck, pulling his shirt off and I'm ready to climb him like a tree, but that's not his intention. He brings the soft fabric to my face, wiping off the mess as he kneels in front of me, both concern and awe etched onto his face.

I smile at him, running my tongue along my bottom lip and tasting him. He continues to use his shirt to wipe my face and neck, letting out a low groan. "You're so much trouble."

I shrug. "The best kind."

He nods, smiling. "Definitely the best kind."

My eyes roam over his body, the chest hair dusting his pecs and the hard planes of muscles flex, and I have to bite back a moan. I'm so incredibly turned on I feel like he could touch a single part of me and I'm going to combust.

"Don't worry, baby, I'm going to take care of you."

I shake my head. "No, it's fine you don't have to."

He furrows his brows at me, shaking his head. "You don't get it. I *want* to take care of you."

"I didn't do that because I wanted something from you," I insist.

"I know, but it doesn't change that I want to. I want to do so much with you. You have no idea."

I close my mouth, unsure how to reply because part of me wants to run. To thank him for the good time and get out of here. But I know I can't always do that. Running isn't the answer. Sometimes I need to let things happen, and maybe I need to let him in. Even if it's just a little bit.

"Then show me," I say softly.

He scoops me up and carries me around the back of the barn to an old tractor. He sets me down and cups my face. "I want nothing more than to strip you down and properly worship your body, but I don't think I can wait to get you back to my house to do that."

"I don't either," I tell him honestly, hooking my thumbs in my waistband so he knows he's not the only one that's desperate. I want to feel his hands on me. I need to. I feel like I might scream if I have to wait any longer to have him touch me.

He helps push the jeans off my legs, and I didn't even notice that he fixed his, but they're hanging loosely around his hips. He picks me up again, carrying me up onto the tractor with him so I'm straddling his lap.

"Hope you weren't done riding because I'm going to need you to show me what you learned today."

I reach down to push his jeans off enough to free his cock again, and I'm almost ashamed at how desperate I am to feel him inside me. He reaches down, sliding his fingers through my slickness and the second his fingertips graze my clit I moan, bucking my hips against him, seeking more.

"I'm already so hard for you again. What're you doing to me?"

I can feel how true that is and I want to be impressed, but I'm so turned on that desperation is overtaking everything else. He plunges a finger into me and I gasp, wrapping my arms around his neck and crashing our mouths together.

He pushes my shirt up, using his free hand to pull down my bra before moving his mouth down to my newly freed breast. He licks my nipple before sucking it into his mouth roughly at the same time he pushes another finger into me. I'm rocking into him, seeking so much more as I gasp and cling to him tightly.

He pulls back from my nipple letting it go with a pop. "You're so wet for me, baby. Did sucking my dick do this to you?"

I mewl in agreement, nodding as I buck against him. "More, Jameson, please."

"*Fuck*, you're so perfect."

My thighs are already screaming from sitting in the saddle, but I shove it all away because he's moving me above him, positioning the head of him at my entrance and I don't waste any time dropping down so he's filling me completely.

Jameson muffles my cry at the sudden stretch with his mouth on mine again. He swallows the noise and his tongue invades my mouth as I rock over him. There's not a lot of room on this single seat, and my legs already hurt, but the beautiful pain only adds to the intense pleasure making its way through me. It's so forceful; I know my release isn't going to take long to take over completely.

He kisses me with the same ferocity as he fucks me, and I can only hold on. I rub against him every time he thrusts up into me, providing the perfect pressure to my clit while he hits a spot inside me that leaves me gasping for air.

"Come for me. I need to feel the way you squeeze and soak me. It's your turn to mark me." He practically growls against my lips and that's what does it for me.

I explode around him with a sharp squeal as I tighten around him, grasping onto him as tightly as I can. I hear his words of encouragement as my orgasm racks through me. His thrusts increase in intensity as he groans, holding me tighter against him.

My release seems to go on forever, and he's holding me so

tightly, I can feel when his crashes into him, filling me up. We're both breathing heavily, skin slicked with sweat and I don't want to move. I drop my forehead against his, not meeting his eyes as we both catch our breath.

His hands tighten on my hips and he flexes slightly, even though I know he's softening inside me. I'm so sensitive I let out a little sound that he catches.

"Are you okay?"

I hum in agreement, nodding against his head because I don't think I can actually speak. Even if I could, I wouldn't trust my voice or whatever may come out of my mouth. I'm sated, dazed, and I feel like I may end up saying something I'll regret. About him, and about how it feels when we're together.

"As much as I would love to stay here like this for the rest of the day, I think I'd prefer to take you back to my place and help you get cleaned up." He squeezes my hips again and I groan. I don't want to move, but I know that the longer we stay like this the more likely we are to get caught.

I lean back and see the way he's looking at me, like he's worried to see my reaction, and it leaves my heart cracking in my chest. All I've done is run from him when he hasn't given me a reason to. It's not fair to take my own trust issues out on him when all he's done is shown me what a good guy he is.

I place my hands on his cheeks, feeling the stubble I've noticed he grows out when he's not on shift, going for a clean shaven look when he is. The roughness tickles my palm and my lips lift in a small smile. "We should clean up, then maybe I'll let you get me messy again."

He groans, leaning into my touch. "Dammit, Sutton, you're going to be the death of me."

I lean forward, pressing our lips together. It should scare me how good I feel in this moment. How happy I am to be here with him, touching him, feeling him, wanting to continue spending time with him. But I don't. Right now all I feel is content.

CHAPTER 32

Jameson

I MAKE sure Sutton is comfortable as I help her pull her clothes back on. My shirt is ruined for the time being, so I keep an eye out for the prying eyes of my mother as we walk back to my house. Bennet and Duke stay close by, following us while they play around and I'm not sure how they have this much energy after all this time.

I'm also not sure how I have this much energy either. The fact that she made me fall apart with her mouth, then again in her perfect pussy back to back is new for me. And the fact that I feel like I could do it again right now if she asked is completely unheard of.

We get back to my house and I'm anticipating the moment Sutton closes up and runs away again. But even as I start the shower, she continues to look at me with wide green eyes, and there's no sign of her closing off. Not as she reaches down, pulling off her shirt, all while holding our gaze steady. I swallow roughly as I take in her standing in front of me like this.

The small bathroom begins to fill with steam as the water gets hotter, and she reaches behind her back to unhook her bra, letting it fall onto the floor in front of her. Neither of us say anything, I'm not about to break whatever spell she's under and ruin this for either of us. She pushes her pants down and I bite back a groan. My pants are tightening against my erection that's somehow present once again, and I think she may actually kill me if this continues.

She steps toward me, her bare chest brushing against mine as she steps into the shower. Once she's under the water, she smiles. "Are you going to join me or just stand there staring?"

I don't think I've ever moved faster than I do in this moment after hearing her say that, shedding my clothes and even though the shower is not big enough to fit the both of us, I'm not going to deny her. She giggles at both of us squished into the small stall, and I help clean her before doing exactly what she said and getting dirty once again.

AFTER AN AMAZING DAY TOGETHER, I thought Sutton may stay the night with me, but she doesn't and I don't push. Especially because as she left she kissed me like she never wanted to stop and as she drove away it felt different this time.

The next day, I'm at Ma's, cleaning up her house while she naps and can't yell at me for it, when I get a text. A smile instantly spreads on my face the second I see her name. Happy that she reached out first.

My hands are wet from doing the dishes, but I wipe them on my jeans quickly so I can open her text. I should probably try to play it cool, but I'm not going to do that. Not when she's letting me in. I'm not going to screw that up.

Sutton: Bennet just brought Captain Cuddles to me. I think he's trying to tell me something.

Jameson: What do you think he's trying to tell you?

Sutton: Either he misses you...

Sutton: Or he wants to play. It's 50/50.

I chuckle at my screen, typing back to her.

Jameson: I think it's the first one, should I come over to see him?

Sutton: If you want to. Then he won't be lonely while I'm out tonight.

Jameson: Out? Where are you going?

Sutton: Jealous? *wink emoji*

Jameson: Concerned. I just want to make sure you're safe.

Sutton: I'm going with Bailey. I'll be safe.

I know Bailey is the neighbor she went to the rodeo with. I wasn't here when she moved into town, but I know she isn't from here. Everyone in Amity knows everyone and everything, including if you leave or arrive.

In fact, it's only a matter of time before someone catches wind of what's going on between Sutton and me. I'm a little surprised that the rumor mill hasn't started already, or maybe it has and I just haven't heard anything yet.

Jameson: Let me know if you need anything.

Sutton: Don't worry, I will, cowboy.

I shake my head, then I hear my mom's voice behind me saying my name softly and I put my phone away.

"What do you think you're doing?" she asks, her voice groggy with exhaustion, and her eyes match. Seeing her like this hurts my heart.

"Are you okay?"

She smiles softly. "Yes, I'm okay. But I'm not going to be if I find out you're doing things around here for me when you shouldn't be."

"Ma, can you just accept that I want to help you?"

She sighs, looking around the kitchen and clearly noticing everything I did to clean up and narrows her eyes at me. She doesn't say anything about it and I'm not sure if I should call that a win or be worried that she's not putting any energy into her playful fights with me.

"I saw Sutton leave yesterday."

"Did you?"

"I like her."

I chuckle. "I know you do."

"Did she have a good time? Was Sandy good to her?"

I fight the blush that wants to cover my cheeks when I think about the good time we had that had nothing to do with the horses.

"Of course she was. That horse is an angel, you know that."

"She is," she agrees with a smile. "They all are. we have a good herd."

"We do. You trained them really well."

She waves me off as she always does and I catch how unsteady she is. I don't like how weak she seems, and I step toward her. "Come on, Ma, I want to help with dinner tonight and I don't want to fight about it."

"Fine," she sighs and that also has me a little worried. "Have you seen your father?"

"No." I know what's going to come next, and because it's her I'm going to do it.

"I'll let you help with dinner if you ask him to join us."

I nod. "Anything for you, Ma." Turning to go find him, she calls out my name again and I face her.

"Then, you go have a nice time with Sutton."

I shake my head. "She's going out with a friend of hers tonight."

"Hm." She smiles.

"What is that?"

"Hm, oh nothing."

I think about letting it go, but the way she's reacting has me wondering what she's thinking. This is how she sounds when she knows something. I should let it go, but there's a chance that she may actually be thinking something I want to hear.

"What is it?" I finally question before opening the door to leave.

"Did she tell you she didn't want you to join her?"

"No, but she didn't invite me either."

"Maybe she wants you to surprise her."

"Ma, I think you're wanting to cause trouble."

She just smiles, and I continue to leave to find my dad, hoping that this isn't going to lead to a fight with him. I just want to make Ma happy, and I hope he wants the same, at least before it's too late.

CHAPTER 33

Sutton

"HAVE you ever been line dancing before?" Bailey asks as we both get into her car to go wherever it is she's taking me.

"No, I can't say that I have."

"I hadn't either before I came here, but it's something to do around here that's actually kind of fun." Bailey starts driving and she seems like she's in a pretty good mood.

Something I've learned about Bailey is that she's extremely closed off. She doesn't show emotion easily, including happiness. She's nice enough except to Wes, who I have yet to meet. But she hates him.

"Cool, so what is this place?"

"It's just a bar, but a couple times a week they do this and they're good with beginners."

I nod, hoping I don't regret this; my legs are still sore from the horse riding lesson and then the other kind of riding I participated in afterwards. The spot between my thighs also remembers what happened afterwards.

That part isn't something I'm going to forget for a long time. Or ever. And I'm fighting every urge telling me to shut down and push him away, to just let things fizzle out. I texted him earlier just because I wanted to. I second guessed myself as I paced around waiting to see what he would say.

And because he's Jameson Turner, he replied right away. Every worry I had faded so easily. That's one of his super powers, I think. At least when it comes to me. But tonight is about hanging out with my friend. If I'm going to be better about letting people into my life again, then I should do it with more than just Jameson.

Bailey is more reserved than I am and for some reason that makes me trust her. At least enough not to worry that she would betray me. We end up at the bar at the edge of town and the parking lot is so busy, every single person in Amity must be here. Maybe even from neighboring towns.

"Are you sure this is for beginners?" I ask through a nervous laugh.

"Oh yeah, trust me, you want it to be crowded like this. That's when you know no one is watching you."

She has a point.

We get inside and the music is so loud I can feel it vibrating the floor. There's a large open area ahead of us that's full of people moving along to the beat. The bar on the left is fairly busy, and on the right there's an area of tables that are mostly empty.

"Do you want to get a drink first or just dive in?" Bailey asks, leaning close, and speaking loudly so I can hear her over the music.

"Definitely a drink." I look at the dancing and while it doesn't seem incredibly difficult, I don't have very much rhythm so I'm not confident that I'll be good at this at all. Liquid courage might help me. It may also make me worse, but hey, if I'm unaware of how bad I am then I can't be embarrassed about it.

We make our way to the bar, squeezing between people to get a spot and wait for the bartender to get to us. Bailey towers over most people here, she's probably close to six feet tall and I wonder if she's ever played basketball.

I order a vodka Red Bull with a splash of cranberry and Bailey gets a cider. We grab a table to get away from the crowd at the bar and I'm watching the people dancing, wondering how I'll ever manage to do that.

I take a big sip from my drink and Bailey notices. "You nervous?"

I nod. "Is it that obvious?"

"Only a little bit, don't worry if you don't want to. You can just watch this time if you want."

"Did you join in your first time here?"

Bailey shakes her head. "Fuck no. I watched a few times before I finally joined in."

"What made you decide to finally do it?"

She looks out at the crowd and shrugs. "Sometimes I realize that I have to throw caution to the wind and do something even if it scares me."

I understand her more than she even knows. It's exactly how I'm feeling about Jameson. It's also how I'm feeling about being here as well. I bring my drink to my lips, downing it quickly, reveling as the cold liquid burns slightly as it goes down my throat.

"You may have to show me what to do, but let's go," I announce.

We walk out onto the dance floor, and I do my best to follow along with everyone. It's difficult at first, but several minutes later I'm caring less about getting the moves right and more about having a good time.

I end up ordering two more drinks in between songs, and each one has me caring less and less about looking like an idiot. I'm dancing, laughing and having a great time. Bailey seems to as well, even though she hasn't gotten any more drinks other than water.

After a while we go back to the table to sit because I need a break. I make sure to get another drink and it's making my head feel fuzzy, and my filter non existent.

"This is so fun. Thank you for bringing me here," I tell my new friend.

"I'm glad you like it. Sometimes we need to get out of our own heads and just...live."

I raise my glass in her direction. "You got that right. You come here to escape a shitty situation, too?"

She snorts. "You have no idea."

"To shitty people," I announce, and she clinks her glass of water against mine in a cheer.

Mid sip my gaze locks on a familiar figure standing by the bar and I fight choking on my drink.

"What's he doing here?"

Bailey follows where I'm looking, and turns back to me with a smirk. "Your stalker strikes again, huh?"

I make a dramatic noise. "Hardly my stalker at this point."

"Why's that?"

I mumble, "I may have slept with him...multiple times."

Bailey chuckles. "Ah, yeah. Well, he's coming this way."

Sure enough he approaches the table and as I look up at him, I feel the way my gaze softens and my entire body gravitates toward him instantly. "What're you doing here?"

"I obviously came for the line dancing." He gestures toward the dancefloor.

"Wait, how'd you know I was here?"

"Baby, this is where anyone comes in this town."

Him calling me baby right now is not something I can handle. The only other time he's said that is when he's inside me, and it brings me right back to how that feels. Add in the alcohol running through my system and I feel like I'm going to end up back in his bed tonight.

Or the tractor again. Or his truck, or even the bar bathroom if I can't control myself.

I need to calm down.

"Bailey, nice to see you again," Jameson greets my friend, and it distracts me from the dirty place my mind went.

"You too. Hope you're being nice to my friend."

I smile at her referring to me as her friend, and it seems silly, but everything is heightened right now apparently.

"Are you telling stories about me?" Jameson teases.

"No," I deny easily.

"Good, have you done any dancing?"

"Oh yeah. Bailey has basically turned me into a pro."

"That so? You going to show me the ropes then?"

I look at Bailey, not wanting to ditch her again just because Jameson showed up. She looks behind us and her face that was smiling and light drops into a frown. "No, you go ahead, this place just got less fun."

I turn to see what she's looking at and see Wes standing at the bar. I can't contain the laughter bursting out of me. "Maybe you two need to do something to clear the air."

She looks at me deadpan. "The only thing I'm going to do is disconnect his engine so he can't wake up the entire neighborhood."

I don't dare tell her I think she's being a bit dramatic. I still think there's more to that story than she's saying, but my tongue feels heavy in my mouth and my body is reacting to the man standing in such close proximity.

"I think I'm going to head home anyway; I'm tired. Do you want a ride, or are you good?" she asks.

I should probably go home with her and turn in for the night. But Jameson's hand is on my arm, and I lose all the reasons why I should go and decide to stay. Him and I end up on the dancefloor, but the line dancing is over and he pulls me against him so our bodies move together.

My arms drape around his shoulders as we sway and I feel myself sinking into him more. My walls are breaking down and I want to let him in even just a little more.

"I don't want to get close to anyone again," I murmur.

"Why not?" he asks gently.

"Because the people closest to me betrayed me."

He leans back slightly to look at me. We aren't moving anymore and his eyes search mine. I shouldn't have said anything. The alcohol running through my veins is making me less reserved and I regret it. He doesn't need to know what happened. Maybe my reaction was dramatic, maybe I'm ridiculous. It was a betrayal from my parents and one of my best friends, but telling him won't change anything because it still happened and I still ran from it.

"Tell me what you mean, baby. Who hurt you?"

I shake my head. "It's not what you think. Forget I said anything. Just dance with me."

He doesn't ask me anything else, just pulls me closer as we start swaying again. I close my eyes, blocking out everything else and just being here in this moment with him. He's the only one I'm paying attention to. The only one I'm feeling. He might as well be the only other person in this whole place with me.

And when his lips find mine as we dance, I lose every other sense I have. His tongue finds mine and I'm completely lost. No one else exists around me anymore.

It's just us.

EVERYTHING HAS BEEN GOING PERFECTLY LATELY. EVER since the day Sutton came over that ended with me fucking her in the seat of the tractor, things have shifted between us. We text every day, and I've seen her a handful of times. Every time we talk, she asks about Ma and it's only made me fall for her even more.

I still don't know what it is that brought her here, but she's alluded to something being the catalyst, she just hasn't revealed what exactly it is. I want to know, because I want to help her through whatever it is, but I'll never push. She'll tell me when she's ready.

Ma's been sleeping a lot and I want to be optimistic that it means her body is trying to heal and give her energy. The reality is that I'm sure she's slowing down as the disease progresses and I can't even bear to think of the time she may have left. Of course she continues to act like everything is okay and that she's fine.

She tries to get my dad and I to talk, and pushes us together in situations more, but it never ends how she wants. He barely says anything to me and our relationship continues to be just as strained as always.

"Jameson, you're up," Dave calls out as soon as I enter the common area and I look at him, then everyone else, confused because I haven't been involved in whatever they're talking about.

"Up for what?"

"Embarrassing stories."

"Why am I involved in this?" I just walked in here and now I'm regretting it.

"Good point, you just came down here, Parker you go." Dave slaps the back of his hand against Parker's shoulder.

"I've never been embarrassed." He shrugs. "It's a gift."

I scoff.

"I bet Lily has some embarrassing stories about you, should we go over there and ask her?" Jo chimes in.

"She wishes. The worst she has is when her mom showed up the first time we...you know."

"What do you mean she showed up?" I ask, already horrified at the thought of my parents ever catching me with a girl.

"We were in the middle of it, and someone was outside calling her name. I looked out the window and saw that her mom was there."

"What did you do?" I'm not entirely sure I want to know, but I can't help but wonder.

"Well, the window was open so we were pretty sure she heard us. Then she screamed at Lily to come outside and it kind of ruined the mood."

Jo is the first to start laughing, and then one by one, we all join in at his expense. I feel bad for the girl he was with, but that's quite the story for them to be able to tell.

"Your turn." Parker nods toward me.

I shake my head. "No way. I can't compete with that."

"Hold on, that's not fair."

"That's too bad for you then." I shrug.

"Wait, what the fuck?"

I just chuckle and head out to work on some of the chores around the station while the rest of my coworkers play their weird little game.

I open the bay doors to get some air flow while I do inventory on the truck.

"Hey there," a familiar voice calls out.

I turn around, seeing the most beautiful woman I've ever met. And she's finally giving me the time of day. But the best part is that she's smiling at me right now. Something she's done a lot more often lately. Her eyes are bright, the green even more prominent in the sunlight while her brown hair swishes over her shoulders.

Without hesitation, I step toward her and wrap my arms around her body, pulling her into me and she goes easily, letting me drop my mouth to hers in a gentle kiss. Her lips are soft against mine and I fight a groan, especially when her tongue teases the seam of mine and I'm about to push it further when she pulls back.

"Not that I'm going to complain about the surprise, but what're you doing here?"

"I pulled up to work and saw you out here so thought I would stop by really quick."

"Well, please feel free to do this any time." I lean down to kiss her again, but our lips barely brush before the call sound goes off and I rest my forehead against hers.

"I think you have to go," she teases.

"Guess so." I don't move away from her yet. I have a few more seconds to hold her in my arms and I'm not going to let go any earlier than I have to.

"Yo, Jameson! Gotta go, your girlfriend called."

Sutton tenses in my arms, looking at me with furrowed brows. "Girlfriend?"

I shake my head. "Must be Margaret. Sorry, baby. I got a hot date, I'll come by and see you later."

She backs away from me, shaking her head. "Yeah, uh don't worry about it."

"Sutton." I start to follow her, but I'm stopped by Dave clapping a hand on my shoulder.

"Come on, man, we gotta go."

Sutton walks back over to the salon and I watch her enter the door as we drive away, though I'm annoyed we have to go out on this false alarm when she's clearly upset. Everything was fine and she shut down just as fast as she had in the past. I know when we get back I'm going to have to do some damage control.

Once we get to Margaret's I'm annoyed and already know I won't be playing as nice as I usually do when we go on these calls. She comes out in one of her elaborate robes, hair curled and makeup done. My coworkers can sense how annoyed I am, so Jo is the one that takes the lead this time.

"Hello, Margaret, how can we help you today?"

Her eyes lock on me, but I stand back as close to the truck as possible. When she speaks it seems like it's only to me. "I'm worried that I have a gas leak."

"Why do you think that?" Jo asks, but Margaret still won't look at anyone else besides me.

"Because I can smell it, why do you think?" she snaps, side eyeing Jo.

"Alright, we'll take a look. Do you have a carbon monoxide alarm?" Dave asks her.

"No, why would I have one of those? They're ugly." She grimaces.

"You don't have an alarm because it's...ugly?" Parker chimes in. "Do you have fire alarms?"

"If there's a fire in my house, I'm going to know it," she says deadpan and I just shake my head.

Parker won't let it go. "What about if you're sleeping or—"

"Jameson, are you going to check if I have a gas leak or not?" she cuts him off.

"My team and I will check," I tell her, emotionless.

We all head inside, and to the surprise of no one, there's no gas leak. As we leave, she attempts to get me to stay as she usually does.

On our way back to the station everyone wants to stop and get lunch, though I want to get back and talk to Sutton. I'm unable to argue since everyone else is on the same page and I have no choice but to go along.

Once we finally get back, I walk over to the grooming salon to fix whatever I may have just messed up with Sutton. I'm instantly greeted by my best friend, the bird, as usual.

"Hot guy, Jameson."

"Hey there."

I hear a muffled, "fuck," and I would know my girl's voice

anywhere. I follow it, only to find her in the middle of grooming a large dog on the table in front of her.

"Not happy to see me?" I tease.

"How was seeing *Margaret?*" I hear the disdain in her tone and realize instantly she didn't take that entire interaction as the joke it was intended to be.

"Hold on." I step around to the other side of the table so I'm standing next to her. "You didn't think we were serious about me having a date did you?"

She shrugs. "You've dated her before, haven't you? It's not like we're serious. You're free to do whatever you want."

I narrow my eyes at her, and gently place my hand on top of hers so she pauses what she's doing and guides her full attention to me.

"I've never dated Margaret. I don't know what makes you think we aren't serious, because I've been serious about you since the moment I laid my eyes on you in that parking lot."

Her breath hitches and she finally looks up at me.

"She said you dated, though." She doesn't acknowledge the other part of what I said, which doesn't surprise me.

"When have you met her?"

"She brought her dog in when I first moved here and made sure to...stake her claim on you."

I rack my brain trying to figure out what she could mean, Margaret doesn't have a dog. Then who she's really talking about hits me.

"You're talking about *Mallory*. Not Margaret." I can't help but chuckle softly at her mix up, but I can't blame her.

"Oh." Her cheeks flame and she tries to look away from me again, but I don't let her, guiding her gaze back to mine with a finger under her chin instead.

"Margaret is an older woman who's been a little obsessed with me. But even if it was Mallory on that call today, it wouldn't have mattered. We dated forever ago and it was never anything serious to me. She didn't mean a fraction of what you do to me."

"I...I have to get back to work and finish this dog," she says softly.

I nod. "Come by the station before you leave later."

She smirks. "Maybe."

I drop a quick kiss to her cheek, and start walking toward the door. "I mean it, Sutton. I need to see your gorgeous face one more time today to get me through the night."

"You're ridiculous," she tells me.

"You like it."

"Shut up, Vern."

"You like it."

I laugh while leaving and I swear I hear the bird call out, "*jizz,*" but I don't think I'm going to question that one.

CHAPTER 35

Sutton

LILY PEAKS around the corner after Jameson is gone, and sighs. "I didn't want to interrupt, but I take it you two figured out your little lovers quarrel?"

"That's not what it was," I deny, trying to focus back on finishing the dog on my table.

"Right, that's what they all say. But a 'not lovers quarrel' was how I ended up at a male strip club with a group of friends one weekend last term."

Here we go.

"One of the guy's had a dick piercing, which I've never seen before and it looks pretty scary. But he was hitting it against the pole, so the music was playing while he just swung his dick and it made a sound every time the metal hit the metal."

Part of me wants to ask how this is where her brain went, the other part of me is curious where else the story is going to go. If there's one thing about Lily, it's that whatever she's going to say, it's never anything you expect. I have a feeling this won't be any different.

"Another guy came out with an electric skillet and started doing this like fire dance around it."

My point exactly.

"One of my friends, not the one who was in the fight with her situationship, but another one that was with us, ended up fucking that guy in the bathroom."

"Was it the same one that ducked the duck man?" I can't help myself, she's rubbing off on me.

"No, she wasn't with us. But she said he had a massive dick and ended up going to a hotel with him. Once they got there he expected her to pay for half and she actually did. And still had sex with him."

"The bathroom wasn't enough for her?" I bite back my laughter.

"Apparently not, though she said his dick was painfully big so I'm shocked she went back for seconds."

That comment gets me and the laugh bursts out of me. It also makes me think of my own...situation with Jameson and how I'm impressed I went back for seconds as well with him considering his size. But it's not just about that with him, he makes it impossible to want to stay away completely.

"Did she see him again?"

"Of course not, he had her pay for half the hotel. That was for a good time, not a long time."

Yet again, I don't know how we got here, but I appreciate the insane story. There's never a dull day with Lily and it helps me get through the rest of my work day without constantly looking over to watch Jameson.

Once I'm done for the day, I head home to let Bennet out. I know Jameson asked me to come back to see him, but I don't want to disturb him at work. I'll call him later.

I'm not even home for five minutes before I see his name lighting up my phone, and I answer as I let Bennet outside.

"Hello?" I answer.

"You didn't come by and see me before you went home."

"I didn't want to bother you; I'll see you when you're off work."

"Come back."

I chuckle, shaking my head, though he can't see me. "Jameson, I'll see you when you're not working."

"I told you, I need to see you in order to get through the night. You're really going to make me wait and just hope I manage to get through?" he says dramatically.

"I think you'll be just fine."

"You really want to risk that? I may just have to make an excuse to come to your house. I just don't think I'll be able to get through, Sutton, please."

I giggle. "You're something else, you know that?"

"Tell me what else I am then because all I want to be is yours."

I gasp softly, possessive talk during a heated moment is one thing, but this just flowed, and it has my heart racing in my chest. It has me feeling all sorts of feelings that have been dormant for too long.

"All I want is a goodnight kiss from you," he pleads.

I find myself unable to say no to him, and that's something I worry will come back to bite me one of these days, but instead, I agree.

After I let Bennet back inside, I change out of my gross grooming clothes and since the summer evening is warm I pull on a simple T-shirt dress and some tennis shoes. I'm just running over to say goodnight to Jameson; I won't be gone long and that's exactly what I tell Bennet as he looks at me oddly when I grab my keys to leave again.

Once I park, I pull my phone out to text Jameson because I'm not about to walk right up to the door. The only reason I did earlier was because it was open and I knew it was him.

Sutton: I'm parked outside.

Jameson: I'll come out.

I wait until I see him step outside before I get out of my car and can't help but speed walk over to him. He pulls me into a tight hug the second I'm within arms reach and I melt into him just like I always do the second his arms are around me.

"I want to show you something," he tells me, pulling back slightly.

"I'm just here to say goodnight; you didn't tell me you had other plans for us."

"Do you have a hot date you need to get to?"

"What if I do?" I raise my chin.

"Then I'll make sure to keep you here so you can't go because the only one that gets to take you on a date is me."

"I'm surprisingly okay with that," I admit.

"Good." He presses a chaste kiss to my lips. "Come on, I'm going to show you around the station."

He pulls me inside, and I'm worried about what his coworkers may say if they see us. I'm sure they'll wonder why I'm here right now. I'm not even sure if I'm technically allowed to be. He doesn't hesitate as he brings me inside, but instead of going to where everyone else is, he brings me to the oversized garage where the firetruck and ambulance are parked.

"You drive this giant thing?" I ask, looking up at the firetruck. I've never been this close to one before and never realized how tall they are.

"Yeah, do you want to sit in it?"

"Are we going to get in trouble for this?"

Jameson chuckles. "No, we do tours all the time. But if we get a call then we're going to have to go."

He leads me to the driver's side, opening the door and helping me climb up onto the seat. I grip the giant steering wheel in front of me and hold onto it and pretend to steer.

"Think you could drive this around?" he asks.

"No way, I wouldn't trust myself."

"Would you trust me?"

"Yeah, I would," I tell him softly. He helps me down and brings me over to the passenger side.

"We call this the Officer seat, it's where all the controls are." He tells me climbing in first, stretching out his hand to help me up. There's not much room for both of us as he lifts me up into his lap.

I swivel slightly and he grunts underneath me. I feel why as I notice him starting to harden, and I suck my bottom lip into my mouth. This isn't the time or place for us to do anything about that, but it makes me feel really good that I have such an effect on him. I move again just to mess with him, and he clamps his hands on my hips to get me to stop.

"You know I would never let anything happen to you, right?" He moves one of his hands onto my thigh, rubbing gentle circles there while I look at all the controls and panels in front of me.

"What does that do?" I point to some buttons, trying not to pay attention to the way he's touching me.

"That controls the lights." His hand continues to move on my thigh, moving up closer to the spot that's growing increasingly wetter with each inch he gets closer.

"What, um, what about that button?" I continue to try and distract us both because there's no way he's going to touch me right now, not when we're out here where we're sure to be caught.

He moves my hair off my shoulder, pressing his lips to the spot where my neck meets my shoulder and asks, "What button, baby?"

To be honest, I don't even know what button I was asking about, or if I actually pointed to anything. All my attention is on the places he's touching me. His hand climbs up my dress and I gasp when his fingers graze my underwear. I grab his arm, digging my fingers in and stopping his movement.

"This is a bad idea," I whisper.

"Do you want me to stop?"

He doesn't move, and neither do I because no, I don't want him to stop. I don't want to be caught either, but something about the possibility is exhilarating. Just like that day in the barn. It shouldn't make me want to continue, but it does.

I let go of the grip I have on his arm and tell him, "Keep going."

And he does. His lips are on my neck, kissing and sucking lightly as his hand moves between my thighs, rubbing me over the fabric there. I buck up against his fingers, leaning my head to the side to give his mouth better access.

"I want more," I moan.

"You want more, baby?"

"Yes, please."

"You can have it, you can have it all."

I nod while he moves my underwear to the side and plunges a finger into me. I gasp, arching back against him, moving my hips and trying to get him to give me even more. He does just that without me having to ask again. He fucks me with his finger, adding another one and I moan, dropping my head back against his shoulder. He brings his other hand up to wrap around the front of my throat. Not squeezing, just resting it there like he's claiming me, not trying to hurt me.

The simple move along with his talented fingers has my orgasm barreling toward me. I'm grappling for anything to hold onto while the force of it feels like it's going to completely consume me. My body thrashes and I call out Jameson's name.

Right as I feel the peak approaching and I'm on the precipice, I thrash and my foot catches on something. I press down as I buck up into Jameson's hand. The sharp sound of a siren pierces the air and I gasp, pushing myself away from Jameson as quickly as possible.

When I look back at him he's laughing and the siren stops. My chest is heaving as I look at his face, looking way too giddy.

"Everything okay?" someone asks from outside the truck, and my face flames. I quickly fling myself onto the drivers seat as Jameson opens up the door, and steps out.

"Yeah, I was giving Sutton a tour, and she didn't realize there's a foot pedal for the siren," he replies easily, and I see he's talking to Parker. The guy that Lily seems to have a problem with.

Between her and Bailey, there seems to be more than a few stories around here that I want to know more about.

"Ah, happens to the best of us, Sutton," he calls out, and I just give him a thumbs up because I don't trust my voice. My body is still reeling from the loss of the orgasm I was so close to having.

"Let everyone know it's all good," Jameson tells him, and I don't miss the smirk on Parker's face as he walks away.

I turn my head to look at Jameson who has a raised eyebrow, trying to bite back his smile.

"What?" I whisper.

"We were interrupted, which means now I owe you an extra one."

CHAPTER 36

Sutton

JAMESON MANEUVERS my legs so they're off the side of the seat and I don't have time to question what he's doing before he yanks the panties off my body, and buries his face between my thighs under my dress.

I drop back, barely catching myself on my elbows as he thrusts his tongue inside me roughly and I have to hold back my screams of pleasure. I use the back of my hand over my mouth to hide any noise that may slip through as he moves up to my clit, flicking it with his talented tongue. The second he sucks it into his mouth, I detonate.

I've hardly had a chance to come down when Jameson pulls me down from the seat, keeping me steady on weak legs as he walks me toward the side of the truck and bends me forward. I have to catch myself before I face plant into the metal, but I know he won't let me fall.

The sound of his belt buckle being undone behind me is followed by the weight of Jameson pressing against my back as he leans over me, his hand pushing up my dress and kneading my ass.

"Better stay quiet. I know you don't want to be caught with my cock buried deep inside your sweet pussy." He presses the tip of himself against my entrance and I clench around nothing, and he must feel the way I tense at his words because he groans. "You like the idea of it though, don't you, baby?"

I don't want to be caught, I really don't, but the anticipation around it does add to my arousal for some reason. Luckily, I don't have much time to dwell on it because Jameson's pushing inside me, and I muffle my gasp against my arm as he sinks in inch by inch. There's a pinch of pain but it's overwhelmed by the amount of pleasure he brings me with how he fills me, stretching me so perfectly.

He pulls back slightly before pushing into the hilt, roughly and this time I'm unable to do anything to hide my sounds of pleasure. He reaches around, covering my mouth with his hand.

"I want to hear you screaming for me, but that's going to have to wait. I'm not going to take it easy on you, but I know you can take it."

He shows me just how true that is when he pulls back and slams into me again, keeping his hand over my mouth tight enough that I know I can scream and no one will hear me. That's a good thing too, because I wouldn't be able to control myself even if I wanted to with the way he's fucking me. One hand holds my hip tightly as he slams into me over and over again.

"Come for me, baby. You owe me another one and you're going to give it to me."

I shake my head against his hand, feeling the telltale signs of my release starting and the only way that it can be stopped would be if Jameson stopped what he was doing, but I know he won't. Even if someone came down here I don't think he would let up. Right now, it feels like we're the only two in the world and nothing can break us apart.

He moves his hand from my hip to my clit and all it takes is a couple tight circles before I lose my balance as the orgasm racks through me. He keeps me standing as my body gives into pleasure. I swear I black out from it. It doesn't take long before I hear Jameson's groan behind me and he pushes himself as deep as my body will allow and fills me with his own release.

Our bodies part and I feel his cum starting to leak out of me. I feel the pressure of his finger pushing back into me, and I gasp. He helps me stand up straight, turning me around to face him, cupping my face, and pressing a chaste kiss to my lips.

"Thanks for coming by to say goodnight," he says against my mouth.

I chuckle, fisting his shirt and shaking my head against his forehead. "I thought you were going to say thanks for coming."

He smiles, pressing his lips to mine again. "That too."

He pulls back, and I just look at him, his blue eyes, the way his jaw is clean shaven right now, showcasing his strong jawline. His dark hair was styled, but is now perfectly messy. I bring my hand up to run my thumb along his jaw, feeling the sharp beginnings of scruff there.

"Goodnight Sutton," he rasps quietly.

"Goodnight Jameson." I smile right before his lips are on mine again and I know I have to go and that we aren't able to spend tonight together, but there will be another night when we can. Because I'm done fighting this. He has me, he has all of me.

BENNET and I get to the Turner's property and I see his dad on a riding mower as I drive to Jameson's house. He doesn't acknowledge me with a wave or anything, though I try to give him the benefit of the doubt, because maybe he didn't see me.

Duke greets Bennet and Jameson greets me, and when the dogs start chasing each other, Jameson pulls me into him immediately kissing me senseless.

"Well hi." I smile when he lets me up for air.

"I missed you."

"It's been like twenty-four hours."

"Yeah, a whole twenty-four hours since I kissed you. You're lucky I survived it."

I laugh. "Oh I'm lucky you survived it?"

"Yeah, I know that it was just as difficult for you."

"You're right." I launch myself into his arms with another kiss.

Once we finally break apart again, I tell him that I saw his dad on my way over. Jameson scrunches his nose slightly at the mention of him.

"I take it that means things haven't been getting better," I assume.

"Unfortunately not. You know how some people just don't seem like they ever want to fix things?"

"Oh yeah, I have a few of those in my life."

Jameson looks at me, wide eyed.

"What?" I ask through a laugh.

"Did you just reveal something about yourself?"

I roll my eyes. "I've told you things about myself before."

"Nothing about your past, your family, or what brought you here," he goads.

I pull my bottom lip in between my teeth, suddenly feeling a pang of guilt that he's right. He's been open with me, brought me into his life and never asked for more than I'm willing to give. Yet, I haven't given him much about my past, or what brought us together.

"Hey." He grips my chin, forcing me to look up at him, and pulling my lip from between my teeth with his thumb. "I'm not complaining. You can tell me or not tell me anything you want. I'm here."

I fall into him, wrapping my arms around his back, and burying my face in his chest. He smells like the mountain air mixed with a scent that's purely Jameson and I want to bathe in it. "I want to tell you," I say against his chest, unable to look up at him.

I know he still hears me, because he holds my cheeks, pulling me back to look up at him. "What do you want to tell me?"

I sigh. "Can we go for a walk?"

He nods. "Of course."

We get the dogs to join us, and they run ahead of us as we keep our pace slow. We aren't walking toward the barn this time and I find myself wanting to see more of the property that's surrounded by tree covered mountains. It's warm, but there's the breeze from the ocean that makes it feel cooler. Jameson doesn't rush me to start talking as we walk, but the moment he inter-twines our fingers I feel myself sigh and find the confidence to tell him the insane story that led me here.

"I was living with my parents because I was saving up to buy a house and Los Angeles is expensive as I'm sure you know," I start, knowing I'm going to over explain just so I can delay the inevitable of telling him the worst parts of the story.

And because Jameson is beyond perfect, he doesn't say anything to rush me or move the story along, he just holds my hand. We both look ahead of us as I continue. "I have this friend —my best friend, really—and we were basically inseparable since we met at the first grooming salon where we started at eighteen. She started acting weird toward me. She started avoiding me and not wanting to hang out as much which I thought was weird, but figured she would tell me what was going on when she was ready. I ended up figuring out it was because she was seeing someone."

I pause as Bennet and Duke zoom by us and I can't help my laughter when they tumble slightly in the grass.

"I came home from work one day and learned very quickly who it was that she was seeing."

Jameson tenses. "No."

"Yup, but it's so much worse. Not only did I catch her and my dad together on the couch mid...act"—I fight off the gag—"my mom was there, too. So she knew about it and wasn't"—another gag—"involved in that moment but I wasn't going to ask any questions. I grabbed my dog and left."

Jameson finally speaks, "You really just grabbed Bennet and left? No plan or anything else?"

"Well, I went back later that night to get some stuff while everyone was sleeping, but I haven't seen them and they haven't seen me since that day I walked in."

"That's insane. How does anyone do that to their best friend, or their daughter?"

I shrug. "I have no idea, but I wasn't about to sit down with them and unpack it all. I just had to leave."

"I don't blame you." He doesn't try to apologize or placate me. He doesn't say I should talk to them, or that I should try to work past it because we're family. He just accepts my choices, and the relief that gives me makes me feel even better about this thing between us.

"Thank you." I squeeze his hand, and look over at him. He smiles down at me, showing his white teeth against the lips that I want to attack with my own. He really is perfect. I didn't think it was possible for anyone to be, but he is. I've been waiting for the other shoe to drop, to see a flaw of his and ruin this illusion of him.

But I don't think it's an illusion. I don't think there's another shoe. I think this is just him.

He leads me to an open area we haven't gone before, and I look around the field, wondering why we're out here. Jameson doesn't say anything, just pulls me down with him so I'm between his legs while the dogs run around together.

Jameson just holds me like this. The fresh mountain air blowing around us, and the secret I've been too afraid to tell anyone is finally off my chest. I feel lighter and more content than I have in a long time.

"Do you think you and your dad will ever have a better relationship?" I run my fingers along his arm that's draped around me; there's a prominent vein in his muscular forearm that I trace.

"If he made an effort then maybe, but I've tried, Ma is trying. The only one that isn't is him."

"Why do you think that is?"

"Because he's a stubborn man stuck in his ways and for some reason, me chasing a dream off this land was too much for him to ever forgive, apparently."

I continue trailing my fingers along his skin, the soft hair dusting his tan skin. There's a couple of scars from years of working on the ranch I'm sure. "Maybe he just isn't good at expressing how he feels."

"I'm sure that's part of it, but he could at least do something.

You'd think with Ma being so sick it would make him realize how finite time is."

I nod, thinking about that for my own situation. It's a different circumstance, but it makes me consider if I should try to make amends. It's not my amends to make, though and I shake the thought away.

"He seems to really love your mom." I bring his hand up to my lips brushing them against his rough skin.

"He always has. I just think she takes it too easy on him."

I lean my head back to look up at him. "Why do you say that?"

"She's always understanding. Of everyone. She's the sweetest person I know, but maybe my dad needs more tough love to get it through his head."

"What about you? What is it that you need?"

Jameson looks down at me, tightening his hold on me. "Right now? All I need is you."

CHAPTER 37

Jameson

WE HAVE a call to Sutton's neighborhood, and when it comes through I hear Scenic drive and am instantly on edge. Luckily, the house number is different so I'm able to keep my calm as we head out. Once we get there I realize it's one of the houses across the street from Sutton. I knock on the door and Wes is the one that answers.

"What's going on?" he asks, confused.

"Uh, we had a call for this address about a possible fire," I answer, now just as confused as him.

"My fire alarm went off, but I didn't call..." His voice trails off and I see him look toward the neighbors house next to him. "Sorry guys, it's a false alarm. If you excuse me I need to have a talk with my overbearing neighbor."

"Just to be clear, you don't want us to check anything out?" I clarify because we can't leave until a scene is cleared.

"No, you're off the hook." Wes is already walking out toward his next door neighbor.

I nod to my coworkers and we load back up to go back to the station. Just as I'm climbing into the truck, the yelling starts.

"Why did you call them, it was just a fire alarm?" Wes snaps.

"I'm not going to have my house burn down because you're incapable of cooking and started a damned fire." I look over and see it's Bailey, Sutton's friend, yelling back at him.

"It went off for ten seconds. If you would just mind your own business, you wouldn't even hear it. Actually, I'm not sure how you hear anything over the sound of your constant bitching."

"I don't know how you hear anything over your inflated ego and that stupid car you drive."

"You know, if you want a ride all you have to do is ask. I mean another one, that is."

She slams the door in his face and I get in the truck, not wanting to be caught eavesdropping, but fully intending on asking Sutton about that once we're back.

"If that isn't some powerful sexual tension, then I don't know what is," Parker asserts.

"Yeah? You would know about that, wouldn't you?" Dave taunts.

"With your mom, yeah I would."

I shake my head, starting the truck and driving us the short distance back to the station while they continue their bickering. I swear, sometimes it's worse than siblings around here.

Once we're back, I text Sutton when I'm able. I could walk over since she's only next door, but I'm not going to bother her again. Plus, I'm sure Parker would want to join and bother Lily, and I'm not going to subject that poor girl to him anymore than she already is.

> Jameson: Do you happen to know why your neighbors want to rip each other's heads off?

Sutton: Is that what you think they want to do? Because I think they want to rip each other's clothes off.

> Jameson: Funny, Parker said the same thing.

Sutton: Great minds think alike, I guess.

> Jameson: You calling Parker a great mind should probably have me a little worried.

Sutton: I think it's because he's young like me, and you don't get it since you're so...

> Jameson: So what?!

Sutton: So much older *laughing emoji*

> Jameson: I'm not that much older than you!

Sutton: Eleven years.

> Jameson: And you're still five years older than Parker.

Sutton: Maybe I should date him, since we are so close in age and have so much in common. Pass my number along to him, would you?

Jameson: I've never been a jealous man, but you're bringing it out of me. Do I need to come over there?

Sutton: What would you do if you did?

I inwardly groan. I like how she's opened up to me. She's more carefree and trusting, but right now, her teasing is going to send me over the edge. I crave her enough as it is, and knowing she's so close, but that there's nothing either of us can do about it, is it's own form of torture.

Jameson: Are you wanting me to tell you how I would drag you into the back room and prove that age only makes everything better? That I can make you come with the simplest touch because I've studied your body and learned all the ways to make it sing for me?

Jameson: Do you want me to tell you that I would do anything for you, including wringing every single orgasm from you, and make you scream my name for so long that your throat is hoarse for days?

Sutton: Oh my God...

Jameson: Would that be enough to prove it to you? Or do I need to tell you how I would tie your hands behind your back as I bend you over, and fuck you hard enough to see stars?

Sutton: Jameson...

Jameson: How does that sound?

Sutton: Sounds like we both need to get off work, so it can be a reality.

I adjust myself in my pants, annoyed with myself that I'm so desperate for her when there's really nothing I can do about it right now. But knowing she wants to fulfill my fantasies with me has to be enough for now.

> Sutton: You know, for how much you've mentioned wanting to tie me up, I'm a little disappointed you haven't done it yet.

Just when I thought I couldn't be harder, she had to go and say that.

> Jameson: Sounds like we have to change that the next time we're alone.

> Sutton: Guess so.

I'm pretty sure I'm in love with this girl.

I think I've loved her since the first moment I saw her, and everything afterwards has only made me fall harder. I know I can't tell her, because she would likely freak out. Admitting it to myself will have to be enough for now. At least until the day I can say the words to her without her freaking out and running away again. If there's one thing I know for sure, it's that I can't ever lose her.

I WALK into my parent's house to get Duke after my shift, and don't see him curled up in his bed in the living room. I also don't see Ma anywhere. I call out for her, but there's no response. I'm immediately on edge. She didn't say she was going anywhere and I don't want her out somewhere no one knows about. She could be hurt or a million other things. I call out for her again, walking deeper into the house.

The bedroom door is shut, and I open it slowly. "Ma?" I hear a snore and a shuffle before the sound of Duke's paws patter across the floor. I open the door wider and see Ma is sleeping, my worry heightening. It's not unusual for her to take a nap, but she's usually quick to wake up if I call for her.

I approach the side of her bed, lightly shaking her and her eyes shoot open. I let out a sigh of relief I didn't realize I was holding.

"Since when are you against me napping? You're the one always telling me to rest," she teases, her voice groggy but she has a small smile on her face.

"I'm not, you should rest."

"Well, now I'm up." She starts to sit up and I help her, though she tries to shake me off.

"Have you seen your dad?"

"Not yet, I just got in."

"I really think you should try talking to him. I know it's hard, Jameson, but I think you both are misunderstanding each other. He said something about needing help with the cattle, maybe you could find common ground like you used to."

I don't have the heart to tell her I've tried and that it's gotten us nowhere. Instead, I nod. "I'll try, Ma."

"Good, and bring Sutton for dinner soon."

I chuckle and repeat, "I'll try."

Duke follows me out, hopping up into my truck with me and I drive us toward my house, making sure to pass by the cattle on the way. If he's not there, then I guess I'll have to try something else.

He's out there, standing by the paddock just looking out like I've seen him do a few times now. Part of me wonders what he's thinking about, why he does this instead of spending time with Ma. If all the work is done why not go be with your wife instead of staring out at the landscape.

I approach him. "Ma said you needed help with something?"

He doesn't even look at me as I step up next to him; he just continues to look out. "I've got it."

I sigh. "Why do you do that?"

"Do what?"

"Shut me out. Not make an effort for our relationship?"

He scoffs.

"What do you think? Do you think you're putting an effort in here? Do you think Ma is happy with the way things have been since I came back? What's the point of being so pissed at me?"

"You don't know anything about what it was like after you left. You couldn't run away fast enough. I wanted this place for you and all you wanted to do was leave it. Now you want everything to be perfect?"

"I want to feel like a family."

"And what does that feel like to you, son? Because you shouldn't have left your family in the first place."

"You'll never get it, will you? You think everything has to be done your way or it was a mistake. Ma wants us to fix our issues, but that's just not possible, is it?"

He's quiet for a few seconds, and I'm about to give up. I try one more time, hoping maybe I could somehow get through to him.

"Can we at least try? For her?"

He grunts, and I take that as his answer.

"Good talk." I shake my head, walking away. I expect him to call after me, to do something to change the wedge shoved between us. To prove that he does care about me, but he doesn't. He just lets me walk away without a single word.

CHAPTER 38

Sutton

WAKING up in Jameson's arms while our dogs both snore on the ground below us is something new, something I would have never expected to happen. But I showed up last night, and now here we are. We've never stayed the night together, but it felt right.

This feels even more right.

I snuggle into him even more and he stirs, pulling me tightly against him. Our naked bodies are pressed together because we didn't bother putting any clothes on last night. I don't usually sleep naked, and I've definitely never felt comfortable enough to do it with someone else.

Jameson isn't just someone else, though. He's become so much more than that.

"How'd you sleep?" His voice is so much deeper in the morning, and I'm a little ashamed at how something as simple as that has me turned on and wanting him again.

"Better than expected," I answer with my lips grazing his skin.

"Any particular reason you think?"

"Hm." I pretend to think. "No, nothing comes to mind."

"Nothing at all?"

"Nope, not a single thing."

He rolls me onto my back as I giggle, feeling his hard length against me and I can't help but roll my hips into him.

"If that's the case, then why're you trying to rub yourself against me?" He raises an eyebrow.

"I don't know what you're talking about." I run my foot up the back of his leg before hooking it around his waist.

"Not at all?"

"Nope."

"So you don't want me to push my dick inside your soaking pussy again?"

I hum, pulling him down with my leg around him. "Why would I want that?"

"Because you love it."

I wrap my arms around his neck, pulling his lips down to mine. "You're right, I do."

AFTER GETTING LOST in each other so many times I finally lose count. We manage to get our clothes on and make some food. I would have been content, not worrying about eating, but Jameson wasn't allowing that. He basically forced me to get dressed and I think it was to stop his own temptation.

"I think Duke needs another bath," he says while frying a grilled cheese.

I look over at the lump curled up with my fluff on the dog bed. "You think he needs to be bathed way more than he does."

"He's not a city dog. He's out here running in the mud and animal poop every day so I think he needs one more often than those dogs you're used to in California," he says with a fake exaggerated country accent that makes me laugh.

"If you say so; you can bring him by whenever I'm working. I'll always squeeze him in."

He plates a sandwich, walks over, setting it in front of me as he leans down so our faces are only inches apart. He looks like he wants to say something, and I just wait to hear what it is. After what seems like forever he bends down so our lips graze. "Thank you."

Some part of me knows that's not what he was wanting to say, but I don't question it. Instead, I lean into his gentle kiss, trying to chase him for more when he pulls away.

"Eat," he instructs, going back to the stove.

"So bossy," I grumble, taking a bite of the hot, perfectly melted sandwich.

"You seem to like it when I'm bossy."

"I also like it when you're sweet."

"Good thing I like being sweet to you, too."

I take another bite. "Good thing."

I DECIDED to surprise Jameson one of the days he's working. It's a bit of a risk, and one that may have me crossing over some lines, but I don't think he'll mind. I go to his parents' place, nervous about being here without him.

I'm parked outside, chewing on my bottom lip, debating whether this is a good idea or not. I'm about to turn around and leave because this was a dumb idea. It feels weird, and I should leave the cute stuff up to him. He's better at being a romantic than I am.

As I turn my car on, Jameson's mom steps out onto the front porch and waves to me. I guess there's no leaving now. Pasting a smile on my face, I step out to greet her.

"Sutton, sweetie, what are you doing here?" She has a wide smile on her face, her eyes are tired and I can tell she's struggling to stand, but hides it by holding onto the doorknob.

"I came by to get Duke, actually," I tell her, walking up onto the porch. "Jameson said he needed a bath and I thought about surprising him while he's at work."

"How nice of you. Come on in for a minute."

"I don't want to impose."

She waves me off. "You could never."

Even though I'm not sure if I should, I follow her inside. That's when I see Duke lying on his back on the couch with his front paws up in the air while he snores loudly.

"Don't tell Jameson I let him sleep on there." She puts her finger up to her mouth.

"Your secret is safe with me."

"I've never seen him so happy, you know," she says, pulling my attention from the sleeping Pit Bull.

"He's probably pretty happy to be back home and spending time with you," I tell her with a smile, but she just snorts out a laugh.

"Oh sweetie, do you really not see it?"

"See what?"

"I know my son, trust me. That man is so head over heels for you. I truly have never seen him like this before."

My cheeks flame and I look down at my feet unsure of what to say to that. "I don't think that has anything to do with me."

She smiles. "It has everything to do with you."

I'm not going to argue with her about this. I want to believe that maybe she's right, but I feel like there has to be more to it.

"I feel bad waking him up." I change the subject back to the reason I'm here in the first place.

"I don't think he's going to mind. His person isn't here anyway."

I nod as she says his name. He perks up, twisting his head to the side, but not moving to get up. "Come on, bud, you're going to get a bath."

He slowly rolls over and gets off the couch with a stretch.

"I'll give you a prime spa treatment," I tell him and he wags his tail. "I'll bring him back once I'm off work."

"Take your time, I'll be here all day."

"Sounds good. Thank you, Mrs. Turner."

"Sweetie, please call me Emily." She pulls me into a hug, and I hesitate for a moment before hugging her back, but there's something about her and Jameson that makes you feel incredibly comfortable.

They make me feel like I'm home. Maybe because I finally am.

I PARK, looking over at the fire station where the bay door is open. I was going to wait to surprise Jameson until after Duke was all clean with a cute bandana, but I want to see him.

Duke and I walk over, and I recognize the tall man who makes my heart skip a beat every time he's around. He's not facing us, so I just stand there, waiting for him to turn and see us. When he finally does his face instantly lights. He looks from me, to Duke, and back to me.

"What are you two doing here?" He approaches us, his smile never dimming.

"I wanted to surprise you. You said he needed a bath and I was going to bring him over here all pretty for you, but I saw the door was open so I just decided to—"

He cuts off my rambling, cupping my face, and pressing his lips to mine. "You're amazing, you know that?"

"It's not a big deal, I just wanted to do something for you."

He looks into my eyes, his blue ones locked onto mine as his thumbs rub my cheeks lightly. "Sutton, I lo—"

He's cut off when a loud siren goes off along with someone talking. I'm too disoriented by the sound to hear what's being said. Jameson's face hardens. "That's a call, I gotta go. I'll see you when we get back."

I nod, and he presses another quick kiss to my lips and then is springing into action. I bring Duke over to the grooming salon, watching as the firetruck and ambulance drive away with their lights and sirens on, and a pit of dread settles in my stomach.

CHAPTER 39

Jameson

SOMETHING ABOUT SEEING Sutton standing there with Duke made my heart feel like it was going to explode in my chest. The fact that she went and got him, that she wanted to surprise me. Having her there, having her be mine was so overwhelming. We may not have established our relationship, but it doesn't matter to me. She's mine and she has been for longer than she even realizes.

It's why I almost told her I love her. The words were slipping out of my mouth without me thinking. It just felt right. The feeling was so overwhelming that I had to tell her, but I was cut off by the sound of a call coming through. It's a car accident, and not only are we being called out, but the neighboring station in the town over is also being called out, which means it's a bad one.

I'm not driving today, Dave is while Jo and Parker are in the ambulance. We speed down the rural roads, trying to get to the scene as quickly as possible. Neither of us say anything, because in moments like this, when we don't know what we are about to come upon, there isn't much to say. I think about Sutton and how I almost told her I love her. I feel like the words are going to explode out of me the next time I lay my eyes on her. Maybe as soon as we get back from the call I'll rush over there and confess it all.

As we get closer, the noise of the siren is drowned out as adrenaline begins to take over. That's when I see it. My stomach drops at what we're coming up on.

I recognize the truck with its side completely smashed and facing the wrong direction. I'm leaping from the truck before it's even completely stopped. My vision is tunneled as I approach the white pick up that's been parked outside my parent's house for as long as I can remember.

"Dad!" I call out. That's when I see him. He's draped over the steering wheel, seatbelt not on, and blood is pouring from his head. I'm ripping at the smashed in door, trying to pry it open. I vaguely register my name being shouted behind me, but I don't respond to them. I'm too busy trying to rip this door off its hinges. There's smoke billowing from the engine and the smell of gasoline and burnt rubber stings my nose.

I hardly even notice that there isn't another car, even though he was clearly hit by someone and it only fuels my rage knowing this is a hit and run. Other sirens approach as I finally manage to rip the door open, but when I go to grab for my dad, I'm stopped.

"You know better than to try to move him right now. Let us take care of him. You can't lose your head," Dave tells me while Jo and Parker approach with the necessary tools to safely move my dad. Rationally, I know his neck needs to be stabilized, but I can't even tell if he's breathing.

Dave holds me back while Jo, Parker, and the other EMTs

work on getting him out. I'm about to ask if he's alive when I hear Jo say, "He has a pulse but it's weak."

The police are here, examining the scene, and I watch as they move my dad onto a stretcher. I break out of Dave's hold to rush over to him. He's completely pale and still. "Are you sure he's alive?" I scream at Jo.

"We have to get him to the hospital," is all she calmly says. We're trained to be calm in the worst situations, to not escalate anything. But I'm unable to do that right now because I've never had a call like this when the patient is my own family.

"I'm coming with," I state firmly as they get him loaded into the ambulance.

"Jameson." Parker sighs.

"No," I snap. "I'm going to the fucking hospital."

"I don't think that's a good idea," Parker tries again.

"I don't care what you think. I'm going," I snap. Normally, I would feel bad about it, but nothing else matters right now. I'm not leaving my dad.

I hop into the ambulance, leaving Parker to get in the fire engine with Dave as Jo starts driving toward the hospital. I will my training to kick in as I take all the proper steps. He's already hooked up to the portable monitor, which only shows how weak his pulse is.

"Come on, Dad. We need you to stay with us," I grit out, right before the monitor flatlines. "Fuck!" I yell out as I start CPR.

I don't notice the tears streaming down my face as I keep the steady rhythm of chest compressions as we get to the hospital. I scream out for Jo to drive faster, but I can't hear her response.

The ambulance stops, and the back opens and the stretcher is being taken out, everyone working quickly to take over for his care. The doctors and nurses take over, putting a mask over his face to force oxygen as they rush him past doors, and I'm stopped from following any further.

I grip my hair, yanking at the strands as I stare at the closed metal in front of me. I barely register being pushed back and voices talking to me, leading me to the waiting area. I'm forced into a chair.

"What happened?" I finally ask.

"They don't know. Hit and run, looked like your dad stopped and took his seatbelt off before the other car hit him." I don't look up to see who's talking to me. I think it's Dave, but it doesn't matter.

"Why would he do that?" I shake my head.

"Might've stopped to help an animal or something."

I rest my elbows on my knees and drop my head into my hands, silently questioning why this happened. What was he thinking? Where is the bastard that hit him and just ran without even trying to help?

I'm not sure how much time passes, completely lost in my mind when I hear my name said through a sob, and my eyes snap up to see Ma rushing toward me and straight into my arms.

Sutton is trailing behind her and I feel myself soften at them both being here.

Sutton hesitates stepping closer, but I don't give her a choice. Stepping toward her the second Ma lets go of me, I pull her into my arms, needing to feel her to ground myself. To give me just a sliver of light in the darkest moment of my life.

"How are you here?" I ask as her hand reaches up and wipes my cheek and I realize it has fresh tears on it.

"Parker called the salon. I rushed to get your mom, then we came straight here."

I drop my forehead to hers, loving her even more, and wanting to tell her, but unable to when everything feels so grim. She deserves to hear those words from me in a better moment, not like this.

"Thank you," I tell her instead. She closes her eyes, gripping the back of my shirt tightly as we hold each other.

I keep her tucked into my side as I go to sit by Ma who's crying. Her red eyes look up at me, and I can see the hope shining through because she's always optimistic. But she didn't see him.

She didn't hear the monitor register that it could no longer pick up his heartbeat.

And I'm glad she didn't.

The door opens several times, but never for us. Time seems to drag on, and I start to gain hope, but then it falls. It's like I'm on a constant rollercoaster of emotion.

Finally it opens and the doctor calls for the Turner family. We all stand, and I have Sutton tucked against my side, and my other arm around Ma's shoulders as she holds her sweater tightly around her. She's always cold lately, and the sterile hospital feels extra cold.

The doctor speaks and I swear the world flips on its axis, because as soon as I hear the first two words I'm lost to the noise of Ma's sobs and the weight of my own emotions as reality barrels into me. Our last interaction. The last words spoken to each other. The fact that I can't ever change them and the last memories I have of my dad will always be of us fighting and seeing him broken in that car.

"I'm sorry. We did everything we could, but he didn't make it."

CHAPTER 40

Sutton

MY EARS ARE RINGING as Emily breaks down and Jameson holds her, making sure she doesn't collapse on the floor. This can't be real. None of this feels real. I'm waiting for the doctor to say he's made a mistake, that he meant to tell that to another family, but he doesn't.

Instead he just repeats, "I'm so sorry."

Jameson holds his mom as they cry, and my own tears fall, but I'm completely silent, feeling out of place and like I'm imposing. Jameson keeps his mom tucked against him as he reaches for me. I almost back away because there's no way he actually wants me to be here right now. His hand finds mine and he pulls me closer, wrapping an arm around my shoulders, tucking me into his side while his mom sobs into his chest.

We all just cry.

At one point Jameson and his mom go back, and I wait, feeling like I should leave, but I'm also the only one that has a car here. I don't want to make things worse or uncomfortable, but I do want to be here for Jameson.

For his mom, too. Even if I don't know her very well, I feel like we've connected in some way. I just can't imagine what Jameson's going through, with his mom being sick, and now losing his dad. And having to see what happened to his dad. My heart aches for him. All I want is to take him in my arms and never let him go. As long as he wants to be there, I want him to be.

Eventually, they come out and we leave the hospital. There's a heaviness surrounding all of us as we walk to the car. No one says anything, and the night feels dull even with the full moon shining in the sky. The emptiness is especially evident as we all climb into my Jeep, and I start to get into the driver's seat, but Jameson silently guides me to the backseat with his mom and gets in to drive instead.

Emily holds onto my hand and I hear her silent sobs. I wish more than anything there was something I could do to make this better, but I know there's not. All I can do is just be here.

The drive back is the quietest, heaviest, and darkest drive I've ever experienced. It doesn't get better once we come back. Jameson cuts the engine on my car, and it's even more silent. No one moves, we all just sit still as if we don't know what to do.

Jameson is the first to get out, and he opens the door to help his mom out. She holds onto him like he's her lifeline. Which I guess he probably is.

He extends his other hand for me, which I take easily. I want to stay, but I need to check on Bennet. As soon as Parker called I grabbed Duke, brought him back here to get Emily, then rushed to the hospital.

After we get inside, Emily quietly says, "I'm going to bed."

"Do you need me to do anything, Ma?" Jameson's voice cracks slightly.

She shakes her head. "I'll see you in the morning."

What do you do after your life gets flipped upside down? How do you keep living and doing things like nothing has changed when in fact, everything has changed.

"I should go home," I whisper once we're alone.

"Please stay," he pleads, pulling me closer.

"I need to check on Bennet," I tell him reluctantly because truly I don't want to leave.

"We can go get him."

"Jameson, you shouldn't leave your mom."

I can tell he wants to argue, but then closes his mouth because he knows I'm right.

"I'll get him, and come back," I compromise.

He cups my face. "I would feel better if I could drive you."

I nod in understanding. "I'll be careful."

He hesitates to let me go, even as he removes his hands from my face, and intertwines our fingers to walk me out to my car. He pulls me in, crashing our lips together. He pours everything into our kiss. His sadness, his fears, his feelings toward me. Everything is said between us without words.

When he finally lets me go, I promise once again to be safe and that I'll be right back. I see him in my rearview mirror as I drive away, and the look on his face has me feeling guilty for the times I've run previously, because it's clear he thinks that's about to happen again.

But it's not. I'm done running.

As quickly and safely as I can, I pick Bennet up and drive back to Jameson's house. The relief on his face when he sees me again is evident and has my shoulders dropping as I let out a sigh. Bennet bounds out of my car, pressing right up to Jameson who greets him with a pat on his head.

"Hi," I breathe, and he immediately pulls me in once again like he needs to constantly be touching me. I let him because I'll give him anything he wants or needs. And I want the physical touch just as much as he does. "How are you doing?"

He drops his lips to the top of my head. "Tired."

I nod, unsure of what to say. There's nothing that can be said at a time like this.

"I was thinking we should stay in the main house so we're close to Ma."

I agree easily. It doesn't feel right to be away from either of them right now. I can't fathom what they are feeling, but I'm going to be here to do what I can.

It feels like the dogs can tell something is wrong too because

Duke doesn't even get up to greet his friend. Bennet doesn't antagonize him, instead opting to lay on the floor next to Duke's dog bed.

Jameson leads me through the unfamiliar house and into what seems like a guest bedroom. The queen bed has a simple duvet and the walls are even more simple with a couple framed landscape pictures.

"This used to be my room," he says, breaking the silence.

I look around at the bareness. "I assume it didn't look like this when you lived in it?"

"No, Ma decided not to subject guests to all my posters."

"Good call on her part," I try to joke.

Jameson strips down to his boxers, and I change into the over-sized T-shirt I brought in the small bag I managed to pack. As soon as we climb into bed, Jameson pulls me against him, resting my head on his chest. His steady heartbeat thrums against my ear as my fingers lightly trace patterns on his skin. I'm tired, but I don't know if I'll be able to fall asleep.

"Sutton?" Jameson's voice is quiet, like he's not sure if I'm sleeping and doesn't want to wake me up if I am.

"Yeah?"

"Thank you for being here."

"I'll always be here for you." And I mean it. What remains unsaid are three certain words that I can't bring myself to say.

Not because I don't feel them, but because I feel them stronger than I've ever felt anything before. But I don't want this to be the night those words are said for the first time. I think he was about to say them earlier, and now I'm glad he didn't.

I don't know how I would have reacted if he had said them at that moment. But if he had, then we would both always know this is the day they were spoken.

So instead of either of us speaking again, we lay in silence, just holding each other. There's nothing more that can be said and we both know that. While tonight has been awful, it only makes me more worried about what tomorrow will bring.

THE LAST WEEK has gone by in a blur. I hardly remember anything that's happened after the night of the accident. My days consist of making sure everything is done around the ranch, helping Ma, and getting all the funeral arrangements done.

Sutton has stuck around to help with everything. She's hardly left my side and I'm beginning to feel like I don't deserve her. She tried to push me away, to fight what was going on between us, and now when she should be fighting it, she isn't. And I don't deserve it.

I can feel how distant I am. I'm a shell of the man I've always been. The loss has hit me harder than anything else I've experienced before and all I know how to do is busy myself to the point of exhaustion so I don't have to think about it.

I can't think about what it was like pulling up to the accident. Seeing my dad and the ambulance ride.

I just can't.

I tried to go back to work, but was promptly yelled at by the chief that I needed to take time off. I wanted to distract myself and get back to my normal routine, even though leaving Ma wasn't ideal. I ended up coming back home only an hour later to her still on the couch, staring at the TV with the sound off.

Sutton was there with her, and didn't seem surprised when I came back. She just gave me a hug that I returned, before mumbling that I had work to do. And I left.

Every night we crawl into bed together, I kiss her goodnight, and we fall asleep in each other's arms. Neither of us say much, because there's still not much for us to say.

The next day we get up and do it all over again.

The funeral is today, I get up extra early while Sutton is still peacefully sleeping so I can get all the morning chores done before the busy day that lies ahead. Of course that isn't the type of busy I want to be right now. Today will be the kind that's going to leave me emotionally exhausted instead of physically. I'd rather my body be so exhausted that I have no choice but to fall asleep instead of leaving my mind to race through the darkness that creeps in.

"Are you almost ready?" Sutton asks, peeking her head into the room we've been sharing.

I adjust the tie I'm not used to wearing. The button down shirt and slacks feel oddly suffocating and it all just feels wrong. I don't think I ever saw my dad wearing an outfit like this and it seems odd to wear this to honor him when he would just show up in jeans and a flannel.

But Ma insisted we all look nice to go to the funeral home

where his service is being held, so I do it for her. Sutton is wearing a black short sleeve dress and low heels. She looks pretty, and I want to tell her that, but for some reason the words get caught in my throat.

I want to tell her everything that I've been feeling. But instead of complimenting her, or telling her how much she means to me or even how much my life shifted in a single night, I just answer her question. "Yeah."

She nods before walking in, shutting the door behind her, and coming up to me, gently wrapping her arms around my waist. I haven't denied her touch, and I never would. But it feels different now and I know she feels it just like I do.

"She's hanging in there pretty well so far." She looks up at me. "What about you?"

I clench my jaw, swallow roughly and look down to her. "I'm hoping to just get through today."

"You will. I'm here for anything you need."

Too good for me.

I lean down to press my lips against hers softly. She sighs at the contact and I hold her a little closer, wanting her to know how much I appreciate everything she's been doing for Ma and me. I may not be able to voice much now, but I want her to know in some way.

We break apart and I tell her, "We should get going."

I drive us to the funeral home. Ma and Sutton are in the back seat just like the night we left the hospital. The car is just as silent as that night, too. Once we get there, I lead Ma inside. She's been weaker since that night, and sleeping more, but I can't tell if it's from the sickness or from her broken heart.

I guess they could go hand in hand. I can't lose her too.

At the root of all of this, that's the fear I can't voice. I can hardly even consider the possibility that I'm going to lose both my parents in such a short amount of time. I want her to keep fighting. I want her to use this as her fuel to fight.

But I worry that this will make her give up. She can't give up.

We get inside the funeral home, and the service goes by in a blur. I sit between Ma and Sutton during the speeches, Ma choosing not to speak. I opt out as well. There's nothing to say that I want these people to know. Anything I want my dad to have known I could have told him. Should have told him.

But I didn't.

We fought instead. The last interaction we had was a fight, a fact that remains unresolved. The tears are back, and I don't wipe them away as I think about the last time I spoke to him. If I could go back and change everything, I would. I wish he was proud of me, and that he understood why I did what I did. I wish we cleared the air before...

"We can stay as long as you need," Sutton's voice breaks through my thoughts and I realize the service is over.

"We can go," I grunt, standing up.

Ma is up by the urn that holds the remains of her husband. Her back is to us, but I can see her shoulders shaking with a sob. I step up to her, wrapping an arm around her shoulders, and she turns into me, crying even harder.

Sutton stands by, ever vigilant, and I just look at her. The woman I've fallen so deep in love with and I'm mad at myself that I'm not giving her everything she deserves.

Some people say if you love someone you should let them go, and I always thought they were full of it because you should fight for your love.

But at what point is that unfair? When is it better to set them free? At what point am I being unfair to Sutton, and should let her go?

As I stand here, looking at her, watching as her bright green eyes shine with tears as she stands with me and the only family I have left. I know there's no way I could be strong enough to let her go myself. But if she wants to leave, I'll have no choice. I'm not going to hold her back.

We leave with Ma hugging Dad's urn tightly, and as we get to the car, she stops Sutton from getting in the backseat with her.

"Sit up front with Jameson, honey."

"Are you sure?"

"Yeah," she says, her voice breaking.

I open the passenger side for Sutton and help her climb inside before we all endure another silent car ride back home. I reach over, placing my hand on Sutton's leg just like I always have when she rides in my car. Immediately, her hand falls to mine, and she holds it tightly.

We say nothing, but the small connection between our hands almost feels like enough.

Almost.

After we get back home, Ma retreats to her room like she's started doing, denying my help. Sutton turns toward me. "Are you okay?"

"I'm as okay as I can be at this moment."

She nods in understanding. There's not much more to say, and suddenly the house feels claustrophobic. It's like I can feel my dad around, sucking the air from the space and making it hard to breathe. Even though he's not here, the weight of his disappointment lingers and I don't want Sutton to see how much it's dragging me down.

"I'm going to go get some work done," I tell her.

She nods, wrapping her arms around herself. I want to pull her into me. To kiss her senseless and lose myself in her for as long as she'll let me. I want to tell her everything I'm thinking and feeling, all my thoughts and fears, and to pour them out to her. I want to bring her into my orbit, but it's not fair to her. I refuse to drag her down with me.

I change before going outside, leaving her in the house while I busy myself with anything and everything I can that needs to be done.

After making sure all the animals have food, cleaning the stalls, and doing some needed maintenance around the property, I'm in the barn. The heat is brutal today, and I take my shirt off to wipe my face and toss it to the side. I'm flinging hay bales around to get them organized and make feeding easier when I hear quiet footsteps approach.

Sutton appears in the entryway of the barn, and I go to meet her. The second I see her face streaked with the remnants of her tears, I break, cupping her face, and bringing her to me. "Baby, what is it? What happened?"

"It's stupid, I just came here to check on you."

"It's not stupid. Nothing you could say to me would be stupid."

"I—I'm—"

I rub my thumbs against her cheek, wiping away the tears that appear there.

"I'm worried you don't want me around. That I'm doing more harm than good."

"No. Why would you think that?"

"I just don't want to be in your way. I know this is a lot for you both, and the last thing I want to do is make it worse."

"You're not making it worse. I'm just...I don't know what to do." I shake my head, dropping my forehead to hers.

"About what? You aren't expected to know what to do."

"It feels like I am. I should be able to handle this and be strong for myself and Ma, but I'm failing at it for her and for you."

"Hey." Sutton places her hands on my cheeks forcing me to look at her. "You're not failing me in any way."

Yes, I am. I'm keeping you here where you feel like you have to be when you shouldn't. I'm selfishly not wanting to let you go.

I can't say any of that. My mouth refuses to form the words, instead it seals over hers, and all the light kisses we've shared are nothing compared to this. This is forceful, demanding, and needy. As soon as my tongue pushes into her mouth she moans, opening up for me. I flick my tongue against hers, then bite her lip and pull it into my mouth.

"I've been failing you, and I'm going to make it up to you right now."

I need to distract myself, pull away from the darkness surrounding my every thoughts. I need to get lost in her, to show her how much she means to me when I can't say the words. I need to feel like I deserve her in some way. To show her that she's helping me more than she can ever know just by being with me. I need to give us both something that will make everything okay if it's only for a little.

CHAPTER 42

Sutton

"HOW'RE you planning on doing that?" I pant against his mouth, my fingers trailing down his sweat covered chest. The hard muscles there tense under my touch as I trace lower, close to his waistband. I don't move to undo them because I'm not sure if that's what he's talking about, and I'm not about to embarrass myself if it's not.

Jameson runs his nose along mine, up to my hairline, his lips touching my forehead. "Remember what I said about tying you up in here?"

I suck in a sharp breath. I remember exactly what he said about that. I remember how much I wanted it as soon as he said it, and how it felt so shocking to come from a man like him. But I know he's been struggling. He's not been the same, and I don't expect him to be.

If this is what he needs, if I can do anything to give him a way to get out of his head, if only for a little, then I'll do that. I always will because somehow I've fallen completely in love with Jameson Turner.

"Yes," I breathe.

"Then I'm going to tell you what I need you to do and you're going to be a good girl for me, and do it."

I bite back a moan at his demanding tone. This isn't the sweet Jameson, this isn't even the Jameson I've experienced in the bedroom before. This is another side to him, one that I want just as much as the others. This one needs something from me and I'll give it to him on a silver platter.

"Take off all your clothes, and go stand over there." He turns me, pointing to the area where the horses get cross tied. "I'm going to get some rope."

He nudges me forward, and I go with a gasp. My underwear is already so wet I should be embarrassed. I work quickly to remove my clothes, knowing the chances of being caught out here this time aren't likely, but the thought still sends a zip of excitement through me.

I've barely stepped out of my underwear, having stripped everything else off already, when I feel the familiar warmth of Jameson's skin at my back.

"Turn around, and put your hands above your head." His voice is deeper than usual, almost cold, but it only makes me feel hotter.

I do what he says, noticing he's still in his jeans, but he has rope in his hand and my heart rate kicks up realizing just how serious he was. He's going to tie me up in here and do whatever he wants to my body, and I won't be able to touch him.

I know if I don't want this or if I need him to stop at any point he would. But I won't. I'm going to give him what he needs. He can use my body however he wants, take whatever he wants, it's his—I'm his.

Once my hands are raised above my head, he crowds me against the wall. My back hits the wood and I gasp, already feeling overwhelmed and overstimulated in the best way without him even touching me yet. The second he starts tying my wrists with the rope it sends a shot of electricity straight between my thighs.

I'm already so desperate for him, so needy for his touch that him simply tying me to a ring attached to the wall has me about to combust. I look up to watch the way his hands move methodically as he ties an expert knot. The rope tightens around my skin and I flinch, but not at the pain.

"Are you okay?" he asks, obviously noticing because he misses nothing.

"More than okay," I answer honestly.

His hands flex, making the veins in his arms pop as he finishes the knots and I swear my knees would give out and I would end up on the floor if I wasn't secured to this wall. When he steps back and I can see all of him, I may actually have some drool pooling at the side of my mouth.

Jameson is a piece of art in human form, and especially like this. Burning blue eyes staring at me with so much heat I swear I'm going to melt from it. The summer night is warm, but the sweat on my skin has nothing to do with it and has everything to do with the way he's looking at me.

His skin shines with the sweat covering him from the work he was just doing, but his chest heaves with heavy breaths I know have nothing to do with exertion. That's all because of me. My eyes find the bulge in his pants, making my mouth water, and I wish he was as naked as me because I want to eat him up with my eyes like he's doing to me.

"You're missing something," he says suddenly, making me snap my eyes up to his once again.

I bite back my retort about the fact that yeah, I'm missing all my clothes, but I stay silent. He goes over to a hook on the wall where his brown cowboy hat is hanging up. He picks it up and puts it on my head before stepping back again. I arch toward him as though my body is a magnet trying to get to him to have him touch me.

"That's better," he growls.

"Does that mean you'll touch me now?" I whimper.

"Impatient. You said you remembered what I told you about tying you up in here."

"I do," I squirm.

"Then what did I say?"

"You, um..." I squeeze my thighs together realizing that can help ease some of the ache and it distracts me slightly because I'm so desperate for him to get his rough hands on me.

"I, what, Sutton?" he snaps. "Don't think you can solve your problem yourself. I'll touch you, but you have to earn it. What did I tell you would happen?"

"You said you would edge me over and over."

"Think you can handle that?"

I part my legs slightly, the air hits the wetness between them. "I can handle anything when it comes to you."

He steps closer to me, hooking his finger underneath my chin and tilting my head back slightly. "You really think so?"

"I know so."

His lips descend on mine again, viciously. He's taking and giving while I do the same. I moan and he swallows it easily while one hand collars my throat, and the other grabs my hip tightly. I want to wrap my arms around him. I want to touch him, but his chest is barely touching mine, just enough for the hair there to graze my nipples and it only makes me want to feel more of him.

"Please," I plead against his lips, my hips bucking forward, trying to get him to touch me.

"I don't think I've ever seen you this needy." His mouth moves to my jaw, kissing and nipping at the skin there, then descends lower. His hand moves from my throat to my chest, pinching my nipples between his thumb and forefinger. I gasp as he rolls the sensitive nub between his fingers, letting out a groan because it's only making the need between my thighs increase. "I like it."

"I don't." My head falls back, the brim of his hat gets caught on my stretched arms. "Jameson, I need more."

"I know you do, baby. I'm going to give it to you, when you're ready for it."

"I'm ready now."

"I'll tell you when you are."

I let out a frustrated groan, but then he sucks my nipple into his mouth roughly and it turns into a cry of both pain and pleasure as he draws it in deeper, his teeth grazing the raised bud and I squeal at the sensation. He lets go with a pop and I look down, but he immediately moves to the other one and does the same thing.

Once he lets go again, I look down to see that my breasts are red and wet with his saliva, and I watch as he drops down onto his knees in front of me. He looks up to me, eyes dark and primal while he runs his tongue along his bottom lip. There's something else there I can't quite name. He's with me, but also not entirely present. There's a coldness to him that I haven't seen before. Though, as soon as he tosses my leg over his shoulder and his mouth is on me, the hunger in his eyes is all I see as he devours me like I'm the greatest thing he's ever tasted.

I pull at the restraints, testing their strength because more than anything, I want to grab onto his hair and keep his mouth against me. But I'm completely at his mercy like this. I both love and hate it because I want to touch him, but being unable to is adding to my pleasure.

His tongue flicks against my clit roughly, then he's pushing it inside me and licking me all over. I'm gasping, bucking against him, and pleading for more.

"I'm so close," I breathe, trying to push myself against him even more so I can get there. Instead of doing one of the many things he knows that would send me over the edge, he pulls back, and I cry out in protest.

"You're still not ready yet."

"I disagree," I pant, my hips bucking, trying to get him to touch me again. I'm so wet and the mixture of my own arousal and his spit only adds to how badly I want him.

"Try again." He dives in once again and as soon as his tongue touches my clit I cry out and almost lose it.

I don't know what he needs from me to show that I'm ready because from where I'm standing right now I feel pretty damn ready to explode. He pulls his mouth away and pushes a finger into me and I moan at the feeling, but it's still not enough.

"You know," he starts and I wish even more now that I had access to my hands so I could muffle his words by holding his head against me, but I can't. All I can do is squirm and whimper as he thrusts his finger slowly, and shallowly. "I think my favorite thing in the world is making you come."

"Great, you should do that then."

"But I think watching you squirm and begging for it might be even better."

I groan, "Jameson."

"Yeah, baby, you'll be screaming my name soon. When I let you come it's going to be on my cock, though."

"Then give it to me now."

He adds another finger pushing it into me roughly, and I cry, looking down, watching how he keeps his eyes locked on what he's doing. The view is almost better than the feeling of those same fingers.

"Why would I do that when I need to taste you some more." Before I'm able to say anything, his mouth is on me again and I'm close to combusting.

The way he's able to play my body like an expert every single time he touches me brings tears to my eyes. Or maybe it's from the orgasm that's lingering just out of reach again, or it's the emotion I'm fighting to suppress. Maybe it's everything from the day, from the past week. It's all overwhelming me and being heightened by the release that's about to completely consume me.

When he pulls back again, I scream in frustration. He has a smirk on his face, lips glistening with my wetness.

"Kiss me," I plead, and that gets him to stand up, crashing our mouths together. I taste myself on his lips, and when his tongue invades my mouth I suck on it, tasting the mixture of us.

I want more.

I need more.

I want to touch him, I want him inside me. I'm losing my mind with the want and need that he's stirring up inside me.

"Jameson, please fuck me, I need you," I plead against his mouth desperately, hoping with every fiber of my being that he won't deny me again.

"I need you too, baby," he confesses and I hook a leg around his hip, pulling him into me even more. The roughness of his jeans against my sensitive core is almost enough to get me there once again.

"Then take me, please." I feel a tear fall from my eye at my desperation. I'm so gone for him in more ways than one. I can't tell him how I feel, he can't know the extent of my feelings right now. I just want to get lost in him and to let him get lost in me.

He pulls away, and must see the tear; he wipes it away with his thumb. "Why're you crying?"

I shake my head. "They're not bad tears, I just..." My voice trails off. *I just love you.*

"I know, I do too," he whispers. I wonder for a second if I said the words out loud, but I didn't. I think he's just feeling everything just as much as I am, but neither of us can put a voice to it.

He pulls back completely, guiding my leg down, and I think he's going to go back to teasing me which may actually make me lose my mind. But then he's unbuttoning his jeans, and pushing them off his legs.

His cock bobs out, hard and pointed directly at me. My mouth waters, aching to have him down my throat again and my pussy clenches, wanting to be filled by him. My body craves him in a way I've never experienced before, but also if he doesn't fuck me in some way in the next couple seconds I may scream.

My body is sweaty, and my arms are numb from being tied up for so long. Even my legs are shaky. Jameson steps forward and grabs my thighs, wrapping them around his hips, positioning himself at my opening and I want to cry with relief.

"The only thing better than seeing you wear my hat is going to be you wearing it while impaled on my cock."

He pushes forward, seating himself in a single thrust and I moan, clenching around him as he fills me in the perfect way only he can. His forehead drops against mine as he lets out his own groan of pleasure.

"How do you do that?" His breath hits my lips, and I try to chase them with my own, but he stays just out of reach.

"Do what?"

"Make me feel like we're the only two people in the entire world. You are everything to me."

He pulls back, and thrusts forward roughly again, then kisses me fiercely. He holds onto my hips as he plows into me while his tongue fucks my mouth. Any thought I had of holding back my orgasm is obliterated because he rubs against my clit every time he pushes fully into me. His thick cock filling me so perfectly and his mouth on mine.

The emotion, the words I can't say, the feeling of being filled by him, it's all too much. I'm not able to hold back anymore and I explode with a loud cry into his mouth. He doesn't let up, his thrusts becoming even more brutal as he fucks me against the wall through my release.

"That's right, baby, squeeze my cock," he growls.

His words and the way he's fucking me prolong my orgasm for so long that I'm not sure if it's just one, or if another one takes over immediately. Tears stream down my face as I buck against him, crying out.

He pushes all the way in once more, groaning out his own release. I feel the way his cum coats my inner walls and it triggers another aftershock of my own orgasm. He kisses me as we both come down, breathing heavily, skin sticky with sweat. He doesn't leave my body yet, his forehead drops to mine and he looks into my eyes. The words we leave unspoken are swimming between us. So much has happened and is felt between us. It's all so overwhelming, but neither of us are putting words to it.

"Are you okay?" he finally asks.

"Always."

And I mean it, but as he separates our bodies I can't help but feel like he's pulling away in more ways than one. A chill coats my skin, and I hope I'm wrong, but this felt a lot like goodbye.

CHAPTER 43

Jameson

I UNTIE Sutton and make sure to give her wrists extra attention to ease the redness. I help her clean up like I always do, making sure she's totally taken care of before we dress enough to go back to the house.

When we lay in bed like we've done every night, I can't go to sleep right away. She's snuggled into my side, and I have my arm wrapped around her. I'm glad she's able to drift off easily, but I lay awake, just as conflicted as before, if not more because of how much she means to me.

She's everything to me and I don't think I'm able to be the man for her. I want to be more than anything, but my life has changed. I have more on my plate than before, and it's not fair to her. I'm going to have to create distance between us, even if it's the last thing I want to do.

I hold her tightly against me because if this is the last night I have her in my arms, I'm going to savor every second of it. Which is also probably why I'm unable to fall asleep, because I know in the morning I'm going to have to tell her goodbye.

THE MORNING COMES TOO SOON and I watch the sunrise through the window while Sutton sleeps peacefully on my chest. When she finally stirs awake, her green eyes look up at me, and my resolve weakens. I graze my lips lightly against her eyelids, her nose, and then down to her lips.

"Morning," she mumbles softly.

"Morning."

Her eyes pop open, and I know she can read me just as easily as I can read her. "What's wrong?"

I swipe her hair off her forehead and don't answer. So many things run through my head, the main one right now being that I don't want to let her go.

"I don't *have* to go to work today if you need me to be here," she offers easily and I shake my head.

"No, we all need to get back to normal," I insist.

"I don't think there's getting back to normal." She runs her hand along my jaw that has more hair on it than I've had in years. I usually avoid shaving on my days off, but haven't been able to have a full beard since I became a firefighter. "But we can start getting used to the new normal."

"Yeah," I agree. There's a pang in my chest even before the next words leave my lips. "Which is why you and Bennet should probably go back home."

Her hand freezes. "You want us to leave? I mean of course, I understand." She moves quickly, getting out of bed, and I want to drag her back.

"Sutton, no. I mean I just don't want you to think you have to stay here. You have your own house and I don't want you to feel trapped."

"No. No, I get it. Obviously you and your mom are grieving. I didn't mean to invade your space." She's gathering her stuff, and I feel like an idiot for thinking letting her go was the smart thing to do when pushing her away feels so wrong. I watch her dress and toss her things into her bag like she's in a rush to leave.

"I didn't mean right now."

"It's fine, I'm going to go to work, and I should drop Bennet off at home first."

I don't like her home not being here with me.

I'm not making sense, and I know it, but I can't seem to find the words to tell her to stop. I can't say the three words that would change what's happening. So instead, I don't say anything. It may be a mistake, but I just let her go. I still walk her to her car, but I can tell she's trying to leave as quickly as possible. I can't help myself as I pull her into me for a soft kiss. She melts into me like she always does.

I still don't say anything because I can't bring myself to tell her goodbye. Neither does she and every second of silence between us has my heart sinking lower and lower in my chest.

The second she's gone I know I've royally messed up, but I also don't know if I'm going to be able to fix it. How I would fix it, or if I even should.

I walk back into the house, and Ma is there which is surprising because I've barely seen her out of bed all week.

"Where did Sutton go?"

"She had to go to work."

"And she took Bennet with?"

I hesitate. "Yeah, she's going to go home for a little while."

I notice the hurt that crosses her face. "Oh. Did she not want to stay here with us anymore?"

"No, that's not it. I told her we should try getting back to normal."

She wraps her sweater around herself tighter and I can see how tired her eyes are and how much weight she's lost. The pain of everything has hit her the hardest. Of course it has. My dad and I had our problems, but he was the love of her life. She's been so busy hiding while I've been busy avoiding...everything. I feel guilty, as though I've neglected her by being so caught up in my own mind.

"What exactly is normal, Jameson?"

I shrug. "Just as normal as we can be considering."

"Normal would be moving on with your life, not ruining it."

"I'm not ruining it, Ma I want to be here for you."

"You are. You always have been," she pauses before continuing, "you also need to let Sutton be there for you."

I shake my head. "I'm not talking about this with you right now. Do you need help with anything before I go feed the animals?"

I can see she wants to argue her point. She probably wants to yell at me, but doesn't have the energy and that thought feels like a slap in the face.

"No, but while you're doing whatever you feel like you need to do, at least think about what you've done. Because pushing that girl away would be the greatest mistake of your life."

"Ma—"

"Jameson," she snaps, loudly. "Think about what your life would look like if you really let that girl go. And don't even try to lie to me about how much she means to you. I've seen it written all over your face. You love her, and you need to realize what losing that kind of love will do to you."

I clench my jaw and shake my head, but before I can say anything she speaks up again.

"You may think your dad didn't care, but he did. More than you know, and trust me when I say that you throwing away love because of him would have him really angry with you."

I have nothing to say now, and I'm not going to argue about it, because I know he didn't care. I know we didn't get any closure and I know he wouldn't have cared if I let Sutton go. He never seemed to have an opinion on anything other than me leaving.

And now he's the one that left us. How horribly ironic.

CHAPTER 44

Sutton

IT'S BEEN a week that I've been living back in my house, and a week since I've spoken to Jameson. I don't want to reach out and overwhelm him because I know he's going through a lot. But when I saw his truck parked at the fire station this morning and realized he's back at work, I thought maybe he would come over here to talk to me like he's done in the past.

I've been here for several hours and that hasn't happened. My stomach sinks and even Lily's insane ramblings aren't enough to break me out of the funk I'm in.

I could tell something was wrong that last night with him. Especially in the morning when he basically kicked me out. Except, deep down, I know he didn't, I just couldn't handle it if he did so I rushed out.

"Hey, are you okay?" Lily asks gently, and the seriousness of her tone takes me off guard because it's Lily.

"I'm..." I sigh. "No. Everything has been rough since, well, you know."

She nods. "I'm sorry about that. Parker tried checking in on Jameson several times and he never got back to him."

I perk up slightly. "Oh, you're talking to Parker?"

"No, I mean, not really. We've known each other forever, but," she waves her hand around, "not the point, this isn't about that."

I sigh, thinking that may have been enough of a distraction, even though it wouldn't have been.

Jerry Lee, with his impeccable timing, chooses right now to grace us with his commentary. *"Shut up, Vern."*

"One day I want to know who Vern is and why he needs to shut up," Lily comments.

"With how much Jerry Lee holds a grudge I don't think he was a very great guy."

"Fair point, but anyway, how's Jameson holding up?"

I fight the tears pricking at the back of my eyes at hearing his name. "I wouldn't really know, he hasn't talked to me in about a week."

"Oh." Her face falls, and I catch the small flinch she tries to hide. "I'm sure he's just really busy, it's not you."

"Right." I look over at the fire station where I know he is. She's trying to make me feel better and I appreciate it, but we both know there's more to it. Especially me.

"What if we have a girls night or something," she suggests and I look back at her.

"I don't think I could keep up with you and your crazy nights out."

"What do you—oh stop. Notice how none of my stories are ever about *me* doing anything. It's my friends that are the crazy ones. We could have a simple night in with some wine and rom coms."

I chew on my bottom lip, looking over at the building where Jameson is again. I'm not going to pine for someone who doesn't want me. Even if it breaks my heart to think about never being with him again. Never getting to talk to him, or feel the way he touches me, or seeing how he looks at me. I blink away the tears threatening to fall.

"Sure, that sounds nice," I tell Lily. "But no men with a duck bondage fetish or strippers with a skillet."

"Don't worry, you're safe from both."

She goes back to work, and I'm cleaning up when the sound of the front door makes my heart start to race. Maybe he's here and came to see me. As soon as I turn around, whatever small amount of hope I had fizzles out instantly when I see that woman he used to date with her little miniature Goldendoodle next to her.

Lily steps out, and her face instantly turns into a glare. "How can we help you?"

"Daisy's due for another haircut."

"Do you have an appointment?"

"No, I'm always able to be squeezed in."

"Not today, we're busy." Lily folds her arms across her chest, and that's when the woman—Mallory—looks over at me.

"Ah, you groomed her last time. You can do it again."

"Uh..." I technically have time, but I'm also pretty sure my brain is short circuiting from the emotional few weeks coupled with the lack of sleep and proper nutrition for myself.

"Hello? I have somewhere to be. Can you take her or not?" she snaps and it somehow brings me back to the present.

It also pisses me off. The sadness I've been feeling fades as anger takes over and I'm done playing nice to people who don't deserve it.

"No. And next time, you can make an appointment, instead of expecting us to work with your schedule."

"Wow, you really won't? So much for the customer always being right. I'm sure Trish will love to hear about this."

"I'm sure she will. Feel free to tell her when you call and make an appointment with her."

She scoffs looking me up and down before turning to leave.

I can't help myself from calling out one last thing. "An Australian Goldendoodle isn't even a real breed!"

The door slams, and I continue to glare at her as she walks out to the parking lot, but instead of going to her car she goes to the fire station and I swear I stop breathing. When she walks in, I feel like I may actually collapse. Lily must see the same thing as me because she lets out a little growling sound.

"That bitch. I'm sure she's just going over there trying to be a desperate little hoebag," she says.

"Sure." I look away, not wanting to see anything else. "I think I may want something stronger than wine for this girls night."

"You got it. You busy tonight?"

"Nope."

I ENDED up inviting Bailey over for the impromptu girls night with Lily. I didn't think too much about it at the time, but now that they're both here in my house, I realize that I couldn't have brought together two more polar opposite humans.

The night started off with some tension because Lily was in the middle of one of her outrageous stories when Bailey got here, and I think hearing about a "cum dumpster" tattoo dare before an introduction was a little much for her. Luckily, after everyone had a drink in their hand the tension dissipated a bit. My anger from earlier has only gotten worse. All the sadness I've been feeling has morphed and I want to call Jameson to scream at him.

I want to ask why he would push me away only to go back to her. Why he wouldn't even have the decency to officially end things with me. How he could claim I'm his, only to turn around and treat me like I'm nothing so easily.

All while I thought he might actually love me.

"What will it be, Sutton?" Lily asks, bouncing on the balls of her feet and I realize I wasn't paying attention.

"Sorry, what?"

"Are we playing never have I ever before or after the first movie?"

"Uh, before," I answer, because all the painful thoughts make me want to drown them out with the alcohol.

"Yay," Lily squeals. "I'll go first. Never have I ever had a one night stand."

I sigh, thinking about lying and taking a sip of my drink, but all my attention is pulled to Bailey when she's the only one who does. I raise an eyebrow, but Lily is a bit more direct.

"Oh, someone here?"

"That's not a part of the game." Bailey diverts, "Never have I ever gone back to my hometown for any reason."

Technically I haven't, and grumble silently about my plan backfiring. Lily takes a sip, but calls it a technicality for some reason.

I decide to throw out the rules to the game, laying it all out on the table and finally take a drink. "Never have I ever walked in on my best friend fucking my dad while my mom watched."

I chug my entire drink while the room remains silent. I slam my cup down, and go to fill it again, not looking at them. Finally Lily breaks the silence.

"Uh, that's not how you play the game, but what the fuck?"

"Yup." I pop the P as I fill my cup to the brim.

"That's so fucked up." Bailey shakes her head. "Is that why you're here?"

I nod. "I lived there, I was working on moving out. Didn't exactly plan on leaving California, but here I am."

Bailey raises her cup. "Never have I ever escaped a shitty past." She takes a big gulp and so do I. It doesn't get past me that Lily does as well, but she doesn't provide any more information.

The alcohol flowing through my bloodstream makes me feel lighter, and at least for now, I forget about the situation with Jameson and the reason these two are here. To make me feel better. I refuse to think about him or what he could be doing. He's probably still working and maybe texting Mallory the way he used to do with me.

Good, she can help him through his grief. Clearly I wasn't good enough, and I'm not going to beg someone to be in my life that doesn't want to be. I knew things were too good to be true with him. No one can be that perfect. It's just another lesson learned. It doesn't matter anyway, I have my friends, my dog and I'll get over it eventually.

I have to.

CHAPTER 45

Jameson

I'VE HARDLY SPOKEN to my coworkers our entire shift. It's been pretty quiet, a couple of false alarm calls and one lift assist. I try not to let it show that every time a call comes in my heart accelerates. I've been trained for so long not to panic, and I've grown used to the sound of a call.

I thought two weeks would be enough time.

Apparently not, but I'm not about to admit that to anyone. I need to get back to normalcy, or the new normal and whatever that looks like. Though, the new normal has looked like not having Sutton around, and not talking to her.

I hate it.

I hate myself for pushing her away, and I'm pretty sure Ma knows what I've done and hates it as well.

I just can't drag her down like this, it's not fair. But it's lonely. Even Duke is depressed and barely looks at me. The horses can feel it, I know they can, and Jasper's about to go back home, and

I've barely been working with him like I was supposed to. I'm sure they'll understand, but I still hate not following through on commitments I made.

Kind of like the commitment I made to Sutton when I told her she was mine. No, it wasn't a proposal or a commitment to anyone else, but to me it was. I've never let a woman wear my hat, never wanted anyone to. No one else has ever been mine in the way she was.

Was.

Because I've lost her.

The amount of times I've wanted to reach out. I've actually stared at my phone for so long I swear I started to see two screens. I've typed out so many messages. I've had her contact pulled up ready to call. I've stopped myself from driving to her house. I just can't do it.

Of course, everything was only made worse earlier when Mallory showed up at the station. Dave, Jo, and Parker watched the entire interaction even though they pretended they weren't.

The worst part is I know Sutton was at work and saw her come in here. All I wanted to do was rush over and tell her that I didn't give her the time of day and sent her away because the only woman in the entire world I want is her.

"If you need anything at all I'm here," Mallory said, reaching for me. I stepped back away from her.

"I don't."

"If that changes, you can call me," she tried again.

"I don't have your number and no, I don't want it. Please, leave."

"Jameson." I think she thinks she's being flirty, but it only makes me grimace. "We used to have fun. We could have that type of fun again, you know."

I scoff. "Not interested and never will be. Bye, Mallory."

Without giving her any more of my time, attention, or energy, I walked away and heard her pout and throw a hissy fit as she left.

My shift ends before Sutton is at work, so I'm not tempted to walk in there, and instead drive home. I've still been staying in the main house, but the bed in my old room feels so much colder without the other body next to me. My pain has multiplied and I know it's all my fault, but I can't bring myself to do anything to fix it either.

I walk in, and Duke doesn't even greet me, doesn't even lift his head. I go to find Ma to check in on her like I always do. The only reason I went back to work was because she practically forced me to. I didn't want to leave her, but she won't let me stay around here.

Her door is cracked, and when I knock softly, she invites me in. We have an appointment for her tomorrow, and I'm terrified we're about to get more bad news. The remnants of our family are barely hanging on as it is and I can't handle any more negative news.

Ma has some boxes on her bed with her, and papers spread out in front of her.

"What are you doing?" I ask, finding a small open spot on the mattress to sit down.

"Going through some of your dad's things," she sniffs.

"Ma, why would you try to do that without me here?"

"You're here now, aren't you?"

I sigh. "How long have you been doing this? Have you even slept?"

"I sleep."

I start to tell her that's not really answering my question, but she doesn't let me because she's holding up an old picture I don't think I've ever seen before.

"What's this?" I take it from her, seeing a younger version of my dad holding me up on a horse. I'm a baby, there's no way I'm more than two years old and he's beaming wider than I ever saw him smile.

My heart cracks in my chest.

"He was so excited when I found out I was pregnant with you," Ma starts, her voice already watery. "I remember asking him if he was hoping for a girl or a boy, and do you know what he said?"

I shake my head, still looking down at the picture and barely holding back the tears forming in my eyes.

"He said it didn't matter as long as they had my heart, that's all he wanted."

The first tear falls before I'm able to stop it, dropping onto the picture in my hands, right on my dad's smiling face.

"Guess he was disappointed that didn't happen," I murmur.

She takes the picture from me. "I know you two had your disagreements, and he was never someone who shared his emotions easily. Do you know how long it took him to tell me he loved me?"

I shake my head again, realizing how little I know about their relationship beyond how they met and what I saw growing up.

"A year! He kept me waiting for a year, and every time I thought it was coming, he would say something else ridiculous. I knew he did though, so I never gave up on him. You probably don't remember his parents, but they weren't the overly affectionate type, and neither was he. I didn't mind. He showed me in other ways, and I knew he was my person."

I swallow roughly, knowing the feeling she's talking about. I know who my person is, too, and I've lost her.

She places her hand on top of mine. "He loved you so much Jameson. I don't think you realize how important you were to him. I know he never really told you and I wish you knew sooner how he really felt."

"Yeah, well he had a funny way of showing it, and I'm sorry it hurts you, Ma, but I just don't think I was the son he wanted. He wanted someone who wanted to stay here forever. He wanted someone to be just like him and I was too different. Did he tell you about our fight we had right before..." I'm not able to say the words *he died.*

"He did."

"Really? What did he say?"

"He said he didn't know how to talk to you."

"That's true."

"Not how you're thinking. He felt like he always said the wrong thing to you, and didn't know how to make it better. Yes, he could come off abrasive, but honey, that's how he always was. He wanted you to know how he felt, but couldn't ever get his point across in a way that worked for the both of you." She pauses and I can tell she's close to crying. "He got his one wish when it came to you. You got my heart. You always see the good in everyone, but it also made you more sensitive than you want to let on."

I can't argue with her, it's true. And of course she knows it.

"I've loved your father for the majority of my life, and the way he showed his love for me was different, it took getting used to, but I did. With you it's like he never quite figured out a way to show you in a way you both understood." She pulls out another piece of paper, this one is an envelope and hands it to me.

I furrow my brows looking at the envelope addressed to me. "What's this?"

"Read it when you want to hear from him again."

"What?"

"Not now. Go get some rest, and then go sit somewhere that makes you feel connected to him, and read it."

I clutch the envelope tightly and nod, standing up because the exhaustion is hitting me even more now.

Duke is curled up on his bed by the wall, I nod toward him. "Do you think he's okay? Should I take him to the vet to check him out?"

"I think he knows his favorite person isn't around anymore, and he's just as sad as us."

My eyes shoot back over to her. "His favorite person? I thought that was you and that's why he always wanted to be over here."

She laughs softly. "Oh no, honey. Duke latched onto your dad right away when you weren't around. He would follow him around when you were working, he was his shadow."

The guilt stabs me in the gut, I didn't even notice how much my own dog liked him. I nod, not sure what to say. I turn to leave, but she stops me, calling my name gently.

"I don't know what is going on between you and Sutton, but don't let your pain push her away completely."

I give her a soft smile, not having the heart to tell her that I think I already have. When I go up to my room, Duke chooses to stay where he's already settled and that's okay because as soon as my head hits the pillow I'm asleep, still clutching the envelope Ma gave me.

CHAPTER 46

Jameson

AFTER SLEEPING for so long I question what day it is when I finally wake up. I panic about needing to take care of the animals and if I missed Ma's appointment. But when I realize it's dark out and I just slept the day away I calm down a bit. Though, I hate that my schedule is about to be messed up. I get dressed to go out to do all the chores I neglected all day.

I'm about to walk out my bedroom door when I see the envelope lying on the bed that I almost forgot about. I debate with myself for a moment before picking it up and putting it in my back pocket. I don't know if I'm going to read it now, or ever, but at least I'll have it with me.

Duke doesn't follow me out, and I don't blame him, it's late after all, but the other animals are hungry and I'm sure the horses aren't too happy that their stalls are dirty.

Once I get down to the barn, I turn the lights on and take a peek in Sandy's stall first, only to see it's almost completely clean. It definitely has been mucked today at least. I check all the others and it's the same. Ma shouldn't be down here doing this, and I feel even worse that she felt the need to. I hope she didn't feed them.

My eyes catch on a small whiteboard we have hung up that we used to use, but lately it's just been covered in dirt and I didn't even know we had a dry erase marker for it. There's a note, and I'm surprised to see who it's from.

> Cleaned up the stalls, didn't feed them though. Thought you might need the help.
> -Wes

I'll have to thank him the next time I see him. I wonder if Ma knows that he came down here or not, but I guess it doesn't matter. I feed them all and then leave for the night, going to the cattle next. The goats, who make it known they aren't happy with the late dinner come next, and thankfully the chickens are all back in their coop, so I lock them inside, and finally feed the pigs.

I look up at the sky and the stars seem extra bright tonight and I remember the envelope burning a hole in my back pocket. Thinking back to what Ma said about reading it when I wanted to hear from him again. On one hand I don't know if I'm ready to, and on the other I'm so curious what he could possibly say that would change what I've thought about our relationship for years.

I walk through the open fields weighing my options until I reach the spot I came to with Sutton, and as soon as I'm down on the grass I wish she was here with me. My arms feel empty without her in them. My ears miss the sound of her voice, my nose misses the sweet floral scent she always had. My lips miss the taste of her. I just miss her.

Pulling out the envelope, I stare at it for a minute, still debating what to do. I could refuse to read it, let our last interaction be the final one between us. I could wait for another time.

A breeze hits me, and for some reason it makes me feel guilty for even considering putting it off. I may not know what it is I'm holding, but it's my dad's words, it has to be. And maybe for once I should hear him out.

So that's exactly what I do.

Slipping my finger under the flap, I gently tear the envelope open and unfold the paper inside, revealing the hardly legible handwriting of my dad. I pull my phone out and turn the flashlight on so I can actually read the black ink scribbled on the paper.

JAMESON,
I DON'T KNOW HOW TO START THIS OTHER THAN TO SAY I KNOW YOU AND I DON'T ALWAYS AGREE ON MANY THINGS. I KNOW YOU DON'T UNDERSTAND HOW I AM A LOT OF THE TIME, AND THAT'S OKAY. I DON'T UNDERSTAND WHY YOU WANTED TO LEAVE, BUT I'M PROUD OF YOU FOR DOING IT. I'VE NEVER KNOWN HOW TO TELL YOU BECAUSE IT HURT, BUT I KNOW YOU HAD TO DO IT. YOU HAD TO FIND YOUR OWN LIFE. AND YOUR MOM HAS ALWAYS BEEN SO HAPPY FOR YOU, WE BOTH HAVE.

WE GOT HER DIAGNOSIS TODAY AND YOU SAID YOU'RE COMING BACK. I DON'T WANT YOU COMING BACK BECAUSE YOU FEEL LIKE YOU HAVE TO. I DON'T WANT YOU UPROOTING THE LIFE YOU BUILT OUT OF OBLIGATION. WE'LL BE HAPPY TO HAVE YOU, BUT I KNOW YOU'RE LEAVING YOUR LIFE BEHIND.

OF COURSE I WISH YOU WOULD HAVE VISITED MORE, BUT WE COULD HAVE AS WELL. I'M SORRY MY PRIDE HAS ALWAYS STOOD IN THE WAY. I'M SORRY I'M NOT ABLE TO VOICE EVERYTHING I'M FEELING ALL THE TIME. I'M SO PROUD OF YOU. I LOVE YOU. I DON'T KNOW IF YOU'LL EVER GET THIS LETTER, WE JUST GOT OFF THE PHONE AND I KNOW YOU WERE UPSET. I DIDN'T MEAN TO DO THAT, I JUST NEVER SAY THE RIGHT THING TO YOU. YOU'RE SO MUCH LIKE YOUR MOTHER, YOU AND HER HAVE ALWAYS BEEN CLOSER THAN US. I WISH THAT WERE DIFFERENT AND I SHOULD PUT MORE OF AN EFFORT IN TO CHANGE IT.

I'M SORRY. JAMESON, I'M SCARED ABOUT WHAT THIS MEANS FOR YOUR MOTHER, AND FOR OUR FAMILY. SHE'S THE GLUE AND I FEAR, WITHOUT HER, YOU'LL NEVER SPEAK TO ME. I DON'T WANT THAT. PLEASE FORGIVE ME ONE DAY, AND I HOPE WE CAN WORK THROUGH THIS TOGETHER. I DON'T KNOW WHAT THE FUTURE LOOKS LIKE BUT WE'RE FAMILY AND I WANT TO MAKE SURE WE STAY THAT WAY.

I LOVE YOU
–DAD

I don't notice how hard I'm crying as I read the last words on the page, and tipping my head back, I look up toward the sky. "Why couldn't you say any of this to me before?"

Another breeze goes by as if in answer and I look down at the paper again. It gives me one glaring thought. He ran out of time and we weren't able to work through our problems before he was gone and I'm not about to make the same mistake.

I know I'm going to have to be on my knees for awhile, begging Sutton for forgiveness. I know it won't be easy, nothing with her has been. But that's one of the things I love about her the most. She makes me work for her and she's worth every single second of it.

That breeze goes by again. "I don't know if I'm insane, or if that really is you, Dad. But I'm sorry too."

Everything seems to calm, and I take a deep breath, looking at a particularly bright star. "I love you, too. If somehow you are listening and can help me get my girl back, I would appreciate it."

It's almost like I can hear his chuckle at that, and I know everything is going to be okay. But first I'm going to have to beg for forgiveness. Which means I need a plan on how to do just that.

CHAPTER 47

Sutton

BEFRIENDING Lily and Bailey has probably been the best thing I've done since moving to Amity. Our girls night was a success that ended with me crying into my popcorn while we watched movies, but I blamed it on the alcohol we consumed. I think it was the exact emotional break I needed. A chance to get it all out, everything that led me here with my family. Everything with Jameson, it all hit me during the third act breakup of the movie we were watching.

But now, I'm refreshed and slightly hungover, but mostly feeling better and ready to move on. I'm going back to how I was when I first came here, focusing on myself and not letting anyone derail that.

After I pull myself out of bed and see what a nice day it is, I call Bennet over to put his leash on and take him for a walk. I don't work today, which is good because I don't want to chance seeing Jameson, or even his truck.

We start to walk down the street and I look over when I hear a door opening, expecting it to be Bailey's but it turns out to be her neighbor.

"Hey," he greets.

I'm so caught off guard, I just give him a wave. I expect that to be it, but he starts walking toward me, and I'm conflicted on how to feel or if I should run in the other direction. The giant, intimidating man approaches. I stay frozen and try to paste a smile on my face that I hope is believable and doesn't look like I'm grimacing.

"We've never officially met, I'm Wes." He stretches his large hand out toward me.

"Oh, uh, yeah. Hi, I'm Sutton and this is Bennet." We shake hands, and I find it really interesting that he's introducing himself now when I've lived here for a couple of months.

"It seems like you and Bailey are friends, so I'm sure she's given you some horror stories about me." He chuckles.

"She actually hasn't said too much about you." I could tell him that I've seen some of their spats, but I don't have anything personal against him, so there's no point in telling him anything.

"That's surprising. Well, I wanted you to know I'm not all bad, and if you need help with anything, I'm around."

I nod. "Thanks, Wes. It was nice to meet you."

"You, too."

He heads back to his house, and I continue on my walk with Bennet, surprised to have had a pleasant interaction with him.

Maybe things will start looking up. At least it's not like it can get much worse.

When we get back home I notice something sitting on my front porch, it's a single flower. A daisy, I think, with a note attached to it. I look around to see if anyone is nearby, a car driving away or someone hiding in the bushes, but I don't see anyone.

Bennet and I walk inside and that's when I open up the note. It's simple. So simple that I reread it a few times, just in case I somehow missed something within it.

I remember the first time I saw you. There hasn't been a day you haven't been on my mind since. I'm going to show you how much you mean to me.

I know who this is from even though he didn't sign it. Unless I have some stalker that's been really good at keeping himself hidden. But I know who this is from.

Part of me wants to crumple up the paper, shred it to pieces, and throw it away. But I just can't bring myself to do it. I pick up the daisy and smell it. I want to know why he picked this flower.

Maybe he was hoping I would reach out and ask. I'm not going to. I'm going to stay strong. He lost his chance with me and he's not going to get another one. Maybe I hold grudges a little too easily, but it's the same reason I'll never forgive my parents or Cassie. No matter how many times they reach out and try to mend things, there's no coming back from that.

Jameson will move on as well. We both will.

THINGS GET WEIRDER the next time I'm at work. Jerry Lee is always a loud mouth with his constant barking, and telling Vern to shut up. Plus, I can't forget some of the newer words he picked up recently thanks to Lily.

Even though she somehow blames me for that one, I'm not sure how.

Today, for some reason Jerry Lee's fixation is on the man I'm trying to forget. It seems like every few minutes he's calling out *"Hot guy, Jameson."* Every time he does it my head shoots up because I feel like I'm going to see him walking through the door. He's not and I have yet to see him at all so I don't know why Jerry Lee keeps announcing him.

"Jerry Lee, if you say his name one more time I'm seriously setting you free."

He barks in response, then goes through his entire repertoire. *"Shut up, Vern. Jizz. Hot guy, Jameson."*

I groan, regretting not having some noise canceling head-phones with me. You'd think I would've learned by now, but Lily has been entertaining enough to justify not getting them. She's not here today, and Trish already left for the day so it's just me, my thoughts, and the annoying bird who is still barking.

"That's it, you're at least going to bed." I storm toward his cage and he squawks again, but I lure him inside with a treat, tossing a towel over the top so he'll think it's nighttime.

I notice another envelope with a flower sitting on the windowsill by his cage. This time it's a carnation. I pick both things up, and see the envelope is addressed to me in the same handwriting.

Maybe I should wait until I'm home to open it, but I can't help myself. I'm too curious. This one is a lot simpler.

I'm lost without you.

I sigh, shaking my head. He's not going to make it easy to not think about him, but I have to. Though I can't bring myself to get rid of the letter or the flower, so instead, it comes home with me to join the daisy in my kitchen.

My phone goes off and I expect to see it's Jameson, but when it says "Mom," I think about throwing it across the room. I've been dodging all their phone calls and texts since I got here. I'm not ready to talk to any of them, but I'm also so fired up because of everything else going on in my life. And maybe closing that door will help me feel some semblance of peace.

That's why for the first time since I walked out of their house after witnessing the worst thing I've ever seen in my entire life, I answer the phone. I don't say anything, I just put it on speaker and leave it on the counter, staring at the screen.

"Sutton?" Her voice comes through the speaker and it's the first time I've heard her since that day.

I don't say anything right away. She says my name again, this time a little louder.

"What do you want?" I finally snap.

"To talk to you. To explain. To find out where you are. There's a lot I want as your mother, Sutton."

I scoff. "Yeah, well maybe you should've thought about that before."

"What do you mean? I don't know what you think you saw, but it's not—"

"Fuck that." I never curse at my mom, but that has officially changed. "You're not going to gaslight me. I unfortunately know what I saw and while I don't know, nor do I want to know, the full extent of the situation, you're not going to tell me it's not what I think."

She's silent other than a deep sigh. "I don't know what you want me to say."

"There's nothing you can say. You guys can be swingers or whatever the hell you do, but Cassie was my best friend and that's a line you don't cross."

"I'm sorry you found out that way."

"But not sorry it happened."

Again, she's silent and I shake my head. I may not have expected this to go any differently, but it's almost worse than I thought.

She finally speaks. "Will you at least tell me where you are? I'm your mother, Sutton."

"I'm safe and I'm happy." *Kinda.* "You don't need to know where."

She sighs again. "I wish there was a way to fix this."

"Well, there's not. And that's really too bad. I've seen what happens when you lose someone before you're able to fix a relationship, and it sucks. But I also think that some relationships aren't worth fixing. Just because we're family doesn't mean we need to be close."

She sniffs and I can tell she's crying, but I'm not going to back down. "If that's what you want."

"It is."

"Okay. Well, goodbye." I hear her tear filled voice.

"Bye." I hang up and hardly notice that I started crying as well. I'm angry at myself as I wipe the tears away. I was hoping that getting this closure would make me feel better, but it hasn't.

The worst part is that it just created an ache in my gut that feels a lot like loneliness and it makes me want to call Jameson. I know he would make it all better. I know he would stand beside me and validate what I did and said.

But then I remember how he pushed me away, and those feelings dissipate. The flowers on the counter tell a different story, but if he was able to push me away once, he could do it again. And I refuse to put myself in a position to get hurt again.

CHAPTER 48

Sutton

EVERY DAY I find a note with a different type of flower. Sometimes it's at work, on my car, or outside of my house. The notes have continued to be simple, mentioning a memory he has of us together. Or something about me that he can't stop thinking about. They're sweet and my resolve is weakening every time I find one, but I continue to stay strong.

Each new flower is added to my collection, and even as they fade I'm unable to throw any of them away. I'm also unable to part with the notes that have started piling up on my counter.

I know I should throw it all away—out of sight, out of mind—but I don't. He also doesn't reach out any other way. I have yet to see him or his name pop up on my phone.

Just the notes he never signs with his name and a flower.

I hate that I've come to anticipate them. When I get to work, I search high and low for one. If there's nothing there, I look around when I get home. Once I didn't find anything right away, then, I saw it was tucked and somewhat hidden off to the side and the relief I felt has me worried because this whole moving on thing is clearly not going well.

I'm greeted by both Jerry Lee and Lily when I get to work, and I wish I could say the bird has let up on screaming Jameson's name, but he hasn't and I think he may actually be a little obsessed with the man.

I suggested an exorcist to Trish. She laughed it off, and I didn't take that as a no. It turns out bird exorcisms are hard to come by, so I'll be on the hunt to figure that out for a while.

"Your first appointment is already here," Lily tells me over Jerry Lee's barks.

"Wait what? I didn't think I had a dog until ten thirty." I grab my phone to check my schedule because I prefer to be here when my clients drop off, and I know it's on me for not being early enough.

"Oh, this one wasn't on your schedule." Lily is biting back a smile and I narrow my eyes at her.

"What's going on?"

"Nothing." Her tone is not believable at all.

"Mhm," I hum.

"Hot guy, Jameson," Jerry Lee calls out, and Lily immediately turns toward him, murmuring threats of his imminent death and I have to laugh because I do the exact same thing.

"What're you not telling me?" I question.

"Nothing. Oh, look at the time. I have work to do." She rushes off into one of the other rooms in the salon and I know she's hiding something.

I go back to the room with kennels and I see Duke's familiar face. His tail wags as soon as he sees me and I shake my head, unable to hold back my smile at seeing him. I pet him, and he leans against me completely as I scratch his belly. "What do you have here, buddy?"

I take the note off his collar, similarly to what Jameson has done before. I'm a little hurt that there isn't a flower to go along with this one, but I push that thought away. I unfold it, unable to wait to read more from the man I swear I'm going to forget at some point.

Duke loves and misses you. He would never forgive me if I didn't do everything possible to try and get You to forgive me.

"Your dad is crazy, you know that?" I ask the sweet eyed Pit Bull.

I call out for Lily who peeks her head around the corner with a smirk. "Yes?"

"Did Jameson drop off his dog earlier?"

"I have no idea what you're talking about. I'm sworn to secrecy."

"*You?*" I gasp in disbelief.

"Yes, me. I can keep a secret, believe it or not."

I just give her an incredulous look.

"What?" she gasps. "I can. Like right now. Bye!"

I shake my head and look down at Duke. I might as well get him nice and pretty, but I don't know if I'll be able to be around when Jameson picks him up. As much as I'm insisting that I can move on from him, I feel like the second I see him, any hope of that will go out the window.

"Shut up, Vern!"

"Shut up, Jerry Lee!" Lily yells back and I sputter out a laugh.

Never a dull moment around here.

I CAN'T BRING myself to reach out to Jameson once Duke is freshly bathed. His nails that had barely grown out are now as short as possible and I even put a cute flannel bandana on him. And just like the strong independent woman I am, I asked Lily to reach out to him.

Of course as the mature woman I am, as soon as the door opens and Jerry Lee greets whoever it is, I rush to the back. My excuse is to get Duke, but I fully intend on just letting him out to go to Jameson without me having to see him.

"Sutton, come out here," Lily calls and I bite back a groan. I didn't hear Jerry Lee announce the man's presence, which is new for him.

"How do I look?" I ask Duke, but then shake my head. "Never mind, it doesn't matter. You're my moral support, got it?"

He just looks up at me with his tongue sticking out. I give him a thumbs up and open the door. He rushes out, and I take my time. Though once I turn the corner, fully anticipating to see the tall, broad shouldered man who broke my heart, I'm met with a different firefighter. This one is younger with sandy colored hair and a mustache he's clearly attempting to grow that isn't fully in.

"Uh, hi, Parker. What're you doing here?" I look from him to Lily in confusion.

"I came to pick up this guy right here." He pats Duke on the head, and my shoulders fall.

"Oh, why couldn't Jameson?"

"Sorry if you were expecting him. He had some things to take care of, but he did want me to give you something." He pulls out an azalea and hands it to me.

I can't help my happy reaction to getting a flower, even though I shouldn't be. I shut down that train of thought before it has a chance to spiral.

"This doesn't count as payment, you know?"

He chuckles. "I know, he also sent cash."

Parker hands over way too much, and I try to give back the extra, but he refuses to take it. I sigh, giving in once he's practically out of the door. As soon as it closes, Lily looks at me with a mischievous look on her face.

"Please tell me he didn't involve everyone in this town for whatever scheme he's planning."

"Like I said, I can keep some secrets," she singsongs, practically skipping away from me.

The worst part is I'm already anticipating what note and flower tomorrow may bring.

IT'S BEEN a week since the first note and flower. Today is day eight and I'm officially conditioned to search for them. There was nothing at work today, so I anticipate when I get home what I'll find, but there's nothing. Unless he hid it extremely well.

I search for a decent amount of time and still find nothing. I guess a week of trying was his limit. Seven letters and seven flowers is where he draws the line. At first I'm disappointed he wouldn't try a little more, but then I'm annoyed that's all the time he was willing to give me.

Oh well, now I can really focus on actually moving on like I should have anyway.

My phone starts to ring and it's an unfamiliar Washington number. I assume it's a client wanting to make an appointment so I answer professionally.

"Hello, this is Sutton."

"Hi, Sutton, honey." The voice is one I recognize instantly as Emily. I'm instantly on alert, wondering why she would be calling me. Just like her son, she instantly eases my panic. "He's fine, I'm calling for myself. I need some help and he's on shift. I hate to ask, but would you mind coming by?"

"Of course, are you okay?"

"I am. I miss having you around, but I'll see you soon?"

I swallow the lump in my throat. "Yeah, I'll head over."

"Thank you."

I look at Bennet, and even he's been moping around for the last week. "You want to go see your friend?"

He perks up, and I lead him out to my car where I take a deep breath before driving. I'm a little worried about seeing the place where I felt my heart cracking as I left. As I pull up, my nerves kick up even more. I know she said Jameson was on shift, but I can't be here without thinking about him. He's everywhere here, even after I park and step out into the fresh air, the cool weather reminding me how long I've been here as summer is starting to turn into fall. I swear I get the faintest whiff of him, the slightly spicy scent that always clung to him along with the pine from the trees.

Emily steps out onto the porch, greeting me with a smile and I'm in awe of this woman. She's fighting the battle of her life and just lost her husband, but she's here smiling at me, and inviting me into her arms for a hug as soon as I'm up the steps.

"Hi sweetie," she says softly before we part.

Bennet is already walking through the open front door searching for his friend.

"Come on in." She guides me inside.

"What did you need help with?" I look around in case it's completely obvious.

"Actually, it's something out at the barn with the horses if you don't mind."

"Oh, I'm really not a professional with horses, I only rode one once." I shake my head.

"Don't worry, it's nothing you can't handle. I would do it myself, but Jameson would throw a fit if he knew I went down there alone."

"So you just need me with you?" I clarify. "Not that I mind because it's really nice to see you again, but I'm just wondering why it couldn't wait until he came back home."

"We've been caring for a friend's horse for the summer and they're coming to get him tomorrow morning so I just want to make sure everything is together for him, and that he's all clean and ready to go home." She smiles, and I can see how genuine she is.

"Okay, do you want me to drive us down there?"

She waves me off. "Nonsense, it's not that far of a walk and I want the fresh air."

I nod, the sun is setting soon, but it's mild out so the short walk may be pretty nice. As we walk at her pace, she tells me stories about her and her late husband. I bite back the tears that want to come, but she's happily reminiscing so I let her. I didn't know the man very well and when I met him he seemed cold and detached, but hearing from her it's obvious he was anything but when it came to his wife.

And somehow that gives me hope that everything is going to be okay for everyone.

As we approach the barn, she pauses her story. "Oh, I have something for you." She reaches into the pocket of her cardigan and pulls out an envelope. My heart instantly kicks up in my chest as I look at the white piece of paper addressed to me.

"What's that?"

"Open it and find out."

I swallow, taking the paper with shaky hands and open it slowly. We're almost at the door to the barn, and all I can focus on is the paper. The eighth letter I didn't think I would be getting. She steps ahead into the building, probably to get started on whatever it is she needs to do. For some reason it doesn't even cross my mind that this is a set up. Not until I see the two words written on the paper.

Look Up.

When I do, all I see is Jameson.

He's standing in the aisle of the barn, looking better than I even remember which seems impossible. He's in dark jeans, a black T-shirt, with that familiar brown cowboy hat on his head, and a red rose in his hands. He steps toward me and I'm actually starting to wonder if I'm hallucinating.

"Sutton," he says my name in that way he always does, his deep voice wrapping around the single word like it's his favorite thing to say, and I love to hear it every single time he does.

I open my mouth to speak, but nothing comes out. He's even closer now, so close I could reach out and touch him, but I won't. I can't. Somehow I find the ability to use my voice. "What're you doing?"

"Have you been getting my notes?"

I nod, clutching the one I'm currently holding so I don't do something crazy like grab him and slam our mouths together. But I won't.

"How many have you gotten?" he questions.

"Um, eight." I hold up the latest one.

"Have you noticed anything about these eight notes?"

I look down at the one in my hand, rereading it, trying to find some secret message hidden within the letters, but there's nothing. I shake my head when I look back up to him.

He smirks. "That's okay, put them together in order and see if you notice anything when you get back home." He hands me the rose, and I take it trying to hide my trembling hand.

"Was this the only reason you got your mom to lure me out here?" I look down at the flower, the red petals looking healthy and vibrant.

"No. I wanted to tell you in person how sorry I am for pushing you away. I'm an idiot, and I knew the second you drove away I was making a mistake, but I just couldn't bring myself to do anything about it. I convinced myself it was best for you. That I wasn't going to drag you down with me as I spiraled."

Somehow I find my strength once again, standing tall when I respond, "And who's to say you won't do that again the next time things get hard?"

"Me. I'm sorry that I made you question how I felt about you or doubt what we have between us. I didn't mean to hurt you. I really was convinced I was doing what's best for you, but maybe I'm selfish. Because even if being apart is what's best for you, I can't do it. I need you in my life, baby. You are everything to me."

"Jameson." I shake my head, and he cups my face, forcing me to look up to him.

"Put the notes together. Take the night to think about it, and if you don't think we can make this work, then I'll accept it. But if there's even a chance of us being together, I'll grab it with both hands and hold on for the rest of my life, because you're it for me."

"I'll think about it, but you hurt me," I tell him.

"I know, I'm so sorry. My fear was that I didn't deserve you, and I know I don't, especially not now. If you let me, I'll spend the rest of my life working to make sure I do."

"No promises."

"Not asking for any. Yet."

The three of us walk back to the main house, Jameson's hand

grazes mine as we walk, but he doesn't make a move to touch me. He walks me to my car, Bennet jumping in and we say goodbye.

And still he doesn't touch me. Not even as I climb into my driver's seat and he shuts my door for me. I watch him in my rearview mirror as I drive away and unlike the last time I had this view, he doesn't look worried or upset.

This time he has hope.

And yet as I leave, I notice the only thing he didn't say were the three words that may have been the thing to completely win me over.

"DO you think she'll be back?" Ma asks as Sutton's car fades from view.

I'm surprisingly confident with my response. "Yeah, I do."

There's eight notes, each one has a letter I made a bit more obvious and when she puts them together she'll see what they spell. I wanted to tell her that I loved her as soon as I saw her today. It took everything in me to hold back and stick to my plan.

I've hated this time without her, I wish I could go back to that day and hold her tighter instead of pushing her away. I know I'll regret it for the rest of my life, but I wasn't kidding when I said I'd spend forever making it up to her if she'll let me.

And she will.

Things are finally starting to look up. Ma got into a trial that's not guaranteed to help, but something makes me feel like it's the hope that we needed. Maybe something can go right, and the sun is finally going to come out.

I just have to wait a little bit longer.

I GAVE SUTTON THE NIGHT, but I wasn't going to wait for her to come to me. I've been chasing her since I met her and that's not going to stop. I'm the one that pushed her away. I'm the one that would have been to blame if I lost her. Which means I'm the one that's going to fight for her.

Collecting the bouquet of flowers off my passenger seat, I check the bundle of blooms—all of them different—just like I've been leaving with the notes. There's no note this time because I'm going to tell her everything. Even if she hasn't figured out the secret message I left in the notes, I have to tell her.

I notice Wes leaving his house as I walk around the front of my truck, and we give each other a head nod before he gets in his loud sports car. He drives off as I knock on Sutton's door. It takes her a minute before she swings it open, her eyes wide as she looks from me to the flowers, then back to me.

"Good morning." I smile, extending the flowers toward her.

"Morning, what're you doing here?"

"Did you think I was joking? I told you to take the night. Did you figure it out?"

"Uh, well." She opens the door a little more. "You can come in."

Her tone is unsure, and for a second I'm worried she did figure it out and doesn't feel the same way. I've been so sure we were on the same page with our feelings, but for the first time I'm not entirely sure. I don't let my nerves show as I step inside. Bennet greets me with a nudge to my hand, which I return with a pat on his head.

"So, I can't remember the order of the notes," she admits, nervously.

I chuckle lightly as she leads me to her living room where the pieces of paper are spread out on the floor.

"Want me to show you or tell you?"

"Show me," she says softly, looking down at the flowers in her hand.

I know exactly what order they go in, so I drop down and organize them for her to see. I made a single letter darker on every one to spell out my message. It's not overly obvious, but I wanted to tell her in some way before I had the opportunity to speak the words.

I LOVE YOU.

"Why are all the flowers different?" she questions.

I stand up in front of her, and she looks up into my eyes. The mossy green I've missed seeing just about brings me down to my knees. I lift my hand, tracing my finger along her jaw when I answer, "I realized I didn't know your favorite flower, so I tried a different one every day, hoping one would be right. And if I wasn't, then I hoped one of these would be." I point to the variety I've brought her today.

She bites back a smile, and then looks down at the notes. The second she gets it, her breath hitches, and I crowd her back. I push her hair over her shoulder, and graze my lips against her ear.

"I love you, Sutton. You're everything to me. You are my first thought in the morning, my last thought at night. I could never go on without you, and I hope you'll take me back because I'm going to hold onto you so tight and never let you go."

I grip her hip, and turn her toward me, she's clutching the flowers like a lifeline, so I gently remove them from her hands and set them down before pulling her against me. One arm wrapped around her back, the other holding her chin to tilt her head back.

"I've been in love with you since before you even gave me the time of day. I know that may sound ridiculous, but I don't care. I'm out of my mind in love with you."

Her eyes search mine, pooling with tears before she finally puts me out of my misery with a wide smile. "Took you long enough to tell me. I love you, too."

Unable to wait any longer, I take her mouth with mine in a heated kiss that I don't plan on stopping ever if I don't have to.

"I missed you so much," she sobs against my lips.

"I missed you too, baby." I drag her with me onto the couch where she straddles my lap, and continues to keep our mouths sealed together.

She opens for me, and the second my tongue touches hers I groan into her mouth and kiss her even deeper. My hand grips the back of her head, tangling in her soft brown hair as I angle her head to where I want her to be.

I kiss along her jaw, and down her neck. She grips my shoulders tightly moaning my name. "Jameson, tell me this is real."

"Of course it's real. *We* are real."

Sutton grips my face and moves me back to face her. We're both breathing heavily, overwhelmed with all the feelings running through us, the emotional release is strong and I want to touch her, look at her, just be with her.

"I don't want to give you everything if you're going to push me away when things get tough again."

"I won't. I never will. I knew as soon as you left I'd made a mistake. It's one I'll never make again. I know you're scared. I understand it, which is why I'll never stop working for your love to make sure I deserve all of you."

"You've always deserved me. We all make mistakes and we're human. I just want to make sure this is as real to you as it is to me."

I nod. "It is. I love you. More than I can even explain with words."

Sutton swivels her hips slightly and hums. "Then don't show me with words, show me in other ways."

I'm instantly hard, and I know she can feel it. My hips flex instinctively, as though my dick knows exactly where it's supposed to be. I take her mouth in a heated kiss once again. She moves against me, rubbing herself on my lap and I wrap an arm around her waist, pulling her into me even more.

"How do you want me to show you, baby? You name it, I'll do it; I'm all yours."

She moans, kissing me harder and with the way she's moving it's like she's trying to fuck me through our clothes. I wish more than anything I could make them disappear instantly because we have to part to remove them, and that's the last thing I want.

"Touch me, fuck me, never let me go," Sutton pleads.

I lift her up and lay her on the couch, covering her body with my own, our lips never parting as our tongues tangle. I'm settled between her parted legs, pressing down onto her and she cries out trying to rub herself against me.

I need to feel more of her so I move down her body, pushing her shirt up, finding that she's not wearing a bra and my mouth instantly latches onto one of her nipples. I suck the hard bud into my mouth and she grips my hair tightly. I let go, doing the same to the other one, before continuing down her stomach. I'm at the waistband of her shorts and I look up at her, silently asking for permission.

She nods subtly and it's all I need to hook my index fingers into the fabric and pull them down. Her hips lift enough to help me ease her out of the shorts and then I look down at her naked body below me. I just stare at her, amazed that she still wants me. Amazed that I'm here with her.

Amazed that she's mine.

She lifts her leg, nudging me with her foot. "Your turn, cowboy."

I reach behind my head to pull my shirt off, dropping it onto the floor next to us. She taps my leg with her foot. "These, too."

I smirk. "I will, but I haven't tasted you in too long, and I need to fix that right now."

I push her thighs apart, settling on my stomach between her legs and tossing them over my shoulders. I reach up with one hand to play with her nipple while the other is banded around her thighs so she's not able to flail them around.

That's when I devour her. The first swipe of my tongue reminds me of how sweet she tastes and I groan, diving back in, needing to taste every inch of her, licking and sucking while she gasps and moans. It's everything I've missed, and what I've needed. Now I have her back, and I plan on being down here for a while.

When I suck her clit into my mouth, I pinch her nipple at the same time and she cries out, arching her back, but she's not able to get far because I'm holding her down. It doesn't take long for me to feel how close she is to her release, and I want it more than I want air.

I stiffen my tongue, pushing it inside her, licking before moving up to flick her clit and push a finger into her tight wet heat and that's all it takes for her. She's coming on my face and I'm licking her as much as I can while she squeezes my finger so tightly my dick jumps, dying to be next.

After she comes down, I climb back up her body and she pulls my mouth onto hers, tasting herself on my tongue. I love when she does that. I thrust against her, wishing we didn't have anything between us so I could sink inside her right now. She pushes on my pants, but I stop her by scooping her up in my arms.

"What're you doing?" she asks as I start to carry her into another room.

"Taking you to bed, because I'm going to make love to you properly."

CHAPTER 50

Sutton

HE EASES me onto the bed and I'm instantly reaching for him, but he's just far enough away that I can't. He removes his pants, and boxers at once. I watch his naked form appear before me. His thick, perfect cock is right in front of me, making my mouth water, and my pussy clench. Even though I just had a powerful orgasm, it's not enough apparently because I'm already desperate for more.

Luckily I don't have to wait long. Jameson covers my body with his own, kissing me again like he can't go more than a few minutes without doing so. And truly neither can I.

My legs spread, making room for him to settle between. I feel his hard length rub my core and I moan at the sensation. When his shaft hits my clit, I bite back a gasp that he muffles with his tongue in my mouth.

"Jameson, please. I need you."

"I need you too, baby." He positions himself at my entrance, and instead of letting him tease me, I wrap my leg around his hip, and urge him to move.

He does, pushing in completely until he's fully seated inside me in a single thrust. The moment we're completely connected, his eyes lock with mine and the moment feels more powerful than any other one between us. There's nothing in the way, emotionally or physically. We're completely connected, our bodies, admitting our love. It's everything I never knew I could feel.

He's everything I never knew I wanted.

"I love you, Sutton," he whispers between us.

"I love you, Jameson," I whisper back.

He pulls back, then pushes in again and we moan in unison at the feeling. This isn't about getting off, this isn't about fucking to feel. This is us connecting in a way that proves we will never be apart again.

Our lips stay locked as he rocks into me, a steady pace that isn't rushed or frenzied. He's still in control as he always is, but this feels deeper in so many ways between us. When he angles his hips slightly I gasp into his mouth.

"That good, baby?" He groans and I nod, crying for more.

"Always," I sigh.

I lock my ankles behind him and hook my arms around his neck, holding him as close to me as possible as he does exactly what he said he would and makes love to me. I love this man in my arms so much and why I thought I would want to give up on him is ridiculous. There's no moving on from him. There's no moving on from us.

This is it for me. He was always going to be it for me.

"I'm close," I cry softly.

"I know, baby. I'll always give you what you need." He pulls back and thrusts in again, harder this time, his pelvis hitting my clit while his cock hits the spot inside me that has me growing desperate for the release that's teasing me just out of reach.

"Please," I plead, arching up into him.

And he knows exactly what I need because he loves me. *Jameson loves me.*

His hands tangle in my hair, pulling on it slightly, and I gasp and his tongue invades my mouth as his hips pick up the pace. With a hard thrust, my orgasm barrels into me. Jameson groans above me, and I feel the second he does the same. His cum fills me and it prolongs my own release feeling the way he claims me.

I've never been into someone possessing me, but with Jameson it just feels right. As we come down, he doesn't leave my body, and his mouth doesn't leave mine. We're just here in our own bubble. Nothing outside of us matters, at least for now. And whatever comes up after this we'll handle it. Together.

"Don't think I'm leaving you again," Jameson says as we break apart, and I bite back a smile remembering the first time we had sex when I thought that's exactly what he was doing.

I giggle as he gets up and quickly returns with a warm washcloth he uses to clean between my legs. I hum at the feeling and how content I feel right now.

"You know," he starts. "One of these days when you're ready I'm going to push all of this back into you to make sure you're nice and full of me so I can get you pregnant."

I squirm slightly because I was not expecting him to say something like that, and also because it instantly makes me want him to make good on that.

"But only when you're ready." He locks his eyes with mine, and I want to tell him I'm ready now with the way he's talking and looking at me like that.

He tosses the washcloth into my hamper, and pulls me against him as we settle onto my bed, skin sticky with sweat but I don't want to move.

"Did you have any other plans today?" he asks.

I shake my head. "I can't remember, but if I did they're cancelled now."

He chuckles. "Good, because I wasn't going to let you leave my side regardless."

"Good thing I never want to."

Epilogue

SUTTON

A YEAR LATER

"You look beautiful, honey," Emily tells me, adjusting the simple veil in my hair.

"Thank you." My face heats with the compliment, even though she's been more of a mom to me than my own for the last year.

My mom and dad aren't present today. I wasn't kidding about cutting them off, though they've tried talking to me over the past year. My mother's confirmation that they weren't sorry about what happened, especially since I'm pretty sure it's still happening, was enough to have me completely done.

The last year also has had its share of problems, and some scares when it came to Emily's health, but Jameson never once wavered with me. He let me be there for both of them, even when things got tough.

The trial she's been in seems to be helping, and it seems like a miracle that she's improved as much as she has. The cancer isn't completely gone, but it's not spreading. She's able to gain weight, and she isn't as tired anymore. She has a glow to her that I'm so happy I get to see.

Especially because she gets to be here for this day. A day I know she's been wanting for so long. I never thought much about my wedding day. I wasn't someone who could picture every detail or knew who I wanted waiting for me at the end of the aisle.

Not until Jameson.

And the day he dropped down to his knee in front of me. He brought me out to the spot on the property where we always go at night to look at the stars. We'd talk about the future and what we wanted out of life. Sometimes, we wouldn't say anything and just sat there with each other while our dogs ran around.

I put him out of his misery and told him what my favorite flower is: sunflowers. And because he's who he is, he surrounded the area with them, and always makes sure I have them in the house.

Saying yes to him was the easiest yes I've ever given.

Now here we are, just a couple months later because neither of us wanted anything big. We decided on a small intimate wedding on the property.

Bailey and Lily are my bridesmaids, even though Lily goes back to college in a week for her senior year. They're both out helping make sure everything is set up the way Jameson and I planned, which is why I'm alone with Emily for now.

She turns me toward her, eyes are already shining with tears, but a smile is on her lips. "I'm so happy for you both. I've wanted this for Jameson for so long and I couldn't have asked for someone better for him."

I return her smile, my own tears threatening to appear. "I'm happy too. You raised such an amazing man."

"Believe it or not, his father was a part of that."

"I do believe it. I just wish he was here today, too." I'm unable to hold back my tears now.

She gives me a watery smile. "Me too. He would be so proud, but I'm sure he's watching."

She pulls me in for a hug, and I think it's so I don't see her start to cry, which is okay with me because then she won't see me doing the same.

Our sweet moment is interrupted by Bailey and Lily barging in. Well, it's really Lily doing the barging, Bailey is following behind shaking her head. Those two have become my best friends, and even though Lily has only been back for the summer, we keep in touch while she's at school. Bailey is still reserved, but she's been coming out of her shell a bit more.

"You bitches ready?" Lily calls out, and then freezes when she sees Emily's red eyes. "Not you, Mrs. Turner, you're not a bitch."

Emily laughs lightly. "You don't need to censor yourself for me, sweetie."

"Good, because if Sutton would've let me throw her a real bachelorette party, you would have been invited."

I roll my eyes. That was a debate with her for a while. Of course she wanted to throw me a party, and Vegas was mentioned, though the thought of her in Vegas scared me. And I didn't feel the need to have a bachelorette party because it just didn't feel necessary.

I lean down to whisper to Emily, "I saved you from bondage ducks and skillet strippers. Don't ask."

Before she's able to comment, Bailey asks, "Are you ready?"

"I really am," I reply. I worried about being nervous on my wedding day, but I'm just excited. I feel like I may end up running down the short aisle toward him because I just want to be in his arms.

"Well then, let's get this show on the fucking road!" Lily claps her hands together and then one over her mouth. I chuckle and Bailey just shakes her head.

They both head out to the yard, and Emily and I follow slowly behind because she's going to walk me down the aisle. I peek out, seeing the small crowd of people. It's not extravagant, but it's perfect. And when I see Jameson standing at the makeshift altar in his white button down with the sleeves rolled up and no jacket because the August air is hot, I'm about to melt purely from the sight of him.

My own white dress touches the ground, but is light and flowy because I didn't want to feel restricted. Lily described it as "very boho" which I think is because the long sleeves are loose and sheer. I clutch my small bouquet of sunflowers and hook my arm with Emily's.

Bennet and Duke walk down the aisle first, meeting up with Bailey and Lily at the end. Jameson has his coworkers Dave and Parker next to him, and I'm so ready to be close to him.

"Let's go." She smiles widely at me as we step outside.

The second Jameson sees us, his face breaks into a wide smile, and just like I thought, I want to rush toward him. I don't, but it feels like it takes forever for us to walk to the front. By the time we get there I'm about to launch myself at my fiancé. I'm stopped by Wes, who's our officiant speaking.

I was surprised when Jameson said he would do this for us, but apparently they've gotten pretty close over the last year since Wes comes by several times a week to work with the horses.

Jameson takes my hand into his own, and he's beaming and I'm unable to hold back my own smile.

"You look absolutely breathtaking," he says just between the two of us as his mom goes to sit down.

"You don't look so bad yourself. But I'm missing the hat," I tease.

"You should be wearing it, looks better on you."

Wes clears his throat. "Are you ready to start?"

Bailey scoffs behind me, "Don't be a mood killer."

I bite back my smirk, especially when he sends a subtle glare in her direction and Jameson and I just smile at each other. Their... *feud* has always been interesting to both of us, but it's become even more amusing after she revealed that they hooked up before. She wouldn't tell me more than that it happened once and will never happen again.

Jameson and I don't believe her, but I guess we'll just have to wait and see.

Our ceremony is short, just like we wanted, and I'm hardly paying attention because the thing I'm waiting for is the moment when he finally says, "You may kiss your—"

"Hot guy, Jameson!" The familiar screech of Jerry Lee calls out, and I hear Trish shush him.

I barely contain my laughter. Jameson's shoulders shake with his own and it brings me back to when Jerry Lee would say that as soon as Jameson walked in. Who am I kidding, he still does, but now it's much less embarrassing.

Wes clears his throat, and tries again. "You may now kiss your wife."

Jameson doesn't waste any time grabbing my face and slamming our mouths together in a kiss that is definitely not appropriate to happen in front of people. But it doesn't matter because everyone else around us fades away. I wrap my arms around his neck, pulling him against me completely as his tongue plunges into my mouth.

I hear a whoop come from someone, and we laugh against each other's mouths. I know exactly who that came from. We break apart and I drop my head to Jameson's chest while he kisses the top of my head.

Lily starts the cheering, the small crowd joining in as we walk down the aisle hand in hand. At the end of the aisle Jameson grabs me and kisses me again. I smile into the kiss, because I don't think I've ever been happier than I am at this moment.

"You ready?" he asks.

"For what?"

"The rest of our lives."

The End

Scars of You is coming

Curious about Bailey and Wes? Read their bonus scene before Scars of You.

READ IT HERE

Acknowledgments

Not many people realize that this book has been in the works for over two and a half years. Believe it or not, I started this *before* I wrote The Hat Trick. This book was supposed to be next, but then these three hockey players and their girl popped into my head instead. That book ended up being the one to change my life and I'll forever be grateful for it.

Now, here we are, Jameson and Sutton are finally ready to be shared! So to my Booha, Ashley, here you go! You've been waiting for them the longest and I hope they are everything you wanted and more.

Chelsey - you are the greatest bestie and PA I could ever ask for, I'm so glad we found each other and you're never getting rid of me!

Maeghen - Thank you for helping me through my spirals and talking through the plot over and over...and over. And yet it still making you cry.

Anja- your unhingedness matches mine and it keeps me going, I'll write you a daddy at some point don't you worry.

Sarah - As always thank you for being with me from the very beginning. I will make you cry no matter what it takes. I will kill off a love interest if I need to!

Kay - Forever grateful for you and that we've been able to work together through so many books. I hope you know there's many more to come!

Kim - This. Cover. This is the cover that made me find you and fall in love with what you create so the fact that we are finally using it makes me so happy. I love everything you create and I'm so thankful for you!

Angie - Thank you for believing in me, giving my books and me a chance. Already you've helped make dreams come true for me, and I know it's only up from here.

Thank you Genna Black and Randi for reading to check for accuracy on the firefighter aspect! And how realistic it is to have sex in a firetruck!

Thank you to my beta readers Emily, Lanae, Jaeann, Jessica, Courtney, Katelyn, and Leslie your comments always make me feel so much better about these stories!

Of course thank you to my ARC readers and every single person who has read my books, who continues to read my books. Everyone who shares the love of my stories and characters it's because of you I'm able to do this and there's not enough words to describe how thankful I am for all of you!

Next up is Bailey and Wes, get ready and buckle in because those two are a bumpy ride, but I promise it's worth it.

Also by Madi Danielle

Amity

Small town romances

Embers of You - A firefighter romance

Scars of You - A neighbors enemies to lovers romance

Memories of You - A second chance romance

Denver Dragons Series:

Hockey romances

The Hat Trick - A why choose romance

The Power Play - A forced proximity cam girl romance

Cross Checked - A friends to lovers novella

The Break Out -An enemies to lovers brother's teammate romance

Uncaged Duet

A dark MMA why choose romance

Uncaged Desires

Uncaged Obsessions

The Falling series

When They Fell - A friends to lovers romance

Who They Are - A cop romance

What They Feel - An enemies to lovers age gap romance

Signed Books available on my website:

www.madidaniellewrites.com

About the Author

Madi is a romance author, wife and mother to one daughter and several animals. When she isn't reading or writing you may find her watching hockey or some cheesy movie. Madi has been writing since she was a teenager, but it took a backseat when she went to college and got her degree in Family and Human Services. After working as a social worker, she got back into writing as an escape and hasn't looked back since. Madi is originally from Arizona, but moved to Oregon to attend UO, which is where she still resides with her family.

instagram.com/madidaniellewrites
tiktok.com/@madidaniellewrites
threads.net/@madidaniellewrites